THE STEPPING MAZE

A DAN KOTLER ARCHAEOLOGICAL THRILLER

J. KEVIN TUMLINSON

KNOVELTON

THE STEPPING MAZE

For Brandon Barr and his family.
I only knew you briefly, but I'll remember you forever. Your story
goes on.

PROLOGUE

UNDISCLOSED LOCATION

Dr. Leopold Marvin fell face-first to the smooth, cement floor, sliding a bit from the momentum of being shoved into the room.

He couldn't see. The weave of the hood over his head let in only a tiny fraction of light. He could hear sounds, mostly the shuffling of feet and then a metallic click. It sounded ominous, but he couldn't imagine what it might be. He waited.

Gloved hands took hold of his forearms, which were pinned behind his back and bound with rough twine.

There were two men, large, strong. Stronger than he was, at least, though that wasn't admitting much. One of the men held him while the other slipped a blade between his wrists and cut the twine.

They dropped him to the floor again, knocking the wind out of him. In a few moments, there was the sound of a very large and heavy door being swung closed. The thud of it was loud and solid and imposing, giving Dr. Marvin a clear mental image of it despite the hood. He pictured the massive thickness of a stone being rolled in front of a tomb.

A series of loud clacks followed, and then silence.

Dr. Marvin lay on his stomach, not sure if he should move. Eventually, he raised his hands to the hood, tugging the drawstring loose and pulling the material away from his eyes. He worked the gag out of his mouth and took a deep breath.

He was in a room. It looked like an office—but everything seemed a few generations removed from present day. Something out of the fifties, maybe? There were desks, tables, chairs, old lamps with leaded glass shades. There were bookcases filled with unmarked spines. There was an ancient looking refrigerator and sink at one end of the room, and a hot plate on the counter.

It was like being kidnapped and thrown into the past. What was this place, a bomb shelter?

"Leo?" a familiar male voice echoed dimly from one darkened corner of the room.

Dr. Marvin rose to his feet, reaching for the edge of a desk to steady himself. He felt his heart pounding, and he wanted to throw up. He was scuffed and bruised, and a bit cold. They had grabbed him from his bedroom, his wife screaming and attacking them until they knocked her unconscious. God, he hoped she was just unconscious.

He looked into the darkness, at the figure across the room, recognizing him instantly as he stepped into the light.

"Bob?"

Dr. Robert Wiley was likewise dressed in his pajamas, and he padded forward in bare feet. "Leo, they got you too?"

"Who are they?" Leo asked, shaking.

Bob shook his head. "I have no idea. I woke up with one of them standing over me. He shoved a rag in my mouth, and then the two of them tied me up and brought me here."

Leo nodded. "Same with me. Did they say anything? Do ... do you know what they want?"

Bob shook his head. "No idea. I've been here for hours, and

until they brought you in a guy was standing in the doorway, blocking me from getting out. He didn't say a word. Wouldn't answer any questions. I started calling him Gill, trying to ... I don't know, humanize him? Get a rise out of him?"

"Did it work?" Leo asked, pulling an old wooden, rolling office chair over and taking a seat. He was rubbing his bruised knees.

"He wouldn't react. I eventually just found a spot in the back and hid out. I don't know what I thought would happen, but then you were here."

Leo nodded. He was trying not to think of his wife. Thank God his daughter and his son were out of the house these days. They should be safe. He hoped.

He looked up. "What about you, Bob? What about your family?"

"Vacation," Bob said. "Lillie and Jeannie went to the lake house two days ago. I was supposed to join them in the morning. I had to wrap up some grading, and I met with some students to discuss their dissertations. I could have just skipped it," he said, looking away. Quietly he said, "Now I wish I'd gone."

Leo nodded, but he was already thinking about their predicament. He rose from the office chair and went to the large, steel door, putting his hands on it. The metal was cold, and it reminded him that there was a slight chill in the room. He held his arms to his chest.

"Yeah," Bob said. "Kind of cold. I found a couple of cots and blankets in the back. Not much, but it'll help."

"Any way out?"

Bob rolled his eyes. "Sure, Leo. I left hours ago."

"I mean, any *potential* way out?"

Bob shook his head. "None I've found. I haven't found any other doors or windows. But we can look together. I have a feeling we're going to be here for a while."

Leo nodded. He looked around and frowned. "What the hell is this place?"

"It seems to be some kind of old office," Bob replied. "Government stuff, I think. Most of the books I've found are manuals. There's some stuff about cryptography. References."

"Cryptography?" Leo asked. "Codebreaking?"

Bob nodded.

What the hell was going on here? Why were he and Bob trapped here? What was this place?

He turned again to the door and started pounding on it, yelling for help. His hands became sore after a moment, and he stopped.

"That door is thick," Bob said from behind him. "About six feet, I think. Steel."

"Six foot of steel? What is this, a bank vault?"

"Could be," Bob said. "No windows. Steel walls. No other exits. It could definitely be a bank vault."

"But why would anyone kidnap us and put us in a bank vault?" Leo asked, his voice going up an octave as the panic started to rise again.

Bob shook his head. "I don't know, Leo. But this is where we are." He said this last calmly, looking Leo in the eye. It was the way Bob had delivered bad news to students, about grades or about the reality of the state of their dissertations. Leo had sat alongside him and several other professors at enough dissertation reviews to know the look and what it meant. Be calm. Accept reality. Be ready to work past this.

He was right. Leo had to calm down. Relax. Center himself. His blood pressure was on the rise, he could tell.

He sat back down, and Bob disappeared only to return after a moment with the blankets. Leo thanked him, absently, and allowed Bob to drape a blanket over his shoulders as he stared wide-eyed down at the floor.

"It's going to be ok," Bob said, pulling up an office chair next to his colleague.

The two of them had taught in the same department for the past thirty years, imparting the intricacies of physics and quantum mechanics to graduate students who were, as far as Leo could tell, getting dumber with each new incoming class. They were more concerned about safe spaces and cry closets and using jazz hands instead of giving applause than they'd ever been about the intricacies of quantum mechanics. No one cared about the science anymore.

Leo had been thinking of retiring. Bob, he knew, was supposed to leave at the end of the following semester.

Two fewer conservative old white men in positions of authority on an increasingly liberal campus. They'd probably be cheered out of the building. No one would be more thrilled to leave all the insanity behind than Leo.

He and Bob weren't friends. Not really. Bob was a nice enough guy, but he drove Leo nuts half the time. The two of them disagreed on nearly everything that wasn't explicitly outlined in a textbook and sometimes went on a row over the textbooks themselves. They argued, but Leo found that he was ultimately the only one who got truly angry and irritated, while Bob seemed to smile through it all, taking everything in small steps, coming through their disagreements as if he was oblivious to their disagreeing at all. It was infuriating. Leo wanted to tie him to a chair and strap explosives to him, half the time.

But the point was that they were not friends, and really had little to do with each other, outside of their work at the university.

They spent no time together. They shared no projects or papers. As far as Leo could recall, neither of them had ever visited the other at home, unless there was some sort of obligatory social event. Even then, conversations were kept to socially benign topics. There was no bonding.

So their jobs—that had to be the reason they were grabbed.

What did these people want with a couple of old, retiring physics professors?

Why bring them here, to some weirdly anachronistic government office, crammed full of code-breaking manuals?

What was it these people hoped to gain? And would they come back to let the two of them out, or leave them to die here?

The questions were piling up, and Leo wasn't getting any closer to the answers.

He turned to Bob. "What if we die here?"

Bob considered the question, nodded, and said, "That would be terrible. But heck, it'd almost be like therapy, wouldn't it? Nothing puts the petty problems of life into perspective like the prospect of dying."

Leo stared at the man for a moment, wanting to shout at him for his optimism as they huddled under blankets in this terrifying space.

He huffed and slumped in the chair.

Bob was right. It would be terrible. And there was really nothing they could do about any of it. All they could do was wait.

NEW YORK, GOVERNMENT-SEALED APARTMENT

Dust drifted in motes through shafts of artificial light, joining its brethren on the piles of books and antique objects. The room was packed with the accoutrement of science, though a couple of generations removed from modern day.

Agent Roland Denzel had seen rooms like this before. A lot more of them, in fact, since taking on Dr. Dan Kotler as his partner.

Kotler wasn't here, though. And it was left to Denzel and Dr.

Liz Ludlum to go over the scene, to try to find some hint of what was going on.

"Shouldn't we call Dr. Kotler?" Ludlum asked. She nodded to the piles of papers, the antiquated scientific instruments, and the artifacts that were clearly from another era. "This is kind of his thing."

Denzel shook his head. "He's at a dig site ... somewhere. I don't have all the details. He's taking a sabbatical."

Ludlum squinted. "A sabbatical? But he's still at a dig site?"

"A sabbatical from Historic Crimes," Denzel said.

Ludlum picked up the stress and irritation in his voice and didn't push.

They turned back to the scene in front of them.

"Two people, trapped in ..." Denzel hesitated and looked at Ludlum. "What would you say that thing is?"

"A vault, maybe?" Ludlum shrugged.

"We can't afford to wait for Kotler to get here anyway," Denzel said. "Who knows how much time they have?"

Two other agents entered the room, each carrying a forensics kit, taking samples and photographs, noting anything they found. Liz Ludlum's new team. Now that she was officially the Lead Forensic Specialist for Historic Crimes, she'd been given some leeway and a bit more authority than she'd enjoyed with the NYPD.

Ludlum carried an antique doctor's bag—something left to her by her grandfather. It had her own kit inside, and she opened the bag to fish out a notebook.

"We're at the right address, and this is pretty much what the letter described. 'To open the door, run the Stepping Maze. Your tools await in the room where it all started.' A riddle, I think."

"Mean anything to you?" Denzel asked.

Ludlum shook her head. "Not really. This really isn't my area. This is more ..."

"Dr. Kotler's thing, I know," Denzel grumbled.

Ludlum was quiet for a moment. She folded the notebook closed and slipped it into her pocket, snapped the doctor's bag shut and left it at her feet.

"Careful with that," Denzel groused. "Someone might think it's evidence, in this place."

"No chance," Ludlum said, shaking her head. "First thing I taught my team was to never touch my bag." She looked at Denzel, sighed, and asked, "What happened, in Antarctica?"

Denzel shrugged. "Nothing that doesn't happen all the time. We stopped the bad guy. Bad *girl*. Sorry," he said, giving Ludlum a sheepish grin as if he'd committed a *faux pas* against her entire gender. "Got cold, got shot, rested up and came home."

"Gail McCarthy," Ludlum nodded. "Seems like Dan hasn't gotten over it."

"Kotler will be fine," Denzel said, an edge coming back to his voice. "Let's focus on figuring this out, so two more people don't end up dead."

Ludlum couldn't argue with that. But she was having trouble figuring what this room and its contents, as interesting and unusual as they were, had to do with two prominent physicists being kidnapped and locked in an impenetrable cell buried under New York City. She did know that the note that had led them here had been addressed to Denzel specifically.

It had not mentioned Kotler. Which was, in itself, pretty strange. Because this had Kotler written all over it.

One of Ludlum's team called to them from across the room, and she and Denzel made their way through the antiques and artifacts and equipment. *Maybe this place is the Stepping Maze,* Ludlum thought, high-stepping over a stack of slide projector carousels that looked as if they dated to the 50s.

This place was going to take a year to catalog.

"Dr. Ludlum, we've found a reference to 'stepping maze.' It's written on this." In a blue-gloved hand, he held up a small ream of aged typewriter paper bound with three brass brads.

Ludlum pulled on gloves of her own and took the manuscript, holding it up to inspect under the work lights the team had brought in. Denzel crowded her a little, looking over her shoulder.

On the cover of the manuscript, in neat type, were the words "Cryptographic Applications of Heisenberg's Theory." In one corner of the page, in a scrawl of handwritten characters, was a note: "Could apply to 'stepping maze.'"

They had their thread. This had to be what the mysterious letter writer had intended them to find. It was a thick tome and flipping through the first few pages, Ludlum could tell it was going to be out of her league. She recognized some of the science, but it quickly got to a level at which she was only an amateur. Notations from high-level quantum physics and mathematics adorned nearly every page. They'd need to bring in some experts to run through this.

"Has to be it," she said, glancing at Denzel.

The agent looked startled and took the manuscript from her in his own gloved hands. "You see this?" he asked, holding it up and turning it to keep the cover in the light.

Her hands had obscured the small print at the bottom of the cover as she'd held it, and she had overlooked something in her casual inspection. But now it stood out like a neon sign.

Dr. Daniel F. Kotler

The author's name in crisp, typed letters.

"That's ..." Ludlum started.

"How old would you say this is?" Denzel asked her.

She shook her head. "I could get a sample, and have it dated. The paper looks aged, though. Yellowed. And it's definitely a typewriter, not a printer. Look at the indentions. I'd say it's at least thirty years old, maybe more."

"This room has been sealed for seventy years," Denzel said. "I had to get special permission just to open it."

"Roland, anyone could have gotten in here at any time and left that," she said. "The person who wrote the letter ..."

"I know that," he waved. "They knew it was here, so the likely explanation is that they put it here. Or they've at least been in this room. Have we seen any evidence that anyone was in this room before we got here? Aside from whoever left it this way?"

She shook her head. "Not that I'm aware. The locks and the seals were all intact. There are no windows. There's ventilation, but it was added when the doors were sealed. The vents are maybe six inches wide, if that." She looked around the room, taking in the piles of boxes, desktops covered in scientific equipment, shelves crammed with reference books. "We're just getting started here. Maybe there's some other way in?"

Denzel called for one of the field agents to bag and catalog the manuscript. "When this is done, I want that at the top of the pile. Whatever else you find, I want that examined first. And I want it scanned and sent to my phone."

He turned, pulling off his gloves as he moved to the door.

Ludlum followed, just on his heels. "O-ok ... But Roland ... Agent Denzel!" She hadn't meant to shout, but it was the only thing that made Denzel stop short and turn to face her. "Where are you going?"

"To get Kotler," Denzel said. "This literally has his name written all over it."

1

TJARU DIG SITE, EGYPT

Dan Kotler was thrilled to be covered in sweat and grime and sand. He was happy to have a trowel and a set of brushes at the ready. He busied himself with gently brushing loose soil from the details of a fallen fragment of limestone, revealing a cartouche bearing the name of Thutmose III—an eighteenth dynasty Egyptian ruler, and the current focus of Kotler's unwavering interest.

He hadn't been this hands-on with a site for a couple of years now—at least, not without a few figurative and literal guns to his head—and it felt good to be back. It reminded him of his grad school days, where exploring the ancient world might have its dangers and risks, but typically didn't involve kidnappings, getting shot, or having your head messed with by a brilliant villainess with the world's most advanced smuggling empire at her disposal.

Dust the cartouche, forget the lady.

Kotler finished up and took a moment to make some notes in his field journal. He used a small, plastic marker to indicate his find, purposefully ignoring its similarity to the flags used to mark crime scenes.

He was charged with just one square of one grid of this site —a task typically left to grad students and apprentices—and he was taking his duties very seriously. This was good, honest work, and could provide some seriously intriguing insight into ancient Egyptian culture. As well as a much-needed distraction.

He left his square in search of some lunch, dusting himself off as he went.

There was a tent set up as a sort of mess hall, and thanks to a very generous grant from Kotler himself it was well-stocked with all the necessities of life. Especially coffee and scotch. But fresh food was transported to the site almost daily, and Kotler was more than ready to dig in.

He prepared a plate, poured himself a glass of iced tea, and took a seat in a back corner of the tent. The shade and the light breeze coming off of the desert helped to wick the sweat from his neck and face. He used a handkerchief soaked in water to wash away the dirt from his face, inspecting the results in a small pocket mirror he was carrying in his kit.

He sighed. He sipped. He nibbled. He kept his mind off of Gail McCarthy and Nazi U-boats and ...

"Roland?" he asked, not quite sure he was seeing who he was seeing.

Agent Denzel, dressed in khaki fatigues and shouldering a desert camo backpack, stepped into the mess tent and let the flap drop back into place. The effect was a brief burst of sunlight followed by the relative shade of the tent as if Denzel had appeared in a flash of mystical energy that was now fading.

"Kotler," Denzel said. "Finally. This is the fourth site I've been to today."

AT KOTLER'S INSISTENCE, Denzel made a meal for himself and poured his own glass of iced tea. He downed the tea in a single gulp while standing at the serving table, and refilled his glass before joining Kotler.

A few other people lingered in the mess tent, quietly chatting as they nibbled and refreshed themselves. Officially there were scheduled mealtimes, but people more or less came and went on their own agenda, most preferring to get back to their assignments as quickly as possible rather than linger too long with the lunch and dinner crowds. It was basically a free-for-all after breakfast. The one time of day when everyone gathered, celebrating and sometimes lamenting the labor and what it meant.

"Roland, what are you doing here?" Kotler asked. He'd last seen his friend and partner over two months ago when he'd told Denzel he needed a break. Kotler had initially planned to take a couple of weeks here but had found the whole experience so cathartic and inspiring, he had asked to stay on. He wasn't sure when he expected to come back.

"You're not answering your phone," Denzel grumbled. "Or emails."

"All of my electronics are still in my bag," Kotler said. "I haven't looked at any of it since I got here."

"Kotler, how is anyone supposed to reach you if you're holed up in the desert with no phone?"

Kotler smiled. "The point was for no one to be able to reach me, Roland. I'm taking a hiatus, remember?"

"I thought it was a sabbatical," Denzel asked, puzzled.

"It's both," Kotler smiled lightly. Denzel seemed agitated, his body language making it clear that he was both weary from his travel and irritated at having to hunt Kotler down. But Kotler could see something else in the way his friend hesitated slightly, in how his eyes darted to the side, considering and contemplating. He was concerned for Kotler, which was touching but didn't necessarily change anything.

Whatever his feelings about Kotler's hiatus/sabbatical, Denzel's standard bull-rush approach to personal dynamics took over.

"Well, we have a situation, Kotler. And I have to ask you to come back with me."

Kotler chuckled and shook his head. "Roland, I'm sorry, but no. I told you, I need some time. I'll be back, I promise. I don't know when, but ..."

"You're misunderstanding me," Denzel said, his voice firm. "I'm not asking. I'm telling you that you're coming back with me. We leave today. I have a helicopter and a plane on standby."

Kotler blinked. "Roland, what's happened?"

Denzel took out his phone and flicked the screen a few times before handing it over.

Kotler took it, looking queerly at his friend, and then turning to the screen.

He arched his eyebrows, then laughed.

"We found that at a crime scene," Denzel said, a bit perturbed by Kotler's reaction. "And I need to know why your name is on it."

Again, Kotler chuckled and shook his head as he handed the phone back to Denzel. "Roland, that isn't my name. First of all, I would never use 'Daniel' on anything. I've always preferred Dan. My books, my papers—everything is 'Dan Kotler.' I know that doesn't prove anything, but it's true."

Denzel gave him an odd look. "I ... guess I knew that, about your books. Never hit me. What's the second thing?"

Kotler grinned. "My middle initial isn't 'F.' I don't have a middle initial." He shrugged, his hands out to his sides. "No middle name."

Denzel scoffed. "This is too much to be a coincidence," he

said, sinking back and staring at the phone in one hand as he sipped more iced tea from the other.

"Why don't you tell me what's happened?" Kotler replied "Maybe there's another explanation. Where did you find that manuscript?"

Denzel nodded.

"We got a letter, a few days ago. It was addressed to me." He swiped at his phone again and handed it back to Kotler.

On the phone was a scan of a typed letter, indeed addressed to Agent Denzel. Kotler read through it.

To: Agent Roland Denzel, Historic Crimes, FBI

Two prominent physicists have been abducted and imprisoned in a chamber that lies under the former New York City Commercial Code building, at 225 Broadway. You will find a door made of six feet of tempered steel. The walls are made of the same material. There is no way in or out, beyond the use of that door.

Dr. Leopold Marvin and Dr. Robert Wiley were abducted last night from their respective homes, and deposited into the chamber, sealed in with only enough provisions for approximately a week. The chamber should have enough air for two people to last approximately two weeks. You have time. Do not waste it.

You will find the key to their rescue in a government-sealed apartment located at 1359 Broadway, number 070.

To open the door, run the Stepping Maze. Your tools await in the room where it all started.

Kotler looked up from the letter. "Dr. Marvin and Dr. Wiley," he said.

"You know them?" Denzel asked.

Kotler Nodded. "They were faculty while I was getting my second Ph.D., in Quantum Physics. Dr. Marvin wasn't really one of my biggest fans if I remember. He respected that I already had my doctorate in Anthropology but felt that was where I should stay. He ... wasn't entirely wrong. I was never the best student of quantum mechanics. I took more of a philosophical approach than the hardcore mathematics that Dr. Marvin taught. I'm actually quite bad at math, which really irritated him."

"What about Dr. Wiley?" Denzel asked.

"We got along much better. I liked him. A bit odd, sometimes a little presumptuous, but friendly. He was fascinated with what I was doing. He used to invite me to his student dinners, even though I only had a few low-level classes with him."

"Have you kept in contact with either of them?" Denzel asked.

Kotler thought about it. "No, not really. Dr. Wiley came to one of my lectures, about a year ago, and we had drinks before we both had to leave for other things. I haven't spoken with Dr. Marvin since graduation, I believe."

"So both of these men were professors of yours, both worked in the same field. And then there's this manuscript with your name on it—or something really close to your name." Denzel paused, thinking, and shook his head. "Kotler, that's just too much coincidence," he said.

Kotler agreed, though he couldn't immediately think of a reason for this to be so. Except for the obvious ...

Someone meant for him to be involved in this.

But why go directly to Denzel? If the goal really was to get Kotler tangled up in this, why hadn't they addressed this letter to Kotler himself?

"There's something else bugging me about all of this," Kotler said.

"There should be a lot bugging you about it, but what do you mean?" Denzel asked.

Kotler couldn't say. A lot was happening in the letter, and in conjunction with the manuscript, it merely multiplied. Certain things, however, tumbled together to scream for his attention, and the answers were slow in coming.

"Stepping maze," Kotler said quietly.

"Yeah, we haven't been able to figure out what that means yet. It may have just been the thread this guy wanted us to follow, to find this manuscript."

Kotler shook his head. "It's more than that. May I?" He indicated Denzel's phone, and the Agent nodded.

Kotler opened a map and entered the address for the vault where the physicists were being held. 225 Broadway was still a commercial code building, handling zoning permits for city contractors. The vault must have been built alongside the building's original construction. Its purpose—well, Kotler could only guess at this point. Six-foot-thick steel walls and doors indicated that whatever was kept inside was meant to be as secure as turn-of-the-century technology could make it. A vault like that could survive against explosives and would take considerable time to cut through even with modern technology.

All of this was intriguing, but it didn't generate any ideas.

Kotler tried the address for the locked room, and things got stranger.

"This address ..." Kotler started.

"Yeah, it's not really an apartment building. It's a sealed room under a cosmetics company."

"Yardley of London," Kotler said.

"Yeah, that's it."

"Another coincidence that isn't a coincidence," Kotler mumbled.

"What do you mean?"

"I think I've figured out at least part of this thread," Kotler replied. "The kidnapper is referencing the American Black Chamber."

Denzel frowned. "That's ... isn't that the code-breaking thing?"

Kotler smiled. "Officially it was known as the Cipher Bureau. Herbert Yardley founded it as a code-breaking operation meant to rival the clandestine operations of other governments. It was more or less the forerunner of the National Security Agency. The birth of US intelligence agencies."

"The NSA," Denzel said, shaking his head. "Does this cosmetics company have anything to do with Herbert Yardley?"

Kotler shook his head. "No, I think this was more of a clever joke on someone's part. This room was government sealed?"

"For most of a century," Denzel replied.

"Funny," Kotler said.

"Not to the two scientists suffocating in a vault," Denzel replied.

Kotler nodded. "You're right. Sorry. It's just ... clever. And there's something else bugging me." He peered at the letter, running scenarios through his mind, playing things out. "The address is weird."

"It's also wrong," Denzel said "There is no number 070 in that building. We found the room after a search. The management let us in without having to get a warrant, and some of the employees knew about a locked room no one was ever allowed to enter. They couldn't have if they'd wanted. Thing was sealed tighter than a tomb."

"You'd be surprised how easy it can be to get into a tomb," Kotler said absently, then shook his head. "But I think the address has more significance."

"What are you seeing?"

"An extra zero," Kotler said, looking up. "Why give an address as zero-seven-zero? Why not simply number seventy?"

Denzel shook his head. "I thought that was weird, too. Ludlum thought it might be a hint at what the guy does for a living. Like maybe he's in city planning or something."

Kotler smiled. "How is Liz?"

Denzel rolled his eyes. "She's back home doing her job, which is more than I can say for you, Kotler. Can we focus?"

Kotler chuckled, and using Denzel's phone he brought up a chart and held it up for Denzel to see. "The letter F," Kotler said.

"I don't get it," Denzel replied.

"It's ASCII code. The number 070 translates to the letter F, which happens to correspond with the middle initial of the author's name, on that report."

"What does that mean?"

Kotler shrugged. "I'm not sure yet. But the connections and coincidences are piling up."

Denzel thought about this for a moment. "What does 'stepping maze' mean?" He asked.

Kotler smiled. "Ok, more history. Before there was the NSA, there was the SIS—the Signals Intelligence Service. This operation was run by William Friedman, a geneticist turned cryptoanalyst who was recruited by the Army to head a brand-new code-breaking division. Friedman recruited a team, including a man named Frank Rowlett, to help in his mission to decipher codes intercepted from foreign governments. This was following World War I, with WWII on the horizon, and code-breaking became the purview of the Army after Yardley's Cipher Bureau was shuttered on orders from Secretary of State Henry Stimson."

Denzel nodded. "I remember this from Quantico. Stimson was the one who said, 'gentlemen do not read each other's mail.' He thought it was unethical to spy on communications from other governments outside of wartime."

Kotler smiled. "That quote is a bit apocryphal, but that's it.

Stimson shut down the Cipher Bureau on the grounds of ethics. But the need for intelligence didn't go away, and the Army picked up the slack. Friedman and his wife, Elisabeth, had both been go-to codebreakers for the US military since well before the Great War. William was asked to head this new division because ... well, because he was a man, frankly. Elisabeth had proven herself every bit the codebreaker that William was, and went on to help law enforcement crack down on gangsters and smugglers during Prohibition." Kotler shivered. "Hard to know who the bad guys were, during that point of history."

"Relax," Denzel rolled his eyes. "You have your whiskey. Carousing and legal inebriation won. But bring this thing around for me. What does all of this have to do with the stepping maze?"

"Friedman's protege, Frank Rowlett," Kotler replied. "He came up with a design for ... well, the easiest way to refer to it was an American Enigma Machine. A device built with reversible electric rotors, or stepping motors, which Rowlett himself referred to as a 'stepping maze.' The result was a device called SIGABA. I have no idea what that might be an acronym for, and I'm not sure anyone else does either. But the device itself was a marvel. It was never defeated, Roland. The Nazis, the Japanese, hell the whole of the Axis forces tried and failed, and eventually gave up. The Nazis even stopped bothering to intercept US communications, because they just couldn't crack the code. Until digital encryption took over, SIGABA was the single-most effective encryption and decryption tool ever built."

"So the stepping maze is a reference to this cigar-o?"

"SIGABA," Kotler smiled. "And yes, I'm pretty sure it is."

"And what does that have to do with two kidnapped scientists?"

"Two kidnapped *quantum physicists,* specifically," Kotler

said, bring up the photo of the manuscript's cover. "And the answer is Heisenberg."

"Wasn't that the dead cat guy?"

Kotler laughed loud enough that some of the grad students and anthropologists in the mess tent looked their way. "That was Schrödinger. And no. But close. Sort of. Heisenberg's Uncertainty Principle is one of the foundational concepts of quantum physics. The principle gets confused a lot with the observer effect, but for the sake of simplicity, we'll say that's a fair parallel. Basically, Heisenberg imposes a hypothetical limit to the degree to which certain measures can be known."

"Uh huh," Denzel said, staring.

Kotler smirked. "It means you can't know both the position and the speed of a quantum particle because measuring one alters the other. Leaving some 'uncertainty' in the mix as you observe quantum effects."

"Got it," Denzel said, yawning and then sipping from his iced tea again. He rose from his chair. "Pack your bags."

"Whoa, wait ... " Kotler protested.

He looked around. Through an open flap in the tent, he could see the dig site he'd just left. The work wasn't finished. It was meaningful work. Important work. History lay there, waiting to be unearthed. How could he ...

"Kotler, two lives are in jeopardy here. And whoever did it is playing games. Games you're meant to solve. You get that, right?"

Kotler did get it. He just resented it. No matter how hard he tried, he couldn't seem to pull away from this life for even so much as a breather.

And yet, despite the frustration, he felt a thrill growing within his chest. There were riddles to solve here. There was a mystery, with its roots in a past that Kotler found fascinating.

There were human lives at risk, too, and how could he turn

his back on them? Forget his personal connection to them, these two men needed his help. They needed these riddles solved so they could stand a chance of rescue.

Kotler had to go back.

"I'm already packed," he said. "Just let me grab my bag."

2

FBI OFFICES, MANHATTAN

The Historic Crimes division of Manhattan's FBI headquarters had grown to encompass a floor of its own. Not only were Denzel's agents given office and cubicle space, but one half of the floor was now dedicated to Liz Ludlum's forensic lab.

Kotler marveled at this. Where was the funding coming from? And why was the FBI so enthusiastic about this work? True, Denzel's close rate was incredibly high. Even the cases that Kotler had nothing to do with were typically closed within a month. Historic Crimes was doing good work. Maybe that was all it was.

The name still bugged Kotler, though.

Technically, "historic" meant something was important to history. A landmark or an event could be historic. What the FBI was going for should have been "Historical Crimes," which meant that the cases they investigated had some significance tied to history and the past.

Kotler had brought this up when the department was first named, and Denzel had informed him that first, bureaucracy would make it near impossible to change the name now, and second, "Shut up, Kotler."

The forensic lab was divided into quadrants, and in a clean room Kotler and Denzel entered to find Dr. Ludlum and her team examining the contents of the government-locked room. The steel tables of the lab were practically buckling under the weight of recovered documents, antique instruments of various description, and a bulk of unidentifiable objects.

Both Roland and Kotler were wearing clean suits, masks, and gloves, to prevent any further contamination of the evidence they'd collected.

Ludlum was studying a sample taken from the manuscript.

"Find anything useful?" Denzel asked.

Ludlum motioned them over to her laptop and brought up the results of her analysis of the sample. "The paper itself is just shy of a hundred years old," she said. "There's enough collected dust and pollutants on it to give us a pretty good idea of when this was put in the room. The typed characters were made with a turn-of-the-century typewriter. Strikers on ribbon. I have scans out with a group that might be able to identify the make and model of the typewriter, though I'm not sure that will be very helpful. Other than that, there's some evidence of carbon transfer paper being used with it when we test the back side of these sheets."

"What about the handwritten stuff?" Denzel asked.

"Standard number two lead pencil," Ludlum said. "The handwriting doesn't exactly match anything in our database, which I expected. We've picked up a few fingerprints and some DNA, but nothing helpful so far."

"Hi Liz," Kotler smiled.

"Dan," she said, smiling back.

Denzel coughed. "So we're at another dead end?"

Ludlum looked at him and shook her head. "All I can say for sure is that this manuscript is exactly as old as it should be.

The ribbon ink from Dan's name matches the ink from the rest of the manuscript, so it's reasonable to assume it was written at the same time."

"Just pointing out," Kotler said, "it's not actually my name."

"Noted, Kotler," Denzel said. "But is there anything about this that might give us some clues? I got a team of engineers and experts trying to find a way into that vault, but even our best effort is going to take a lot longer than these two men have."

Kotler huffed, and leaned over the manuscript, turning some of the pages using a pair of tweezers. Ultimately, he flipped back to the cover and examined the handwritten note. "Could apply to stepping maze."

"Anything?" Denzel asked.

Kotler reluctantly shook his head. He looked up at them. "We have a complete scan of this? Something I can take with me, to read?"

Denzel nodded. "It's in your inbox, along with everything else we thought might be part of this."

"I can forward all of the results of the analysis if you want," Ludlum said.

Kotler nodded. "Please. I don't know if it'll do any good, but you never know."

"You think the contents of that thing will be useful?" Denzel asked.

Kotler shrugged. "I think the kidnapper thinks it will," he replied. "Have we found anything on Dr. Daniel F. Kotler?"

"We have," Ludlum said, smiling. "I had someone run a search and background. A lot of his record is classified. We have some of his papers and a government file, but a lot it is redacted. We had better luck running his personal and family history. Turns out he was your Great Grandfather, Dan."

Kotler's eyebrows arched in surprise. "Seriously? I mean, I

assumed we might be related, but that's a pretty direct line. I've never even heard of him."

"Maybe you were named for him?" Denzel asked.

Kotler thought about this. "I really don't know, to be honest. I haven't looked that deeply into my family history."

Now it was Denzel's turn to be surprised. "You? I figured you'd have some kind of pro-level account on Ancestry.com."

Kotler looked from Denzel to Ludlum, shook his head lightly, and sighed. "There's ... a lot about my family history that I've just never wanted to look into."

Denzel and Ludlum both studied him for a moment, and finally, Denzel said, "It looks like you may have to deal with this, though. You good for this?"

"Do you need help?" Ludlum asked.

Kotler looked from one to the other and sighed. "I do," he said. "But I think I'd better start by calling my brother."

FACETIME'S RING was slightly piercing in Kotler's AirPods, but he gritted his teeth and bore it. He wasn't sure if the pain was real, or if it was a psychic translation of the slight anxiety he was feeling about this call.

He was relieved when Alex, his nephew, was the one who answered.

"Uncle Dan!" Alex said.

"Alex! I didn't expect you to answer. I'm calling for your dad."

"I can go get him," Alex said.

"First, tell me what's going on with you," Kotler smiled. "How's the detective business?"

Alex operated what Kotler called a "boy detective agency" out of an outbuilding behind their home. "Any mystery solved, but it'll cost you a buck." He took on local mysteries—stolen bicycles, missing lunch money, that sort of thing. There had been occasional hints of more dangerous cases, and Kotler had lectured Alex at length that he should stick to safe waters. His nephew was a little too like Kotler for anyone's comfort, however.

The boy was brilliant, exuberant, and pretty good with a puzzle. Kotler was constantly sending Alex souvenirs and objects of interest, encouraging the boy to keep pursuing his keen interests in science and mystery.

The two of them had a bond that Kotler knew his brother, Jeffrey, wasn't entirely thrilled about. Kotler tried to respect his brother's preferences, but he adored Alex. He settled for being the distant, occasional influence on the boy, rather than dropping in for visits too often.

"I found a lost book for one of my clients," Alex boasted. "It was an autographed copy of 'The Great Gatsby.' Worth lots of money."

"Good work!" Kotler said earnestly. "I'm sure they were glad to get that back. But you're staying safe when you're on these cases, right? Not putting yourself in danger?"

"Never!" Alex replied, with the sort of enthusiasm that Kotler immediately recognized as complete BS.

Kotler sighed, gave his nephew the usual admonishments about being safe and careful and honest with his parents. "I mean it," he said, and Alex swore he was being safe. Kotler really had no choice but to take his word for it.

Now it was time to get down to business.

"Can you put your dad on?" Kotler asked. "And tell him to use the earbuds."

"You got it, but you know he hates those things," Alex said.

"Tell him it's important," Kotler replied.

He watched the world go chaotic as Alex raced through the house in search of his dad. There was a brief exchange, some grumbling from Jeffrey as he dug the earbuds out of a desk drawer, and finally Kotler saw his brother's face appear as if looking down on him from the other side of the screen.

"Hello, Dan," Jeffrey said.

"Jeffrey," Kotler replied. "You're looking good. I like the beard."

"It itches," Jeffrey said, scratching lightly at one cheek. "But yeah, I like it. So does Christina. What's up?"

Kotler smiled and shook his head. Jeffrey was a nice guy, smart, and very stable. He was the younger of the two of them, but Kotler sometimes felt like Jeffrey was the suffering older brother, tolerating Kotler's childish antics.

Jeffrey had plenty of friends, Kotler knew, and he wasn't afraid to interact with them. When it came to interacting with his brother, though, Jeffrey was guarded. He tended to frown on most of Kotler's life choices. And though he certainly had as much money as Kotler, following the death of their parents, Jeffrey lived in a modest, suburban neighborhood, and worked the sort of job his neighbors might work. A secret multi-millionaire, living next door to guys who worked as plumbers and women who ran floral shops, completely undercover.

Kotler would never admit this to his brother, but he admired him for his lifestyle. Where Kotler had decided to pursue an exploration of humanity through history and science, embracing his wealth and living a life of travel, notoriety, and the occasional torrid affair, Jeffrey lived a quieter life, out of the spotlight and contentedly quiet.

Kotler wished they could have a better interpersonal relationship, but it just wasn't happening. At best they were tolerant of each other. Brotherly love could carry them that far and no further.

"I'm helping the FBI with another case, and something close to home has come up. You're ... well, you're more of a family historian than I am. I was hoping you could help me learn a little more about our Great Grandfather."

Jeffrey nodded. "I can send you something with our family tree if you want. And some bios. I've managed to track the Kotler family back by about twelve generations, if you'd like to see it. Things get a little sketchy from there."

Kotler was surprised. "That'd be great, email me whatever you have. I'd love to take a look at the family line later. But let me ask you, what do you know about Dr. Daniel F. Kotler?"

"Well, other than being our Poppa's father, I know that he was a physicist. He had some ties to the Manhattan Project, actually."

"Really!" Kotler exclaimed. "Wait, you knew this and never mentioned it?"

Jeffrey shrugged. "You don't exactly come over for dinner."

That was fair. Kotler checked in with his brother from time to time, but he didn't make much of a habit of dropping in. Things were ... strained.

He had a pretty good relationship with Christina, his sister-in-law. And Alex was one of his favorite people on Earth—the feeling appeared to be mutual. But Kotler and Jeffrey hadn't spoken much since Kotler had left for college at eighteen. Even before that, they hadn't exactly been best friends. After their parents died, they'd both become wards of Cristoff Valler, their father's research and business partner.

Life became a series of disjointed learning exercises at that point, with Kotler embracing Cristoff's penchant for historical anomalies and ancient mysteries, and Jeffrey pining for a normal childhood of which he felt he was being deprived.

They had drifted apart.

"Daniel has a bigger file than almost everyone else on our family tree," Jeffrey said. "I'll send it over. I have photos, too."

"That would be very helpful, thank you. Did you happen to find anything in your research that would connect Daniel to the Signals Intelligence Service?"

Jeffrey shrugged. "Maybe. I don't remember every detail, Dan. But the file is searchable. Hold on."

He turned away from the phone and Kotler could hear the clacking of keys from that side. He knew that Jeffrey still depended on an aging Windows laptop that Kotler had practically begged him to upgrade. Jeffrey was fine with "good enough," though, and had no interest in doing anything that might be considered trendy, particularly with technology. It had been all Kotler could manage to get his brother to start using an iPhone, to make face-to-face communication a little easier. Kotler suspected Christina and Alex had something to do with Jeffrey caving on that one.

"Ok, I just emailed everything to you. You need anything else?"

Kotler looked at his brother's face, studying him. It struck him, at that moment, how much Jeffrey looked like their mother. It was the eyes. And the nose. The beard obscured things a little, but Kotler could see her there. And maybe a touch of their father, in the brow.

"No, I don't need anything else. But ... how are you? How's work?"

Jeffrey squinted just slightly. Suspicion. Kotler could read it clearly, and it made him a bit sad. There were too many miles and too many walls between him and Jeffrey. And he knew it was his fault. Jeffrey played his part, but it was Kotler who had put the distance between them. It had started after their parents died, and Kotler had just kept running from there.

"Good," Jeffrey said, a little guarded but softer.

Kotler saw something else then, in his brother's eyes. An old hurt. A yearning. A small boy wanting his older brother and his mom and his dad to all just be together again.

"Just good?" Kotler asked.

Jeffrey finally smiled a little. It touched his eyes and

followed to his lips only a moment later. Tight. Guarded. But there. "Dan, things are good. Are you ok? I heard a few things."

Kotler hadn't been prepared for that turn. He laughed lightly. "I'm ... fine. You know me. I'm like a super ball. I bounce back."

"And usually twice as hard and right back to trouble," Jeffrey said, the smile finally breaking out in full.

Again Kotler chuckled. "That's me. Bombastic, with trouble all around. What about Christina? I got a Christmas card. Nice photo."

"She's good. She's doing some volunteer thing, helping with the Historic Preservation Society. We made a big anonymous donation last month, to try to restore the old library. Pretty nice old building and construction starts next month. They're planning to turn it into a community clubhouse with a museum. Pretty nice."

"You have any hand in the design?"

Jeffrey laughed and shook his head. "No, I just wrote a check."

It went on like that for the next fifteen minutes, and Kotler found he was reluctant to end the call. But he remembered that there were two men in grave danger, in a secret vault in New York, and time was short.

It made him feel guilty.

Guilty for having gotten lost in conversation with his brother while two people faced death. Guilty for having to end the call with his brother for any reason whatsoever, after neglecting their relationship for so long. But when he said he had to go, he caught a flash of relief in Jeffrey's expression. Relief, but also a tiny bit of regret. So that was something, at least.

With the call ended, Kotler opened his laptop and brought up the documents that Jeffrey had sent. He filed all of the family stuff, putting it in Dropbox. He'd explore that later. He'd avoided looking at his family's past for a variety of reasons, but knowing his brother had such a keen interest in it, to the point of producing a library of research, made Kotler curious. He wanted to see his brother's work.

For now, though, he focused on Dr. Daniel F. Kotler and his frankly fascinating past.

3

DAN KOTLER'S APARTMENT, MANHATTAN

Daniel Faraday Kotler.

Kotler could hardly believe that anyone would name their kid "Faraday," but he was thrilled to see a thread of scientific interest in his family. It spoke volumes about the influences that had led to Kotler's own life and career choices, which was fascinating and intriguing all at once.

Dr. Daniel Kotler, the man himself, had a fascinating history.

The good doctor was born in 1896, in Catahoula Parish, Louisiana. He'd left Louisiana for Texas, at the age of seventeen, where he enrolled at Texas A&M to pursue an undergraduate degree in agriculture. His education was interrupted, however, as World War I erupted onto the world stage, drawing in all able-bodied and patriotic young men from across the nation.

By all indications, Kotler's Great Grandfather leapt enthusiastically into service.

During the war, Daniel's intelligence and scientific bent was noticed by his superiors, and he was placed into service as a

Communications Technician. He was in charge of intercepting enemy transmissions, mainly by tapping into telegraph cables that stretched across the war-torn landscape of Europe.

It was here that he was first pulled into the world of code-breaking.

It was a minor foray, and Daniel was mostly charged with intercepting and identifying enemy messages so they could be passed on to trained codebreakers. But he was exposed to the process enough that he became intrigued and took on code-breaking as a side hobby. His interest bled over into his official work on occasion. He would sometimes translate enemy encryptions before sending them on to the official code-breakers.

As a rule, this wasn't something the Army wanted him spending his time on. But the backlog of transmissions over the wire meant plenty of lag time, and Daniel was merely doing paper-and-pad translations of less sensitive broadcasts. But it helped, or so Kotler assumed, and Daniel received a commendation for his assistance. Someone had noticed.

When the war ended in 1918, Daniel returned to Texas A&M, where he completed his undergraduate degree in Agriculture. But his wartime experience had changed him, it seemed.

After completing his undergrad, he left Texas A&M to pursue graduate studies at the University of Michigan, turning now to physics.

Why he decided to make this transition was unclear to Kotler, but Daniel obviously had a love and a passion for science. The Great War had shaped the lives and futures of a lot of young men, in myriad ways. Kotler felt it was fortunate that for Daniel the war had nurtured something positive and inspired within him a desire to look deeper into the workings of the universe. Many of those who returned from the battle lines in Europe were not so fortunate.

It was at the University of Michigan that Daniel was first introduced to the work of Thomas Young, the English polymath who performed the original double-slit experiment—firing single particles of light at a phosphorescent sheet of material and noting the results. This experiment revealed that light, bizarrely, behaves as both a particle and a wave, depending on whether it is being observed.

The startling conclusion, that observation changes the outcome of the experiment, would be further scrutinized later, by other prominent researchers. But the revelation that light had some mysterious dual nature was what immediately took the scientific world into a whole new viewpoint of reality.

It was the birth of quantum physics.

Science was now looking deeper into the inner workings of reality than it ever had before, and Daniel was clearly enamored of it. His doctoral thesis was an in-depth exploration of the nature of light at the quantum level, with a proposal that measuring the trajectory of specific light packets, known as *quanta*, as they were fired would allow the observer to pre-model the pattern of particle impacts on a phosphorescent screen, while also determining the nature of the resulting wave pattern, after repeated firing. The double-slit experiment, now used to predict the future. In limited quantities.

It was an ambitious application of Young's experiment and results, and it had some intriguing implications. The science was still young, however, and the results were still uncertain. Daniel's premise had a few holes. But the thesis was enough for him to get his Ph.D. and to continue pursuing the fledgling field of quantum mechanics full-time.

It would be nearly a decade later that Werner Heisenberg would introduce his Uncertainty Principle, completely disproving Daniel's own hypothesis and further enhancing the mystique of Quantum Mechanics as a field of research.

Daniel seemed unperturbed by having his work unraveled.

He went on to publish several papers in prestigious journals, building on the theories of the more prominent physicists in his field, including Heisenberg. The papers were peer-reviewed and well-vetted, by some of the sharpest minds in science at the time. Commentary on Daniel's work was glowing in its praise.

Kotler scanned through Daniel's bibliography, as compiled by Jeffrey, but did not find *Cryptographic Applications of Heisenberg's Theory* anywhere. An indication that the paper was never published if it was ever even submitted.

That was disappointing, and a bit curious. There were some implications, considering how prolific Kotler's Great Grandfather had been with his publications. But the fact that this particular work was found tucked away inside a government-sealed room provided some clues.

Maybe the information in this paper was too sensitive for public release?

Kotler read on, now including the declassified documents that Liz Ludlum had provided.

Daniel's career in physics continued, and he seemed to gain some notoriety in certain circles. As the decades passed, he was tapped by both the military and the government to participate in a variety of fledgling programs, including some off-the-books, black-ops type stuff. Some of this was later declassified. Some remained locked away to this day. Kotler found all of it fascinating.

Then, in 1942, Daniel and his wife were relocated to Los Alamos.

Things went a little strange at this point.

Though Daniel was clearly a part of the original Manhattan Project team, mostly in a support capacity, after around eighteen months he was pulled from the roster and moved offsite. Some of his work on the project was still classified, even today, but that paled in comparison to the level of redaction that took hold of Daniel's work following his move.

According to what public records Jeffrey had been able to cobble together, Daniel was now employed by a city planning office.

Kotler doubled back, checking to make sure he hadn't inadvertently mixed files from some other relative. But it was true. Dr. Daniel F. Kotler, physicist, had worked for city planning in New York City. Specifically, he had worked as a developer of city and zoning codes. He was essentially making the rules that governed building permits within the city.

This made no sense, except ...

There was an address for Daniel's employer, on a bank record that Jeffrey had included. Kotler checked it against his notes and smiled.

It was the same address as the commercial code building, at 225 Broadway.

Things became clear. Daniel had been recruited out of one high-level government program, and into another. He'd gone from the Manhattan Project to, Kotler could only assume, working as a covert codebreaker.

This seemed to be confirmed further when Kotler read about Daniel's next career change, only a few years later. In 1950, Daniel became an employee of the AFSA—the Armed Forces Security Agency. The very program that William Friedman had been running only a short time before the founding of the National Security Agency, at which point he'd taken several of his people, including Daniel, with him.

Dr. Daniel F. Kotler had been a founding member of the NSA.

4

FBI OFFICES, MANHATTAN

"The NSA," Denzel repeated.

"I had no idea," Kotler said, leaning back in his chair and sipping coffee from a sleeved to-go cup. The two of them were in Denzel's office, overlooking the bullpen of agents. Kotler had brought coffee from a new place near his apartment—the sort of café that made Kotler realized he had really missed the city, despite being reluctant to leave his hiatus.

Egypt had a lot of intriguing and incredible things to recommend it, but the desert lacked the variety of cafés and coffee shops that Kotler preferred. In fact, other than what Kotler had ported in, the coffee choices at the dig site had been pretty abysmal.

They were going to miss him.

"How does this help us?" Denzel asked.

"I'm not sure yet, but it's where the information took us. Daniel was an early NSA agent, recruited into the program after working with William Friedman, presumably as a code-breaker."

"There's a thread," Denzel nodded. "And something else

has come up. My people found a compartment, hidden in the wall next to the vault door. It has some kind of device mounted in it. We think it's an early version of a security keypad."

He picked up a remote from his desk and aimed it at the large screen mounted on his wall. He fumbled with it a little, and Kotler hid a smile behind his hand as his partner worked out the intricacies of essentially turning on a television.

After a moment, and a couple of unnecessary whacks of the control against Denzel's palm, an image finally appeared on the screen.

Kotler stood, moving closer to inspect the image. He peered at the photo, making out what looked like a specialized typewriter keyboard. The keys were round and mounted to the sort of levers one would expect on an antique Underwood or similar unit.

On a typical typewriter, pressing a key would cause a bar to strike an ink ribbon, transferring a character to a page.

This device was a bit more complex than the typical typewriter. There was no place to scroll in a sheet of typing paper, for a start. Beyond the keyboard was a dense housing, and from what Kotler could see there were ribbons of cable coming out of it and disappearing into the wall.

"They've managed to get the housing off of the thing, and inside there are a series of rotors. Step motors, just like you were talking about, with the cigar-o."

"SIGABA," Kotler corrected absently. He was studying the device intently, noting every detail, anything that stood out as unusual.

The keys of the device were the first anomaly he noticed. Rather than a single character per key, each had a combination of five characters—alternating sequences of A and B.

From left to right, across what would be the home row of a standard keyboard, the sequence went:

AAAAA BAABA AAABB AABAB AABBA AABBB ABAAB ABABA
ABABB

"SO THE LETTERS," Denzel said. "We figure they correspond to a typical typewriter keyboard, but that's as far as we've gotten."

"Bacon," Kotler said quietly, amazed.

"Er ... are you ... hungry?" Denzel asked.

Kotler chuckled. "Sir Francis Bacon. The playwright. Well, among other things. He was a polymath, possibly on a level with Leonardo da Vinci. He was an author, a statesman, and a scientist. And he had a fascination with cryptology. He even invented his own secret code, known today as the Baconian Cypher." Kotler nodded to the screen.

"And this is it?" Denzel asked.

"I'm pretty sure," Kotler nodded, leaning in once again to study the keys.

He picked up a pen from Denzel's desk and used it to point to the screen. "You've noticed that each key has five characters. Alternating between A and B."

A second later a red dot appeared in the area Kotler was indicating, and he looked up to see that Denzel's remote had a laser pointer, which the agent was using to wobbily highlight the A/B sequences.

"Yeah, hard to miss," Denzel said.

Kotler shook his head, smiling lightly. "*AAAAA* is the letter A. *BAABA* is the letter S. And it continues like this, across the entire home row of the keyboard. ASDFGHJKL."

Denzel looked at the keyboard of his laptop and nodded. "So it's a fancy typewriter."

"Except it connects to a series of rotors, which we have to assume will activate or deactivate something inside the door. The key to the lock," Kotler said.

"That tracks," Denzel nodded. "We can't risk tinkering with it too much until we know more. But my people have traced a line that goes into the wall and is picked up again in the door. Things are on pause while we figure this out. We don't want to risk setting off something nasty."

"Smart," Kotler nodded.

"Do you know anything that could help us solve this?" Denzel asked.

Kotler exhaled. "Maybe. I know the cipher, from a historical perspective at least. The key here is to find the password. Not so different from a modern-day system, really."

"Any clue what that could be?"

Kotler paused, then shook his head. "Not yet. But I'm working on it. Whoever did this clearly meant for me to be involved. It's ... well, in a sense it's personal."

"Your great-grandfather," Denzel nodded.

"Yeah," Kotler said. "And his work, I'm guessing. I've been reading the manuscript you found. Daniel was brilliant. His theories were cutting edge for the time. Even for a couple of decades after. His application of Heisenberg's principles is only now being implemented in digital security. There are quantum encryption methods in use today that could be considered the intellectual grandchildren of Daniel's work if this paper had ever been published. There's a firm in Silicon Valley that was on the verge of developing the ultimate quantum integrated encryption key until something happened with their CEO. I think she was accused of espionage."

"Can any of that help us get into that room?"

Kotler had to admit he wasn't sure. He stepped back, studying the image of the device in the wall, wondering what it meant. What any of it meant.

The red dot reappeared, this time hovering over the digital clock in the upper corner of the screen.

"Time is running out," Denzel said.

Kotler nodded. "I'll double up, Roland. We'll crack this."
Denzel said nothing.

AT SIX-FOOT-FOUR and a muscular 270 pounds, Red Ryba was a noticeable figure, but he knew how to blend in. It helped that it was Fall in Manhattan, and temperatures were low enough that he could layer a long coat over his clothes and wear a scarf and hat. He looked like any other New Yorker, only taller and broader. If one looked closely, they might notice. But in Red's experience, people rarely looked closely.

Since he and his brother, Cameron, had abducted the two professors, they'd been watching the Yardley building, reporting back anything notable. The two of them took turns walking past the cosmetics store, strolling casually and never pausing or looking suspicious. Red listened to audiobooks as he walked, which helped him to stay casual and prevented anyone from trying to talk to him. And, he had to admit, he truly enjoyed the audiobooks.

Red knew that there were FBI agents present, but unless he or Cameron called attention to themselves, they should be fine.

Right now, the task was to observe. Red had made this clear to Cameron, who had the unfortunate tendency to want to take action, and quickly. But the client had given very clear orders. Observe. Do not interfere, unless they were asked. That was what they would do.

Red's phone vibrated. He paused the audiobook and checked.

A text message. From the client.

There's another package. Details are in your inbox. The money has already been transferred.

Red smiled. He'd never met the client in person, never even heard this person's voice. But they were always considerate and always paid on time. They obeyed Red's rules. They were the best kind of client, by Red's estimate.

He'd been doing this work for nearly a decade. His brother had joined him only five years earlier. It hadn't taken long for word of the "Ryba brothers" to reach the criminal underworld, and they never had to spend time looking for clients.

Though their services were not unique, they had a reputation for doing even the most distasteful tasks without question or hesitation, and at reasonable fees. They were fair. And honest—as far as people in their line of work could be honest.

There were rules.

Money was paid upfront. This was non-negotiable. To assuage any worries on the part of the client, the Rybas offered a 200% money-back guarantee—something Red had picked up from reading Tim Ferriss's *The 4-Hour Workweek*. Red was obsessed with self-improvement and found that these popular books lent themselves very well to his less-than-legal career.

The 200% offer was intriguing to clients, but in nearly ten years in the business, the Rybas had never had to pay it. They had a 100% success rate. It was part of their legend.

A second rule: Their business was referral only.

This cut down on the risk of undercover agents discovering or getting to them, and it also served as a simple way to vet new clients. The Rybas only took work once a former client had made introductions. And the former client, by making the referral, was also agreeing to certain penalties if their referral turned out to be less than desirable.

Vouching for someone put the former client on the hook, so it was only fair that they receive a 10% commission. But if anything went wrong, the Rybas would hold the referrer responsible. This was also fair.

The current client came to them from a woman the Rybas had worked for on many occasions. She had vouched for the new client and had even facilitated the initial payment. But shortly after the arrangement, she was either incarcerated or killed. Red wasn't sure which, as details were sketchy.

This made Red nervous, and he was just about to pay the new client the 200% refund when he received another deposit. The new client had doubled the fee, as compensation for the increased risk.

Facing the prospect of a black mark on their reputation, it was much more attractive to keep the client, and the money, and finish the job. No sense ruining a perfect track record, just because someone died. And as a bonus, they could keep the 10% commission.

Everyone was a winner. Except for the dead lady.

Red found a place to sit and get a bite to eat while he read emails. He chose a Turkish place and was enjoying a nice *shawarma* and a thick, syrupy Turkish coffee while he examined the details of their next task.

The woman, their new target, would be challenging to abduct.

Physically she would be only a minor threat, but the problem was access. Her position and her work ethic put her out of reach much of the time.

The client had included some surveillance details. The target was something of a workaholic, spending long hours in the office and returning home late in the evening. Even on weekends, she tended to spend her time working, though she'd lately become better at delegating.

Her hobbies typically put her in crowded places—flea markets and farmer's markets on weekends, theater and the symphony in the evenings. She had a book club but hadn't attended in months. She went to a kickboxing class frequently, but irregularly, likely as she felt she had time or needed the exercise.

Red could see why the client wanted her. Taking her would create a great deal of chaos for Dr. Kotler and Agent Denzel.

There were still plans and actions in motion—Cameron was currently completing part of his assignment, which was a risky but necessary encounter with the doctor and the agent. Risk was part of the job, however, and Red had trained his brother personally.

These actions, alongside the abduction of the woman, might be enough to derail the current investigation, which Red assumed was the point.

He made no pretense at knowing the mind of his client, but he'd been in this business long enough to make some educated guesses. It was pretty clear that the real target in all of this was Dr. Kotler. His name, above all others, had come up most often. These small demonstrations of force, the complications that the Rybas brothers were meant to add, represented some deeper play on the part of the client. Red couldn't know the overall plan, but he had enough of a role in it to guess at some of it. The client was smart, wealthy, and well-connected. What-ever motives might be at play were unclear, but Dr. Kotler was definitely at the heart of it all.

Red checked the accounts. He noted that their full fee had been deposited in the form of cryptocurrency. Untraceable. Universal. Crypto was one of the best things to happen for his business since he'd started this work. It eliminated the need to carry large amounts of cash, to deal with offshore bank accounts, and to endlessly launder his income. Though some laundering was always in order.

Red ran the application that further washed their income, splitting it into multiple crypto accounts, all from automated systems housed in countries around the world. Later these systems would buy into another currency on his behalf, consol-idating it for accessibility, and he and Cameron would be several layers removed from the initial transaction.

The wonders of the internet age.

Alright then, Red thought. He sipped the remainder of his

coffee and consumed the rest of the *shawarma*, then used a VoIP app on his phone to send a text to his brother. He forwarded the details of their new assignment, and then stood and left the café.

The chill in the air was pleasing to him. It was a lovely day in Manhattan.

He popped his earbuds back in and resumed the audiobook where he'd left off.

5

"Let's take a break," Denzel said, standing from behind his desk.

Kotler looked up, surprised. "Roland ... have you been compromised? Blink once for yes ..."

"Kotler, don't be you about this. We've been at it for hours, and we have to eat. And I know you well enough to recognize that a change of scenery can kick things loose for you."

Kotler stared at Denzel for a moment, then stretched, leaning back and feeling a creak in his neck and shoulders and lower back. His partner was right on all counts. He could use a break, and some food. And a change of scenery would definitely be welcome.

It was just surprising that Denzel was the one suggesting it.

They grabbed their coats and left Denzel's office, making their way along the catwalk that overlooked the bullpen. They took the stairs to the cubicle level and were making their way to the elevators when the doors opened. Liz Ludlum rushed out, moving straight ahead at a pace that said she was on a mission.

She was dressed in gym clothes—skin-tight and revealing her midsection.

She was amazingly fit, Kotler noticed immediately. He'd noticed before, but seeing her now, her dark skin glistening and the ripples of a six-pack undulating as she moved, the whole picture came home to him all at once.

She was a phenomenally attractive woman. And perhaps even more attractive, to Kotler, was just how brilliant she was. He'd always had a thing for women who were smarter than he, and Dr. Ludlum was definitely that. She could run circles around him in forensics, for certain. And he was pretty sure that she could master any subject she put her mind to. She was simply stunning.

"Kotler," Denzel muttered. "You're staring."

Ludlum sprinted through the office and into her lab, and Kotler felt himself blush.

He *had* been staring. It was difficult not to, but he felt a bit of shame over it, as if he'd been caught leering or catcalling. He'd just been ... taken.

"Right," he said, as the two of them resumed their walk to the elevator.

"I may have to talk to her about that," Denzel said, frowning and sounding a little bemused.

"Excuse me?" Kotler said, feeling a slight rise of panic.

"The outfit," Denzel said.

Kotler blinked. "Oh. I'm sure she had a good reason. She was probably getting in a workout downstairs and something big came up. Maybe we should check in with her?"

"Nice try, Kotler. But she has my number. She'll reach out if she needs us. You can pass her a note in class later."

"I ..." Kotler started, defensive, and then shook it off. "Right," he said, and ignored Denzel's mirthful expression as the two of them rode the elevator down to the lobby.

"You like her," Denzel said as they descended.

"Of course. She's an amazing woman, for sure. A valuable asset."

"Kotler, you're a grown man. I'm not going to tell you who you can and can't date. If you like her, ask her out. It might help break the tension, and we wouldn't have to go through all the gee-gaw and hormones every time the two of you are in a room together."

Kotler laughed and shook his head. "I appreciate the permission and all, Roland. I'm just ..."

He let it drift, and Denzel seemed to pick up on it immediately, which was a relief. Kotler wasn't entirely sure he could explain what he meant.

"I understand," Denzel said quietly.

They rode the rest of the way in silence.

DENZEL'S CHOICE of café was more about location and convenience than quality.

Just over a block from the FBI's Manhattan offices, Kotler and Denzel settled into a booth with torn vinyl seats and a questionably sanitized Formica tabletop. The place had the vibe of an old-school diner but was small and a little cramped. A waitress handed them two large menus, wedged into plastic sleeves.

"You take me to the nicest places," Kotler said.

"Good tuna melt here," Denzel replied, holding the menu at an angle to the table and studying it like it was the Wall Street Journal.

Kotler smiled and shook his head, opting to try Denzel's suggestion. They ordered when the waitress returned and talked about anything but the case as they ate. Kotler had ordered an iced tea but had to exchange it for a Coke after a couple of sips. The water, clearly, was not filtered.

Denzel chuckled. "You can be kind of a snob," he said.

Kotler arched his eyebrows. "Snob! You wound me, sir!"

The waitress brought the check and two cups of coffee, as requested. Denzel paid with a credit card, and the two of them lingered, chatting quietly. The café had a light crowd, and pop music played from dusty speakers hanging in the corners, near the ceiling.

"I'm getting a little worried," Denzel said as he poured artificial creamer from a tiny plastic cup, stirring it in with a spoon. "The engineers aren't making any progress. There's evidence that the room may be wired with some kind of trap, and it's stalled us."

"I saw the report," Kotler nodded.

"You find anything from your granddad's paper?"

Kotler shook his head. "If there's anything helpful there, I'm just not seeing it. I've read it, highlighted a few things I thought were connected. But in the end, it's really just an idea that Daniel had. A suggestion, with some explanation about how to apply it to encoding and decoding a message."

"What about the Bacon thing? Any idea what the passcode could be?"

Again Kotler shook his head. He sipped the coffee and winced. The same water that had made the tea unpalatable had also made the coffee taste awful, like grounds floating in dishwater. Kotler reluctantly poured in a couple of faux creamers himself.

They both sat, stirring their coffees, each feeling miserable and frustrated.

There was the sound of someone entering the café, triggering the little bell above the door.

Denzel's eyes went wide. "Kotler! Get down!"

The agent rose from the table, and in a smooth motion he drew his weapon from under his coat.

Kotler instinctively turned and saw that a masked man had

just entered and had drawn a weapon of his own. He stood, the door braced open against his back, and held the gun on the two of them.

People screamed and hid behind their booths. The waitress ducked behind the counter.

"A message," the man said, his voice low and gravelly. An affect, Kotler surmised. He was disguising his voice.

He held up a cylinder, something Kotler didn't recognize and tossed it into the café. He then fired two rounds in their direction.

Denzel took cover first, and then returned fire, but the man was already out of the door. Denzel rose and sprinted after him.

Kotler slid out of the booth and was about to join his partner in pursuit but paused when he saw the cylinder. He stooped to pick it up and studied it for a moment.

Denzel burst back into the café. "Call the police," he shouted to the waitress, who immediately fumbled with the phone.

He looked to Kotler, "Was anyone hit?"

Kotler was ashamed to realize he hadn't even checked, but he looked around now and saw that no one had been injured. They were cowering and remaining hidden, frightened out of their minds, but otherwise ok.

He looked up and saw that one of the hanging speakers had been hit by the gunman's fire.

He wasn't aiming at Roland, Kotler thought. *He wasn't here to kill anyone. He was a distraction.*

"Kotler!"

Kotler held up the cylinder. "He said it was a message. He was here to deliver this?"

"What is it?" Denzel asked, moving forward.

Kotler shook his head. He didn't know, but he intended to find out.

Something was going on here, running deeper than the

abduction of two of Kotler's former professors. This had always had the earmarks of being personal, aimed at Kotler somehow. But they had been treating it like any other case. They'd been working the details as if the vault and the encryption device were the mystery.

The real mystery came down to a single question.

Who was behind all of this?

6

HISTORIC CRIMES FORENSIC LAB

Liz Ludlum was frustrated with the pace of progress, and unsure what to do about it.

Her team was working around the clock, sifting through everything they'd recovered from the government-sealed room. What they were finding was fascinating, but most of it didn't seem relevant. Of all the recovered items, only the manuscript appeared to bear directly on this case.

She'd initially had everyone in the department put other work on pause, to prioritize this case and find a way to save those two men. While it was immensely helpful to have more eyes and minds on the problem, it added a great deal of additional pressure to get results quickly. For every hour her team was working this case, another case was growing cold.

She shook her head and made a decision. Turning to her laptop, she sent notices to a few of her people, telling them to return to their prior caseload.

It was a management decision.

It felt almost like giving up.

After days of sifting through this mess, they'd gotten

nowhere. And each of those days was one day less for Dr. Marvin and Dr. Wiley. Reallocating resources might mean the difference between life and death for them, but there was just no way to know. Keeping resources from other cases, however, made those exponentially more challenging to solve, and might lead to things falling through the cracks. In her position, she couldn't allow that. Personally, she couldn't allow it.

She had to make the tough call.

This was a higher-pressure scenario than she'd been used to at the NYPD, despite her FBI title and duties being essentially the same. While running a forensics lab at the NYPD certainly had its challenges, rarely did someone's life depend directly on whether she and her people could quickly uncover key evidence. In most cases, in fact, she was working to solve cases in which the victim was already dead. There was always a time pressure, as Detectives worked to catch the bad guys before they disappeared and took any evidence with them. But this was different. Having two lives depend on her findings was a force multiplier.

Her first instinct was to throw everything she had at this, to solve it with volume and brute force. But there were other crimes to solve, other bad guys to bring to justice, and other victims to avenge. She had to be a leader in this. She had to be smart.

Still, the work had to be done, and her resources were finite. That meant she was taking on more of the work herself.

She decided to approach it strategically.

Since her team was still sifting through everything in search of new clues, Ludlum decided to go back to the evidence they'd already uncovered. She was scrutinizing everything now—double-, triple-, even quadruple-checking previous findings and assertions. She had new notes from Dan Kotler and Agent Denzel that might give some additional light to the situation, and she was reconsidering her analysis with these in mind.

It was tedious. But it was ...

Well, honestly, it was bringing no results whatsoever.

She leaned back and rubbed her eyes with the palms of her hands. She stretched and felt a series of pops in her back and her neck. She was tense. Her muscles sore. She could use some exercise—a few rounds of kickboxing would help. But she barely had the time to go to the restroom.

Still, she knew better than most that revelations and insights usually came in moments of relaxation and activity and distraction. Intensive focus had its place, but sometimes you had to disengage and do something else, to give your brain something else to think about and let new ideas present themselves. There was such a thing as thinking too hard about a problem.

She stood, stretched, and made her way to her locker.

The building had a gym, and it was one of the best that Ludlum had ever used. She grabbed her gym bag and took the elevator down to the workout facility. A quick change, and in moments she was on a treadmill, jogging, focusing on her breathing and form.

Yoga might have been more relaxing, but Ludlum felt some pent-up energy that she needed to burn. Running felt more active and helped bleed off some aggression. Besides, the rhythmic pounding of her feet on the treadmill became hypnotic after a time, making it easier to let her mind wander.

She had run nearly ten miles, according to the treadmill's display, when some of the disparate details of the case started to snap together at random. Some rogue idea dismissed earlier for being implausible, suddenly became significant, after considering Dr. Kotler's notes. Something clicked.

It hit her all at once—she'd been overlooking something. There was a detail that nagged at her, and she'd only now connected the dots.

She stopped the treadmill and paused only long enough to

grab a towel from a set of shelves by the door, wiping sweat from her face and neck as she sprinted to the elevator and rode impatiently back to the Historic Crimes level. The instant the doors opened she sprang forward, quickly navigating the rows of cubicles, intent on reaching her lab.

She got a few quick glances from co-workers as she sprinted through the bullpen. She was wearing tight-fitting workout togs, spandex that stretched over and clung to her curves, and a tank top that revealed her arms, shoulders, and midriff. Not exactly office-appropriate attire, but she was in a hurry. And, to their credit, her co-workers glanced up and then quickly pretended not to notice.

Ludlum burst into her lab and went directly to the manuscript, pulling on gloves and one of the clean suits. She wasn't worried about contamination at this point, but the suit covered her workout clothes—a veneer of modesty that was more for her psychological benefit than the result of protocol. The gloves, however, were always required.

She opened the evidence bag and placed the manuscript on one of the examination tables. She glanced around and spotted a magnifying glass and held this over the manuscript as she turned to the first page.

By this time she'd looked as closely at this thing as she could, using every bit of modern scanning technology at her disposal. There hadn't been much to uncover.

Fingerprints and DNA had proven fruitless. Chemical analysis of the paper, the ink, the graphite of the handwritten message—all had led them in circles for days.

They'd tracked down the typewriter manufacturer, which was a dead end. They had records going back nearly a hundred years, but nothing that would help. The place was practically a museum these days, staying afloat via the collector's market and tourism.

One of Ludlum's staff had managed to date the ink on the

pages to get the age of the manuscript to within a couple of months in a specific year. This was interesting but also proved useless.

There just wasn't much to learn from the components of the thing. They'd analyzed and scrutinized it almost to its atoms and found little to nothing.

What they hadn't done, however, was examine the text itself.

Not the content. Kotler was looking deeper into that, and so far hadn't found anything that might relate directly to the case. His notes were a shorthand version of Daniel Kotler's theories, outlining how the Heisenberg principle might be applied to cryptology. Intriguing. Interesting. But irrelevant, as far as Ludlum could determine.

What Ludlum was looking at now, however, was the physical lettering—the typeface, or what some might call the font, though that wasn't precisely the right term. From a practical and literal perspective, Ludlum was forcing herself to think of the type on the page not as letters, with inherent meanings, but merely as marks that might indicate some hidden data she could uncover. She was looking at them the way she'd look at a DNA sequence or an assembly of bones or blood spatter. She was looking for patterns.

She was seeing anomalies.

The typeface used was fairly standard. A typical serif font, not dissimilar to that used by any other typewriter from the era. It was unremarkable, for its time.

Except there were tiny differences from one instance of a character to another. Small, almost unnoticeable, and only evident once Ludlum started looking at it under magnification. A missing serif here, a slanted character there. Small. Discreet. Very hard to spot.

Unless you were looking for it.

She turned to her lab computer and brought up the scans of the manuscript, then enlarged them onscreen.

The first page—the title page—had no noticeable aberrations. But the first interior page had dozens.

She started highlighting these onscreen, marking them on a separate layer from the scans. It took time, and she often had to double-check, to make sure what she was seeing was real and not some trick her mind was playing. It was tedious work, but unlike the previous tedium, it was producing measurable results. Something was there.

When she finally sat back and looked at what she'd uncovered, she held her breath for a moment and then let it out in a burst.

There was a pattern. There was definitely a pattern.

In fact, now that she was aware of Kotler's discovery, that the strange keyboard they'd found at the vault was employing the Baconian Cipher, the pattern in the manuscript leapt out at her as obvious. There was no question.

She was no expert in Baconian Ciphers, not by miles, but she'd looked into them after reading Kotler's report. They made sense, once she knew the pattern. Not all that dissimilar to looking at DNA notations, written out with the Roman characters G, C, A, and T to represent the different nucleotides. Knowing the nomenclature, the symbols and their meaning, she could determine the sequence, and decipher it.

In a sense, Ludlum herself was a codebreaker. Her job was to spot patterns, or occasionally a break in a pattern, and decode what she saw into a language that others would understand. She could interpret the pattern of blood spatter, could identify a male or female by certain bones, and could determine whether a bullet was fired from a specific gun using striations and rifling marks found on the slug. Code, embedded in the world around her, deciphered into its core meaning. She did this regularly, and she was very good at it.

It wasn't much of a stretch to apply her skills to recognizing and even deciphering a Baconian Cipher. It was also easier to identify the cipher when she saw it. And she was seeing it now, spread like measles in the pages of Dr. Daniel F. Kotler's manuscript, contaminating every page.

The door to her lab opened, and she looked up to see one of the agents from the bullpen. "Just got word. Agent Denzel and Dr. Kotler were involved in a shootout, just down the block."

Shootout? Ludlum felt herself go cold. "Are they ... were they hurt?"

"Negative," the agent replied. "Police are on the way to the scene, and some of us are going to meet them there. Can you spare anyone to tag along?"

She almost volunteered herself but thought better of it. She needed to log what she'd just discovered and didn't want to risk losing any details. She also had a well-qualified team who could handle this, and she needed to trust them to do their jobs, too. She called one of her staff and gave them instructions.

The agent in the door nodded and left her to her work.

She sat for a moment, feeling a strange sort of panic. It was unreasonable, she knew. Kotler was alright. So was Agent Denzel. They were both fine. But for some reason she still wanted to sprint from her lab and run to wherever Kotler was, to see for herself.

She took a breath and turned back to her work. She wrote a report, detailing what she'd found. She saved it to her folder on the FBI's database and sent an email to Agent Denzel.

It had taken half an hour, and she'd felt like jumping out of her own skin for all that time. But it was the right thing to do. It was the job.

She suddenly remembered that she was dressed in gym clothes and a contamination suit, and that her regular clothes and her bag were still in the gym.

She'd left it all behind as she'd rushed to check on her hunch.

Ludlum made her way to the elevator and rode down to the workout room.

Her bag was still where she'd left it, near the treadmill. She snagged it and went into the changing room, giving herself a quick wash from the sink and toweling herself off before getting dressed. She checked the mirror, toyed with reapplying some makeup, and decided she had bigger and better things to worry about. She needed to get back to the lab. Maybe she could get an update on Kotler and Denzel.

She exited the changing room and slammed into someone who was standing in the doorway.

"Oh!" She said. "I'm sorry, I ... this is the ladies changing room," she said, suddenly realizing the figure in front of her was male.

The man, tall and broad, looked down at her and nodded. He was wearing a balaclava, obscuring his face. "Dr. Liz Ludlum," he said.

Ludlum felt the panic suddenly return, too late to do her any good.

7

CAFÉ, NEAR FBI HEADQUARTERS

Extricating themselves from the scene at the café took far longer than Kotler had patience for. Denzel's subordinate agents showed up first and did an admirable job of taking charge of the scene. Witnesses were questioned and then directed to incoming medical personnel. The sidewalk outside of the café was cordoned off, along with part of the street, and agents were directing foot traffic away from the area. The police arrived quickly and took over, and the FBI agents mostly dispersed, returning to headquarters.

Denzel met with the NYPD Detective who was taking over the case, gave his testimony, and offered his card. Kotler was questioned along with every other patron of the café, though he was hoping Denzel would have helped to arrange for some special treatment, to speed things along.

There was just too much happening.

Finally, Kotler was dismissed. He joined Denzel as they walked back to the FBI building.

Kotler took the cylinder out of his coat pocket.

"Kotler," Denzel said, his voice stern and a frown creasing his face. "Why do you have evidence from a crime scene in your pocket?"

"It was a gift," Kotler said, smirking.

"Kotler ..."

"If we hand this over, I can't examine it. We have two men trapped in a vault with only a couple of days of air left. We don't have time to go through protocol on this one." He paused, glancing at his partner. "Do we?"

Denzel had turned to look straight ahead. His expression was still stern, but he wasn't arguing. "What is it?" he asked, his voice tight.

Kotler shook his head. "I haven't had much chance to examine it, but I'm pretty sure it was meant for me."

"Why?" Denzel asked.

"Because it has my name on it," Kotler replied. He held the cylinder up to reveal a series of characters etched into it in rows from end to end, encircling the entire artifact like horizontal stripes. The characters were Roman, both alphabetic and numeric. But they were complete gibberish, forming no words that Kotler could recognize.

Except for the six characters that ran in a line at what Kotler now thought of as the "top" of the cylinder.

K-O-T-L-E-R

He showed this to Denzel.

"Ok," Denzel nodded, eyeing the cylinder as they walked. "I'll give you that. So what does it mean?"

"I think it's a cipher key." He thought for a moment, the brisk walk helping him think. "I'm not sure what it is, exactly, but it seems familiar. When we're back, I'll see if I can find anything that matches."

Denzel was quiet for a moment, but as they entered the FBI

headquarters and showed their IDs, he said, "I'm not happy with you taking evidence from a crime scene."

"I understand," Kotler said, nodding solemnly.

They rode the elevator to the Historic Crimes level, and as the doors opened, they were greeted by a bustle of activity.

"Agent Denzel!" one of the agents called. "We have a situation!"

KOTLER STOOD over Ludlum's gym bag, which had a small, plastic evidence marker on top of it. Another marker sat near the blood.

Agents, many of whom were from Ludlum's own team, were moving all over the gym, taking swabs and prints from the door handles, the equipment, and anything else they could find.

Kotler was wearing a pair of disposable shoe covers and had pulled on a pair of blue rubber gloves. He had been told to stay out of the way, but now that they'd covered the women's changing room, he was allowed to wander in. He didn't know what he was looking for. He felt somehow numb.

"Kotler," Denzel said quietly.

Kotler turned, a bit of life returning to his expression as he raised his eyebrows, hoping.

There was a subtle shake of Denzel's head. "We have footage from the hall and from the gym. A few angles. He took out the cameras in the stairwell just before coming in here. He knew what he was doing."

"What do the other cameras show?" Kotler asked.

"He'd managed to get into the building through the mailroom, in the basement. We have him breaking open a door with a pry bar. He was actually able to make his way to the Historic Crimes level, through the stairwell."

"That easy," Kotler said quietly.

Denzel shook his head. "Not easy. Not exactly. But he used the shootout at the café for cover. He knew about it."

"So we were a distraction?" Kotler asked.

Denzel shrugged. "I can't say for sure, but it seems like it. He made it to our floor, and when Liz took the elevator back down, he took the stairs. He was smart. He'd figured out where she was going and went right to her."

"Smart," Kotler sneered. Everyone was smart. Everyone had things figured out. And once again Kotler was the focus of some game, targeted by someone smart enough and bold enough to be able to get to him and the people he cared about, even here.

Whoever this guy was, he had resources. He'd just nabbed an agent right out of FBI headquarters. It shouldn't have been possible, but there it was.

"Got this, around the time Liz was grabbed," Denzel said, handing over his phone.

Kotler read the email. A short message, only a single line. But there was no mistaking what it meant.

We have her. You have 24 hours.

"Tech guys are tracing it to see what they can find but ..."

"Let me guess," Kotler said bitterly, "it's been bounced through half a dozen VPNs, sent from a throwaway account that was probably stolen from someone else. And there's no way to know who sent it or from where."

"That about sums it up," Denzel nodded. "Kotler, listen ... we'll get her back. I swear we will. She'll be safe."

Kotler looked up at his partner and saw the same frustration, the same anger, the same fear and worry that Kotler himself was feeling. He huffed and shook his head. "It's a goad. They're prodding me."

"I think so too," Denzel said.

Kotler held up the cylinder. "This is a message."

"Then let's solve it."

Kotler nodded, and the two of them left the gym, riding the elevator up to the Historic Crimes floor. Kotler was out of the elevator as soon as the doors were open, and Denzel followed on his heels. The two of them ended up in Ludlum's lab. Kotler lay the cylinder on an exam table, and opened one of the lab's laptops, starting a search.

"What are you looking for?"

"Google," Kotler said. "Six-character cipher. I recognize this. I've seen it before, in the research."

A moment later he turned the laptop for Denzel to see. "ADFGVX," Kotler said.

"Err ... is that supposed to mean anything to me?"

"It's the name of this cipher," Kotler said, gesturing to the cylinder. "Those letters are distinct from each other, in Morse Code. So they're used as part of a binary cipher that relies on a randomized grid of thirty-six characters."

"Ok ..."

"Thirty-six, because there are twenty-six Roman characters in the alphabet, plus ten digits from zero to nine. Together these form a six-by-six grid, with ADFGVX at the top of each column and to the left of each row."

Denzel shook his head. "I'm trying to follow, but I'm not getting it."

Kotler turned the laptop back and started typing, frequently referencing the cylinder as he went. A few minutes later he showed the result to Denzel.

	K	O	T	L	E	R
	A	D	F	G	V	X
A	O	P	1	R	Y	2
D	D	U	I	C	S	J
F	5	N	3	W	7	8
G	E	6	B	F	K	M
V	V	Z	0	9	X	R
X	H	Q	G	T	L	A

Denzel studied the chart. "So what am I looking at, exactly?"

"This is the key for an ADFGVX cipher. I pulled the grid from the rows of characters on the cylinder. I added the ADFGVX headers, top and left." He pointed to the characters at the top and left of the grid, running his finger along them for Denzel to see.

"This type of cipher dates back to World War I, invented by Colonel Fritz Nebel of the German Army. Basically, there's a six-by-six grid of randomized characters, and with the headers on the top and left of the grid you get a binary address for each letter of the alphabet and each number from zero to nine."

Denzel looked at it, and Kotler saw his features light up with recognition. "Ok," he said. "Ok, I see what you're saying. So the letter O would be AA. The number 1 would be AF."

"Right," Kotler said.

"What part does your name play in this?"

Kotler shook his head. "It's a way to address this to me, but it's also a key. This cipher is easy to crack if you keep it in this sequential order. But it becomes a lot tougher when you transpose characters, scrambling them so that anyone trying to crack this will not only have to decipher each character but will have to rearrange what they find into actual words. Add to this the fact that these codes were originally written in German and there are all sorts of challenges."

"But whoever sent this gave you the key," Denzel said.

Kotler nodded. "And I don't know why, unless the goal is to speed things up. But there's a problem."

"More problems?" Denzel asked.

"We have a key, but we don't have a lock."

Denzel considered this and nodded. "Where's the coded message we're meant to unscramble?"

"Exactly," Kotler said. "It's likely that the message will be in this binary format, repeating the characters ADFGVX over again and again. But we haven't seen a pattern like that. We haven't gotten an encoded message."

Denzel quickly raised a hand to his eyes. "We have, actually."

He tapped his phone and handed it to Kotler. "Liz sent that email just before she was abducted. I gave it a look, and I was going to tell you about it, but all of this happened." He gestured to the laptop Kotler was using.

Kotler read through the email, his eyes wide. "She's brilliant," he said.

"So there's something in that manuscript," Denzel said.

"Something I overlooked," Kotler said, mournful.

"But we have it now. Is it connected?"

Kotler opened a PDF of scans that Ludlum had included, noting the highlighted markings. She had gone to the trouble of translating a few of the pages, and the results were encouraging.

"She thought it might just be gibberish," Denzel said. "But it looks like what you're describing."

Kotler agreed. The translations came to long strings of characters, alternating between A, D, F, G, V, and X.

The manuscript contained a code within a code.

Kotler opened a browser tab and did a quick search.

"Now what are you doing?" Denzel asked.

"This cipher has been around for a century. There are

hobbyists out there who know all about it, and I'm betting ..."
he tapped a few keys, then clicked on a link and smiled. Denzel
came around behind him and looked at the screen.

"What is it?" he asked.

"It's a java applet that someone created to decipher this
code. All I have to do is plug in all the variables, including the
keyword."

Kotler typed his own name into the keyword field, then in
another he entered the characters from the six-by-six grid, row
by row. In a final field, he typed the first set of scrambled characters from the manuscript.

The translation appeared instantly.

---

*Yardley's Black Room is secure. Perfect off-site storage for our
backups. All ciphers, references, and materials have been dupli-
cated and stored safely.*

It was a short message, but it had taken a couple of pages to
encode it. Kotler scrolled through the rest of the digitized
manuscript. "Liz marked all of the pages. She did it. She
cracked this. All we have to do is decode the rest and plug it
into this applet." Kotler huffed. "It's going to take hours to do
this manually."

"Let's get the tech guys on this," Denzel said. "Maybe there's
a way to speed this up."

Kotler nodded and stepped aside as Denzel called in their
specialists. In moments, both Kotler and Denzel found themselves superfluous, hanging out in the background as the tech
team attacked a century-old code with modern technology.

"Come on," Denzel said, motioning for Kotler to follow

"Where are we going? Shouldn't we wait here? For the team
to get this translated?"

"They can take care of it, and they'll send it to us when they're done. We need to see what else we can find regarding Liz's abduction."

Kotler considered this and followed without question.

8

THE YARDLEY OF LONDON BUILDING

Kotler hadn't yet seen the Black Chamber.

Technically, he still hadn't seen it, since it was currently locked behind a six-foot-thick steel door. But the space surrounding the vault was intriguing on its own.

The room was on the basement level of the Yardley building, and accessing it had meant winding through some maintenance tunnels, dodging protrusions of pipes and conduits and valves, passing miles of electrical cable and plumbing. It was no wonder the room had stood here undisturbed for so long. Generations of maintenance workers had been the only people to come down here on a regular basis, and they were likely told to leave it be.

It was a bustle down here now, though. There were engineers and agents hard at work on finding a way into the vault, and Kotler and Denzel were ushered in by two men guarding the door. The space was a sort of antechamber, Kotler observed. It looked a bit like the front room of a set of offices from a noir detective film. He could imagine a prim secretary seated at a large, oaken desk, answering phones and clattering away on an old typewriter.

The room had sparse furnishings—a table and a couple of wooden chairs, a desk lamp, a painting of an airship docking at the top of the Empire State building. All of this had been shoved against one wall, the painting hanging above the antechamber's debris like a yard sale sign.

Kotler knew that the idea was to change scenery and thus change perspective, to get his mind off of solving the code that might save Liz's life, and thus give him some chance of actually solving it. The ironic enigma of problem-solving.

It was kind of Denzel to think of it. But from Kotler's perspective, they were facing a nearly identical task here. Two men, both connected to Kotler, were locked in that vault, and could only be saved if someone figured out a century-old code to unlock six feet of steel.

Same problem, different view.

Kotler and Denzel were hanging back, letting the team do its work, and Kotler was feeling more useless by the minute. They were no less in the way here than they had been back in Ludlum's lab, but twice as useless.

But the new environment, the bustle of the agents and engineers, the visceral quality of the antechamber all managed to finally get Kotler thinking in new directions. And something occurred to him.

"We're approaching this in the wrong way," he said, after a long moment.

"How's that?" Denzel asked.

Kotler looked up at his partner. "We're trying to solve all the puzzles, assuming that if we do, we'll win this. But it isn't about that. Or, it isn't entirely about it. There's someone out there, pulling the strings on this. They're connected and powerful, we know that much. But what else do we know?"

Denzel regarded Kotler for a moment. "We need to know their motive."

"Right," Kotler said. "What's driving them to do this? It's pretty clear that they want me involved. So we can assume that whatever the motive, it involves me."

"Unless that's a distraction, too," Denzel said.

Kotler blinked. "You're right." He thought. "What would someone gain by getting me involved?"

"By giving you puzzles to solve," Denzel added.

Kotler nodded. "They clearly know me. Or know enough about me to realize I can be distracted by the codes and puzzles."

"They didn't come to you first, though," Denzel said.

Something sparked in Kotler's brain. "No, they didn't. They came to you."

"So ... what does that mean?" Denzel asked.

"I'm not sure yet. It's clear that this person is smart, that they calculated a lot of variables ahead of time. If I didn't know any better, I'd think ..."

He hesitated, as if saying her name might invoke her, bringing her into the room in a swirl of brimstone.

"Gail McCarthy," Denzel supplied, quietly.

Kotler nodded. "But she's dead. We know that."

"Someone in her organization?"

Kotler considered this. It was possible. Gail had been the protege of her grandfather's business partner, Richard Van Burren. After his death, Gail had seized control of a vast smuggling empire, possibly the most advanced in history. Since her death the law enforcement agencies of the world had been slowly dismantling the organization, taking it down in several successful operations. But it was possible that someone out there, some protege of Gail's, had eluded capture and was seeking revenge. It couldn't be ruled out.

But it didn't feel right.

"We don't have enough information," Kotler said, finally. "We can't know what's driving this person. Not yet."

"So we're back to solving the puzzles," Denzel muttered.

Kotler knew what his partner was feeling. Frustration. Anger. Whoever was behind this was running them like rats in a maze, and they had no choice but to keep looking for the cheese.

The activity in the room was fascinating to watch, and Kotler let his mind wander. He was intrigued by the approach that the engineers were taking with trying to bypass the security panel. He wandered over to get a closer look.

He recognized the keyboard from the photos he'd studied, but it was something else to see it in the real world. He knelt in front of it, leaning in and looking closely.

Each key had its set of five characters. An unusual sight, for sure. But the builder had kept the same QWERTY pattern as a standard typewriter. A touch typist could operate this without hesitation. That was probably for convenience.

Or was it something more?

What if the layout was kept to something familiar to compensate for some other variable?

The code that would unlock this was something of a password, similar to a computer password. Modern security software could encrypt a computer password, replacing characters with hashes—basically masking the character as it was accepted, to avoid prying eyes.

To anyone looking at this keyboard, the Baconian cipher would work as a hash, masking the actual characters. Unless someone was able to see and memorize the exact pattern of keystrokes, they'd have a tough time gleaning the passcode by observation.

Still, even back in the '20s, the security-minded people working for the American Black Chamber would be conscious enough to want to change the password regularly.

Having to remember a new password every month or every week would be challenging enough, even for trained cryptologists. But having to remember the pattern of a scrambled keyboard on top of that would add an unnecessary level of challenge. There was every indication that entering the wrong password might set off booby traps within the walls of the vault. A standardized keyboard would be a safety precaution.

There was no reason to believe that the password used when this room was still in service was the same password in use now. In fact, they knew that whoever was behind all of this had access to the vault. They'd known the original password, and it was likely they would change it.

All part of the game, Kotler thought.

"Roland," Kotler said over his shoulder. "What was the message you got? When you were told about the government-sealed room?"

Denzel took out his notepad and read the message aloud.

"To open the door, run the Stepping Maze. Your tools await in the room where it all started."

"So they knew that the manuscript was in there," Kotler said. "And they knew that there was a reference to the Stepping Maze on its cover. The same mechanism used in this device. Was there any sign that they'd been in that office?"

Denzel shook his head. "There were seals on the door that no one would be able to bypass without disturbing them. We went down that route, looking to find a way someone could have gotten in there, maybe planted that manuscript. But as far as we can tell it's been sealed in there for decades."

"There must be photos of it," Kotler muttered. "Documentation. Somehow they knew." He thought for a moment. "The cipher we found in the manuscript. It mentions the Black Chamber as a backup site. Whoever this is, they somehow found their way into the Black Chamber and discovered that manuscript exists."

Denzel frowned. "Seems likely," he said. "So what does that mean?"

"I'm still putting it together. But I think I know how to open this door."

Denzel stared at him for a moment. "What?"

Kotler looked at one of the engineers, who was probing a set of wires with a meter, tracing it to see if it could be bypassed safely. "Is there any danger of setting something off, if I get the passcode wrong?"

The engineer nodded. "Big danger, yes," he said. "There are explosives in the load-bearing walls. This whole building could come down on us. There's a trigger with three settings. Three tries. But someone set it to one."

"That's our best guess, yeah," the engineer said. "There are also seven step motors in this sequence. That means seven characters in the passcode. That's a lot of variables."

"One," Kotler repeated. "Meaning one try."

"One try, seven characters." Kotler huffed and looked up at Denzel. "I have this," he said.

"Kotler ..."

"Roland, I have it. I know what the passcode is."

Denzel studied him, then turned to one of the agents. "Clear the building," he said.

9

UNDISCLOSED LOCATION

Ludlum had been awake up until she'd been shoved into a metal box.

She'd fallen unconscious then and woke up to a shooting pain in her head and the feeling of something sticky between her cheek and the floor. Her hands and feet were bound, and she was gagged.

She knew she had a head injury. She assessed it the best she could, laying in the dark and unable to reach up and probe the wound. She'd blacked out, and she had a splitting headache, which might mean a concussion. The box was pitch dark, however, and she couldn't test her vision to see if it was blurry.

She was moving.

She felt the vibration of a vehicle rolling. The box she was in seemed relatively soundproof, and the best she could make out was the droning of an engine. She could feel and hear the shift in the transmission, the rumble of the vehicle as it carried her away from FBI headquarters.

A truck, then. Something large, probably commercial.

The information didn't help much, but she was glad for it

all the same. She kept a running tally of new data. It helped to assure her that she didn't have brain damage, that despite the pain in her head she was fine. For now.

This was bad. Going through all of it, running everything back and forth, examining the sequence of events, she came to the very solid conclusion that yes, this was bad.

Someone had somehow managed to snag her right out of the FBI offices. Granted, they'd gotten to her in one of the less secure sections of the building. But how brazen and resourceful would someone have to be to get into FBI headquarters and grab an agent?

This was a professional. There was nothing sloppy or ad hoc about the job, and that said a lot. Mostly it said she was in trouble, with very few options at the moment.

She wriggled, trying to see if she could get some leverage. She managed to get onto her side and feel around to find the binding on her feet. It felt like insulated wire. She ran her fingers over it, finding a complicated knot that would have made any Scout leader proud.

Her hands must be tied in a similar way, though she couldn't find the knot with her fingers. It must be on the back of her wrists.

She started working the knot at her feet, probing and pulling, tugging at anything that might give her a way to loosen it. She wasn't having much luck.

And then the truck stopped.

She froze, waiting for the inevitable.

After a long moment she heard metal on metal, like a door swinging open, and several minutes later the top of the box was lifted. She blinked into the light that poured in.

The man—large, muscular, and still wearing the balaclava —casually reach into the box and picked her up, almost one-handed. He slung her over his shoulder and carried her out of the truck, down a slanted loading ramp.

She made no move to struggle. She would have pretended to be unconscious if she hadn't already blinked up at him from confinement. At this point, she couldn't see any benefit to wriggling free. Her hands and feet were bound up tight, and the best she could achieve would be falling to the hard, cement floor, risking further injury.

She had to let this play out.

She focused on breathing. She had to get her heart rate and adrenaline under control. At the moment, she was furious to the point of chewing through the gag in her mouth, but that wouldn't do her any good. She had to keep cool. She needed her mind clear so she could plan. Save the adrenaline in case she had to fight.

It was just the indignity of all of this.

This man had grabbed her, slammed her head against the frame of the door in the women's changing room, and carried her out as if she were a sack of laundry. He was strong. He was calm. He was in control. And that really pissed her off.

But she'd wait. She'd see what happened next, and she'd keep a clear head.

They were parked in what looked like an abandoned construction site, under a metal cover rooted to a concrete pad. Gravel crunched under the man's feet as he stepped off of the pad and carried her to a trailer, far back from where he'd parked.

Here, amid the detritus and construction equipment of a build site, the trailer was practically invisible. The sounds of the area—boats in the nearby river, vehicles speeding by on an unseen street, construction equipment operating nearby, loud music, the sounds of city life—the white noise of it all would further camouflage this place. She couldn't call for help with any hope of being heard, even if she managed to remove the gag.

Inside the trailer, the man dropped her to the floor, leaving her in one corner as he stepped back out, shutting and locking the door behind him.

That was it. No explanations. No provisions. Nothing to indicate that she would ever be released from this place. She was still bound and gagged and was now locked in a work trailer located God knew where.

Ludlum was calm but still furious. She knew that the odds favored her dying here.

She intended to beat those odds.

10

YARDLEY OF LONDON BUILDING

Every soul had been evacuated from the Yardley of London building, as well as its neighboring buildings, and the streets had been cordoned off for three blocks in all directions.

No pressure, Kotler thought as he stood in front of the antique keyboard.

"Kotler," Denzel said.

"Roland, maybe you should leave? I mean, if I get this wrong ..."

"If you get this wrong this building comes down on both of us and the two men inside this vault. Believe me, it's a better fate than having to stand in front of the Director and an IA team, explaining why I let you do this."

"Won't you have to do that anyway?" Kotler grinned.

Denzel shrugged. "I end up doing it about twice a month these days, and it always goes better when we have a check in the win column."

Kotler nodded. He knew, of course, that Denzel was sticking around out of solidarity and support. He knew, also, that this might backfire on them even if he was right about the passcode.

Time was running out all around, though. The two men inside the vault had less than two days left. Liz had less than one. There were too many codes to break and too many mysteries to solve, and hesitation was a luxury they could no longer afford.

It was time to stop playing it safe.

Kotler puffed his cheeks and shook his hands like a safe-cracker. "Ok then," he said. "Let's get crackin'."

Denzel groaned. "Try not to enjoy this, Kotler."

Kotler chuckled and stepped up to the keyboard, placing his fingers on the home row, inhaling and exhaling once, twice, three times.

He struck the first key—*AABAB*.

He paused, cringing, waiting for the ceiling to cave in. When nothing happened, he struck the next five characters with paced, firm strikes.

AAAAA-BAAAB-AAAAA-AAABB- AAAAA

He stopped, looking up at Denzel. "This is it," he said. "So far, so good. But this is the last character. If I'm right, we're in. If not ..."

"It's been good knowing you, Kotler," Denzel said.

"You too, Roland."

Kotler looked back to the keyboard, took a final breath, and struck the last key—*BBAAA*.

RED LEANED against the aging Chevy pickup, hands shoved into the pockets of his jacket. It was overcast, but occasional breaks in the clouds let rays of sunshine through. The air was crisp, but not overly cold. It was a good day.

He watched through the chain link fence as a motorcycle

slowed and turned into the lot, winding among shipping containers, disappearing briefly and then reappearing as its rider pulled to a stop, taking off the helmet that concealed his features.

Cameron rolled his neck and shoulders and smiled at his brother.

"Done?" Red asked.

Cameron nodded. "I sold it to a Mexican operating out of Jersey. He's taking it South. It'll be in Oklahoma by morning."

"Good," Red said. "And you cleaned it?"

Cameron smiled. "I did everything you taught me, relax."

With the van disposed of there was little evidence that might lead the FBI to where Red had left the woman. The site itself was closed, a lack of funding keeping the project from going forward. Though the owner, one of Red's clients, had his own reasons for keeping the site closed indefinitely.

It would be a good spot to keep her, for now. Depending on how long the current client needed her out of play, plans could change rapidly. Red suspected that Dr. Ludlum might have peered through her last microscope, but he would wait until he was given further instructions.

His brother climbed off of the motorcycle—a classic Indian that Cameron had taken great pride in restoring. It was an expensive hobby. But worse, it was indiscreet. It was a very noticeable bike.

Still, Red liked seeing his brother happy. The risk was slight. And Cameron was smart. He had common sense, unlike their youngest brother. He would be cautious.

"What now?" Cameron asked. "Any word from the client?"

"Only that we should wait," Red said. "Dr. Kotler and Agent Denzel have the cylinder. I'm told to expect him to make rapid progress from here."

"What's the story with him?" Cameron asked. "He's some kind of history buff?"

"An anthropologist," Red said. "He's famous, in his way. Archeology. He goes to sites all over the world, finds artifacts and treasures, and he writes and speaks about his experiences. You can watch some of his speeches on YouTube. Very interesting."

"And now he's an FBI agent?" Cameron asked.

"His work with the FBI is consulting," Red replied. "He's been doing this for the past couple of years, using his expertise in anthropology to help the FBI solve cases with roots in history. All of this is in the dossier, brother. You should read it."

Cameron nodded. "Uh huh," he said.

Red smiled. His younger brother was not patient. He tried. He had improved a great deal since Red had taken him on as a protege. But he was young, impetuous. He hadn't seen the sorts of things that Red had seen. The wars, the action, the results of missions that went off the rails. Red had been forced to overcome his youthful drive for action and adventure, and to learn patience, timing, precision. Cameron would learn these things as well. He knew the consequences of slipping. So far, he had avoided significant mistakes.

Which did not mean that his execution didn't need some work.

"Your delivery today, at the café ..." Red started, pausing to see and gauge his brother's reaction.

Cameron smiled. "A good distraction, just as you asked. Two birds with one stone."

Red nodded. "It allowed me to get into the building. It was good work. It wasn't the plan, however. You were supposed to deliver the cylinder to the FBI building in a package addressed to Agent Denzel. You risked it being seized as evidence when you threw it into the café. If Dr. Kotler hadn't hidden it away, it would be in the hands of the police. There might have been a significant delay to the plan."

Cameron started to say something, to argue and defend himself. He caught the look in Red's eyes and stopped.

This was the condition.

Red had allowed Cameron to join him in this business, but there were rules. One rule governed all others: Cameron would never argue when corrected.

Mistakes, Red knew, would be made. It would take time for Cameron to overcome his nature. It had taken Red, himself, years to get past being impulsive and impatient.

Red would break his brother if he got too far out of line, but it was better if Cameron learned these lessons on his own, as Red had. They would last longer, have deeper roots. If Cameron could make sense of things on his own, it would make him far better at this. Autonomy was valuable, but discipline was even more so.

There could never be any argument. Red's correction was law. An absolute that Cameron could not dispute.

Or there would be consequences.

Cameron paused, took a breath, nodded. "You're right. I went off of the plan."

Red studied him, then finally smiled lightly, cuffing Cameron's shoulder. "I understand. You know that I want you to be autonomous, to think for yourself. It's the only way this can work. You have to be free to adjust the plan as needed. Sometimes it is necessary to throw the plan away and act on your best judgment. Tell me, brother, was this one of those times? Answer honestly."

Cameron said nothing for a moment but ultimately shook his head. "No. I risked the operation with this change."

Red smiled at his brother. The maturity was there. The inner strength that Cameron would need, to keep to this, to do this work. He was very proud of him. The lessons, the training, all of it was paying off.

Red took his other hand from his pocket. He was gripping a

set of brass knuckles, the fingers of his left hand laced through them.

With a quick pulse of his arm, Red punched Cameron in the jaw, knocking his brother back.

Dazed, Cameron stumbled but kept his balance, then stood upright again, swaying slightly.

"Step up," Red said.

Cameron's eyes were wide, a bit dazed, but he stepped forward, waiting.

Once again Red punched his brother, this time in the solar plexus, knocking the wind from him and driving Cameron to his knees.

"The third," Red said.

Cameron coughed and wheezed but managed to get to his feet and stand in front of his brother.

Red once again struck, this time at Cameron's side, bruising his ribs.

Cameron grunted, but stood again, swaying but upright, looking at his brother with a neutral expression.

"Three strikes, as we agreed," Red said.

Cameron nodded. "Thank you for using your left hand."

Red shook his head. "You were doing what you thought was right. You made a mistake, but it cost us nothing, in the end." He dropped the brass knuckles back into his coat pocket and peeled the gloves away from his hands. He reached up, holding Cameron's face, turning it to look at the welt that was rising on his jaw. "A bruise. A couple of days," he slapped Cameron's opposite cheek, lovingly. "Same with your ribs. You may be a bit uncomfortable for a time."

"I'll live," Cameron said, smiling.

Red laughed. "You will," he said, and kissed his brother on the forehead.

"Now we wait. I want you to go to the construction site. The woman is in the survey trailer. It's locked tight, and her hands and feet are bound with 18-gauge electrical wire. It's unlikely she'll be able to get free, but I want you to watch, just in case. Keep anyone from coming around, of course."

Cameron nodded. "What about you? Any orders from the client?"

Red shook his head. "No, not yet. I'll let you know if anything else comes up. But for now, I'm going to the movies."

Cameron laughed. "You and your movies."

"There is a new one, with superheroes. I like superheroes. They're colorful."

"Enjoy, brother," Cameron said as he climbed back on the Indian, gingerly, a hand to his ribs. He pulled on his helmet slowly as well. The Indian's engine started with a loud rumble, and in a moment, Cameron was speeding away toward the construction site.

Red watched him go and shook his head. He was a good kid. He learned fast, and he was dedicated. He would have to overcome this unfortunate tendency to act without thinking, preferably before it got him killed. Red would continue to mold him.

The alternative would be sad, but Red would not hesitate. Everything he'd built was too important to allow it to crumble due to youthful impetuousness. Cameron would learn, or he'd have to be dealt with.

For now, he was a good kid, and he was doing fine work. His mistakes, for the moment, were forgivable.

Red climbed into the Chevy and drove to a movie theater a few blocks away. He parked the rusted pickup in a lot near the theater and walked the rest of the way. He'd bought it for cash, had never bothered to register it, and had only used it a few times. Red no longer needed it and would arrange for a car to take him home after the movie.

Inside the theater, he bought popcorn and a soda large enough to drown in and then found his seat. For the next two hours, he enjoyed the spectacle of super-powered fistfights, high-charged action, and buildings exploding and crumbling to ruin as the heroes made last-minute escapes.

Typical stuff. The kind of thing an audience expected. But no less fun to watch. And Red enjoyed every minute of the suspense.

11

BLACK CHAMBER, MANHATTAN

Leo and Bob were huddled together on one of the bunks. Leo scratched absently at his cheek, where a scruff of gray was starting to blossom into a full-on beard. They had no real toiletries, no way to shave. They'd kept themselves relatively clean with monkey-baths in the kitchenette sink. And thank God there was a toilet. Toilet paper, on the other hand—well, thank God there were also reams and reams of newspapers and other documents.

It might be a blow to archival history, but they were doing what they had to do.

Food was getting short. By Bob's estimate, they might be able to ration and have food for another week. Leo had agreed. But the two of them had kept silent about the real problem they faced.

They had measured the room, as best they could. Close enough to figure its volume, which gave them a way to estimate how much air was in the vault.

It wasn't good news.

Best case scenario, if they stopped using the stove to cook

food and kept themselves relatively still, without talking, they could make the air last another couple of days. Best case.

Worst case, they'd already burned through at least a day's worth of air before realizing their real predicament. It might be too late.

Now they sat, silent and staring at the floor, each sipping cold broth from coffee mugs. Waiting. Waiting for rescue. Waiting to die. Waiting to know which side of the coin was going to land facing up.

Leo didn't want to die here. But what choice did he really have in it all? The choice had been taken from him, and from Bob. And although he'd never considered Bob much of a friend, he found himself glad for the man's company, here at what could be the end. They had their differences, but they also had their similarities. Those similarities may have been the sole reason that Leo found Bob so annoying. But they were past that now.

Death, it seemed, was the best therapy for making two people forget their grievances and bond with each other.

Leo had just taken another sip from his mug when there was a very loud, echoing click from somewhere in the vault. It resonated through the room, echoing from the steel walls. It was a hollow, final sound.

Leo and Bob looked at each other. Could this be it? Was this some final call?

There was another sound. Familiar. The ratcheting of a wheel being turned. The locking mechanism from the door.

Leo and Bob stood, hesitated only a moment, and together they rushed forward, shedding blankets and dropping coffee mugs on the cot. They sprinted past the desks and chairs, the wind from their passage blowing over the playing card tower they'd built and causing loose pages to flit from desktops.

The cards fluttered around their feet like Fall leaves as they stopped in front of the vault door, each swaying a bit, unsteady. They stared, jaws slack. They watched.

The door creaked and opened slowly, and two men were revealed as a shaft of light from the vault fell on their faces.

Leo recognized one of them.

"Mr. Kotler?" he asked.

"Dan?" Bob added.

"Professors," Kotler smiled at them. "You're safe. Let's get you out of here."

PARAMEDICS TENDED to the two professors as Kotler and Denzel hovered close by. They approached the moment the two professors were cleared.

"Dr. Marvin, Dr. Wiley," Denzel said.

They'd been given cups of coffee and had blankets draped over their shoulders as they sat on the bumper of the ambulance. Dr. Wiley nodded and said, "Agent ...?"

"Denzel," he showed his FBI badge.

"Agent Denzel," Wiley said. "Thank you for rescuing us. It was looking pretty grim in there."

"Dr. Kotler was the one who figured out how to get you out of there," Denzel said, nodding to Kotler.

"I see," Wiley said, smiling. "Dan Kotler. It's been a while. Thank you."

"Yes," Dr. Marvin added. "Thank you, Dan. We owe you our lives."

Kotler stood with his hands in his pockets, chin nearly to his chest. "I appreciate it, and I'm very relieved you're both safe. But I think I owe both of you an apology. Whoever did this ..." he gestured vaguely to the Yardley building. "They meant it as some sort of message for me. I'm responsible for the two of you being in there."

Marvin and Wiley glanced at each other, and it was Marvin who responded. "Dan, whoever did this, that's who is responsible." He turned to Denzel. "Do you have any idea who it is?"

Denzel shook his head. "No, but I'd like to ask the two of you some questions, if you're up for it."

"Please do," Wiley said, actually smiling.

"Wait," Marvin said, his expression becoming worried. "My family ... my wife?"

"Your families are both fine," Denzel said reassuringly. "We had them moved to a safe house as soon as we knew what was happening. They know you're safe. We'll take the two you there after you've been cleared by a doctor."

Marvin nodded, accepting this.

"Ask whatever you like," Wiley said.

Denzel started probing, asking questions about what they'd been doing before being kidnapped, who they might have been in contact with, and whether they'd heard or seen anything that might be useful.

Kotler listened for a while but stood back after a time. He was watching the crowds—hundreds of New York citizens and dozens of reporters and news crews had gathered at the barricades. This was the second big event of the morning, involving the same two people, and it wasn't escaping notice. The press was hot on the story, shouting questions and taking photographs. Kotler's face would be in the papers once again. There would be snooping and intrusions.

He took his phone out of his pocket and called his apartment building.

Ernie, the building's doorman, answered, and after a quick greeting Kotler asked, "Has anyone come around, asking for me?"

"No sir," Ernie replied. "Not for some time."

"Some time?" Kotler asked. "When was someone there last?"

There was a pause from the other end of the line, as Ernie either thought it through or checked some record. "About a month ago, I think. You were out of town, still in Egypt I believe. You sure have some adventures, Dr. Kotler! But someone came by to visit. A man. Older gentleman. He didn't leave a name but asked if I knew when you were expected back."

Kotler thought about this, considering.

"I apologize, Dr. Kotler. I should have told you. It slipped my mind."

Kotler smiled. "No, Ernie, it's fine. I appreciate you letting me know. I expect that there will be reporters coming by over the next few days. I wanted you to know that I haven't given anyone permission to come up. And I may stay elsewhere for a week or two."

"Should I tell anyone where you are?" Ernie asked.

"You can say I'm out of town. Let them guess all they like." He paused for a moment. "There's video surveillance on the lobby, isn't there?"

"Yes sir," Ernie replied.

"If I sent an FBI agent over, would you be able to find the footage of the man who came looking for me?"

"I sure can, Dr. Kotler. I'm supposed to ask for a warrant, but since you're giving permission, I think I can fudge it."

Kotler smiled and thanked him, then hung up.

He turned just as Denzel was approaching. "I don't think we're getting anything useful from the good doctors," he said.

"I may have another lead," Kotler said, explaining about the man at his building.

"I'll send someone over to get the footage. You think it might be our mystery figure?" Denzel asked.

"I'll take any lead I can get right now. We're burning through our 24 hours."

"You think that's still in play? You got those men out of the

Black Chamber. Wasn't that what our mystery figure was aiming for?"

Kotler shook his head. "At first I thought this was about getting into the Black Chamber, but it's pretty clear this is about something else."

"Any ideas about what?" Denzel asked.

"I'm working on it."

Denzel thought for a moment. "What was it?" he asked.

"What was what?"

Denzel glanced back at the Yardley building and said, "The passcode. You were so sure you knew it, and you were right. What was it?"

Kotler smiled. "It was right in front of us, but when the engineer said it was a seven-character word I knew I had it."

"And it was?"

"Faraday," Kotler grinned. "My great grandfather's middle name."

12

SURVEY TRAILER

Ludlum struggled for hours and finally made some progress on the knot of wire binding her feet.

It had come at a cost.

Her fingers were sore and bleeding, cut and blistered from the activity of feeling, twisting, pulling, over and again. Her shoulders ached, and her back was cramped and sore. She hurt all over, but she couldn't give up.

Another tug and twist, more pain, but something different finally happened. The wire loosened, the knot released, and she was able to free her feet.

She rolled into a sitting position, stretching her legs and rolling her ankles with relief. She also stretched her neck from side to side, trying to release some of the tension. It felt good, but she only allowed herself a moment.

With her feet free she at least had a bit of mobility. It was the first step, and there was still more work to do.

She braced her feet on the floor, her back pressed against the wall of the trailer, and then pushed herself into a standing position.

So far so good.

Now able to move, she started exploring the trailer, looking for anything that might help.

There was a desk and a couple of tables, some chairs, and scattered piles of blueprints and survey maps. There were also some instruments that Ludlum recognized as survey equipment. That gave her a pretty good idea of what this place was, at least. Though she wasn't sure it helped.

There was a large cabinet in one corner, locked with a padlock. There might be tools in there that she could use, but at the moment she had no way to get to them.

She began pulling open desk drawers, twisting to grab them with her aching hands and yanking them until they caught on unseen stops within the desk. She had hoped they could be dumped onto the floor, but no luck. She'd have to do this the hard way.

She turned her back to the drawers and began feeling her way through the contents, blindly groping, turning to look if she felt something that had any promise.

She had little luck until she pulled open the middle drawer —a tray filled with drafting pencils and plastic templates.

None of this was useful, but as she stooped to peer into the darkened recess of the drawer, she caught a glimpse of something silver and shiny.

She couldn't reach it with her hands bound. It lay tantalizingly out of reach, obscured by a disheveled pile of business cards and crumpled invoices.

She looked around the trailer again, frantically searching, and spotted an empty cardboard tube. It had once held a rolled-up survey map or some other document but had been tossed, empty, to one end of the trailer.

She went to it, turning to face away, and then braced herself against the wall of the trailer, sliding back down to a sitting position. She wriggled over to the tube, scooching until it was in the gap between her lower back and the wall, and fumbled with her fingers until she managed to grasp it. Her prize in hand, she once again pushed against the wall, sliding back up to her feet.

She took the tube with her to the desk drawer and used it to fish around, prodding and turning it to shuffle things out of the way. It was a tedious process, and took time.

Her torso was twisted into an awkward and painful position, but she was able to see over her shoulder well enough to guide the tube. After a moment she smiled as a glint of chrome made its appearance.

She dragged it forward, inch by inch, until it was visible and within reach.

A pair of toenail clippers.

She dropped the tube onto the desktop, just in case she needed it again, and leaned backwards to fish the clippers out of the drawer.

She turned and sat on the edge of the desk. The last thing she needed was to drop these things on the floor and have to work out how to retrieve them. This way, if they fell, she could pick them up off of the desktop.

She fumbled with them, opening them up and working to align them to the wire around her wrists. It wasn't easy. The wire was thicker than the gap in the clippers, and she had to settle for slowly chewing away at her restraints. The process was agonizingly slow, and at times quite painful. It took patience and concentration. She could feel sweat breaking on her forehead, rolling down her cheek, soaking into the gag.

She first cut through the rubber insulation and could feel the twisted threads of metal wire inside. She started on these now.

Her hands cramped several times, and occasionally a strand of wire stabbed at her fingers, causing her to wince. She dropped the clippers once, and she mumbled a muffled curse as she fumbled to pick them up again, to reposition, to start over.

With the gag still in her mouth, she felt a rising dryness and thirst. It was distracting, at first, but she eventually learned to balance it with the work of her hands. One pain distracted from the other, back and forth, over and over, and she made progress.

Feeling the ragged wire with the tip of her fingers, she believed she was getting close. She might have it severed soon. She felt a thrill of hope. With her hands free ...

From outside the trailer, there was a sudden, loud rumble. It started at a distance but was growing persistently closer.

A motorcycle.

The man who had brought her here had driven a van, but that didn't mean he couldn't switch vehicles. It could be him.

Her time could be running out.

She closed her eyes and bit down on the gag. She pictured the wire, imagining it as split nearly to the breaking point. A few strands left, that was all. She could do this. She cut, the strands of wire stabbing into her cuticles and fingertips. She pushed and cut. She pulled. She cut.

The motorcycle engine stopped. It was close.

How far away had the van parked, when she'd been brought here? There was that pad of concrete. Then the gravel. Then the short set of wooden steps. The hasp on the door. She couldn't calculate the time she had left, she had to trust it was enough.

She cut again, and tugged, pulling her wrists apart as hard as she could.

The wire snapped.

The door opened.

GOVERNMENT-SEALED APARTMENT

Kotler looked around, taking in the space that, until this moment, he'd only seen in photographs.

Evidence markers had been removed, and a large portion of the room had been cleared—bagged and tagged and taken back to Liz's lab at Historic Crimes. There was very little here for Kotler to look into. Liz's team had been incredibly thorough and organized, as he would have expected.

"Anything?" Denzel asked.

Kotler shook his head. "I'm not really sure what I'm looking for here, I just wanted to get a better idea of the place. Our mystery figure led us here." He turned to face Denzel, who was standing in the doorway, hands in his pockets. "Why?"

Denzel looked around and shook his head. "We found a photo of this place, in the Black Chamber. It shows the manuscript, right where we found it. It's a fair bet that whoever is behind this relied on what they found in the Black Chamber, to lay a trail of breadcrumbs for us to follow."

"Riddles and puzzles," Kotler said quietly.

"They knew what was here, anyway. Or had a pretty good idea."

Kotler nodded. "And they gave us a clue."

"The stepping maze," Denzel said.

Kotler stepped deeper into the room, turning and taking it in. This space had been sealed by government order before he'd even been born. His great-grandfather may have done some of his work here. This space could well be tied to the birth of the NSA—one of the most powerful clandestine organizations in history.

Part of him mourned that it had been disturbed before he'd gotten here, that he hadn't had the opportunity to see it as it had been found. But he knew that was silly. This was no different than the dig site he'd tended in Egypt, when Denzel had come to retrieve him. The work had been done here, properly and in an organized way. He could reference Liz's notes on this site, as well as those from her team. It was only a petty sort of FOMO—fear of missing out—that made him regret that he hadn't seen it all with his own eyes.

Why had the government sealed this space?

That was an easy question, now that he thought about it. If this really were part of the origin of the NSA, the documents in this room would have been highly classified, sensitive material at the time. It was an archive of cryptology. Secrets about secrets, and the government, in its usual schizophrenic methodology, would want to both keep it and bury it.

As the decades had gone by, the contents of this room would have become a little less relevant. The need for secrecy would be less necessary.

But there still had to be something here. Something that the mysterious figure behind the scenes wanted.

And just like that, it clicked.

"Roland," Kotler said, turning to his partner, smiling, the answer now obvious.

He paused.

He recognized the man immediately. He was hard to forget. Over six-foot-tall, broad shoulders, powerful arms. Even with a balaclava masking his face, there was little doubt that this was the man who had abducted Ludlum.

And at the moment he had one arm around Denzel's throat and a weapon trained on Kotler.

13

GOVERNMENT-SEALED APARTMENT

"Dr. Kotler," the man said quietly.

Kotler raised his hands, slowly. No sudden movements. He was in the middle of the room, with nowhere to duck or hide. The gunman would have a clear shot.

Denzel was held firm, his face blazing red, gripping at the man's arm. The gunman seemed entirely unfazed by it. Nothing Denzel did seemed to bother the man in the least.

Kotler worried that his friend couldn't breathe.

"Please," he said. "Can you ... can you let him breathe? Please?"

The man showed no outward signs of movement but must have relaxed his grip on Denzel's neck. The agent slumped slightly, his chest heaving, his hands still gripping at the gunman's powerful arm.

"Dr. Kotler, we still have Dr. Ludlum. The clock is still ticking. There isn't much time left."

"Who are you?" Kotler asked, not really expecting an answer. He was buying time, trying to figure out what to do.

"Return to FBI headquarters. Retrieve the manuscript and the decoded message it contains."

Kotler nodded. He'd been right. He'd only just put it together a moment earlier, but now it was obvious. The person orchestrating all of this had tagged the manuscript as a clue, having spotted it in the photograph from the Black Chamber. They had been unable to get to it, thanks to the government seal. But an agent of the FBI, properly motivated, could reach it. Especially if that agent's partner had some personal connection to it—if his name were on the cover, for example.

"What do you want with it?" Kotler asked, still stalling, still hoping.

The gunman shifted and now turned his weapon to Denzel's head.

"Ok!" Kotler said, bringing his hands down, palms forward, pleading. "Alright, I'll get it. Please ... just don't hurt him."

He kept the gun to Denzel's head, unmoving, and Kotler watched his partner's face go red again, the struggle renewed.

Kotler yelled but didn't dare move.

It took a moment, but Denzel finally stopped struggling. He slumped, and the man let him fall to the floor. He stepped back then, the gun dropping to his side.

"We will know when you have it. You will receive instructions on where to send it. You have thirty minutes."

At that, he raised the gun and fired.

Kotler ducked, covering his head and diving to the floor. The sound of the shot rang in his ears, but once he realized he hadn't been hit, he looked up.

The man was gone. Denzel lay unconscious on the floor.

He scrambled to his feet and checked Denzel's pulse. Strong. Steady. He was unconscious, and he'd have a hell of a headache later, but he was alive.

Kotler checked his watch.

Thirty minutes.

No time to wait and no time to waste. He rifled through Denzel's coat pocket, then stood and raced into the corridor, down the stairs and out into the street. He found Denzel's sedan parked in front of the building. He had the keys in his hand, and in seconds he was in the driver's seat and speeding toward FBI headquarters.

14

SURVEY TRAILER

Ludlum stood, aching and bleeding hands clutched into fists at her side, gag still in her mouth. She squared off with the man in the doorway.

He was wearing a motorcycle helmet and riding leathers. He hesitated, seeing her there, and his hand shot into his leather jacket, emerging with a gun.

She ran forward, a muffled scream in her throat, and leapt at the man, grabbing him by the collar of his jacket and using her grip and momentum as leverage. She brought her knees up driving them into the man's chest and ribs. The gun flew to one side, bouncing from one of the cabinets and falling to the floor of the trailer.

There was a muffled cry from inside the helmet as the man stumbled backward through the door, tipping from the top step and going down to the concrete walkway, hard.

He was stunned, but Ludlum wasn't much better off. The ordeal of the past several hours had taken a toll, and though her adrenaline was up, she was still feeling the effects of a minor concussion. Her head was pounding, and she was breathing heavily. Sweat soaked her whole body.

The man groaned beneath her, and then made a move. He reached up, taking her arm in an iron grip, and then rolled, trying to pin her to the ground. ·

Her knees were already up, after slamming into him, and she was able to keep some leverage even as she was forced onto her back.

Ludlum had spent the past ten years attending kickboxing classes two to three times per week. The key to defense was distance, which she'd lost in this case. But the advantage of hundreds of hours of kicks to heavy bags, coaches, and opponents was an abundance of leg strength.

She pulled her knees closer to her chest, his weight now pinning them in place, and then jack-kicked upward, driving her feet into the man's solar plexus.

He grunted as he rose into the air, and she twisted to send him tilting to her left as she rolled to the right.

His grip on her arm was firm, but the combination of impact and movement allowed her to pull free.

The two of them were still on the ground, each crouched and staring at each other. Ludlum felt gravel cutting painfully into her palms and knees but held her position.

The man was in a similar pose, and with the polished motorcycle helmet and the riding leathers, he looked like a supernatural creature poised to leap.

Ludlum considered her options, her mind racing. She had trained to defend herself, had put in hundreds of hours of practice, but this was different. This was real life and real death on the line. The adrenaline coursed through her. She got angry.

The man was rising to his feet, and she might have done the same, but she knew it would wick away any advantage she had. Staying low would make attacking her an awkward proposition, but there was also the helmet to consider. It protected his head, so his lower body was her best target. But it also restricted his vision, and staying low would make things more challenging for him.

She bit down on the gag again, wishing she had a moment to pull it free. It was restricting her breathing, forcing her to inhale and exhale through her nose in noisy rasps.

She ignored it.

She squeezed her hands, taking up fistfuls of gravel.

She rushed forward.

The man had only just regained his feet when she hit him, and this time she was aiming to do as much damage as possible. She shoved her hands up and under the faceplate of the helmet, pushing past the chin strap and into the gap where the man's face would be. It was an awkward move, binding her hands and putting her at a disadvantage. But with her hands over his face, she opened her grip and let gravel fall.

The man jerked, turning his head and twisting his upper body. She could hear coughing and sputtering as gravel and dirt fell into his mouth and nose. All of his effort was suddenly concentrated on clearing the debris so he could breathe and see.

Ludlum took advantage of the move to pull her hands free and roll to the side. She couldn't waste this chance. She had to end this, now.

She looked around frantically, hoping to find anything she could use as a weapon.

On the ground, the man clawed at the strap of his helmet.

She only had a moment.

There, next to the trailer, was a broken survey tripod. One leg had been sheared off somehow, and it lay on its side, in the weeds. She raced to it, picked it up, hefted it. The weight wasn't much, as it was made of aluminum, but it was sturdy. The two remaining legs had sharp stakes at their tips, meant to stabilize the tripod on soft ground.

She looked up to see that the man had removed the helmet, and was brushing gravel from his eyes, spitting it out of his mouth. He took off one of his gloves and wiped at his eyes, blinking.

She raced forward

He saw her. His eyes were hard. Angry. And then wide. Shocked.

She plunged into him, driving the sharpened points of the tripod legs into his stomach, tilting, driving upward.

He let out a strange, gurgling noise, between a grunt and a cry. He reached out, gripped her forearms, tried to push her back.

Blood and gore spewed over their hands, coating them, making everything slick and slippery. His hands clutched and flailed a few times, and there was more noise from his throat. Gurgling. Sputtering. Wheezing.

Silence.

He slumped, falling forward. Ludlum shifted the tripod, turning it, dropping the man's body off to one side.

She collapsed to the ground, then scrambled, crawling away until she was leaning against the wooden steps of the trailer. She sobbed, then tore at the gag, reaching behind her head, struggling to untie it and finally casting it away.

The sobs were audible now, and she breathed heavy, ragged breaths, trying to calm down, trying to get a grip.

This wasn't the same man who had brought her here.

That meant she wasn't yet safe.

She rose to her feet and moved cautiously to the body on the ground. The tripod protruded absurdly from his stomach. He was still. She checked his pulse.

Dead.

She needed to get out of here.

Ludlum searched his pockets until she found the keys to the

motorcycle. She glanced at the helmet, laying off to the side. Revulsion shivered through her.

She couldn't have her face in the same space his had occupied. She couldn't breathe air reflected back to her from that faceplate, knowing that his own breath had been doing so just moments ago.

It felt intimate and grotesque. A macabre kiss from a man who had tried to kill her.

She left it laying in the gravel, like an alien skull staring up into the sky. She limped to the motorcycle, parked under a corrugated metal carport, on the same pad of concrete where she had arrived.

It was a nice bike. A vintage Indian that someone, presumably the man, had restored. It had the look of something cared for, and for a strange instant Ludlum felt a spike of regret. She had killed someone. She'd taken a life. It went against who she believed she was, and it made her sick. She wanted to vomit.

She took several breaths, calmed herself, let the feeling of nausea pass.

She climbed on the bike, started the engine, gave it some throttle. The roar of it was loud, almost obnoxious. It was somehow comforting. A feeling of power in a moment where she'd felt at her weakest. A reminder that she was powerful, too.

She looked at the man one last time and felt rage well up again. She rolled forward, brought up the kickstand, and then gave the bike some throttle.

She'd only ridden a motorcycle a couple of times, with some friends during college. She could handle it, but this bike had a level of power she knew she'd have to respect. Still, as she crunched over gravel, she was aware that she was about to do something foolish and a little dangerous. Petty, but necessary.

She gunned the throttle, lurching forward, and then turned the bike so she could throw a shower of gravel over the body of the man. A symbolic burial, maybe. She was the first to throw dirt on his grave.

She kept the bike under control, kept her balance, and righted herself as she raced forward, through the open gate of the construction site and onto the city streets.

15

FBI OFFICES, MANHATTAN

Kotler left the sedan in front of FBI headquarters. He'd take flack for it later, once this was over and Denzel had recovered. First this had to be over. Kotler was up against the clock.

It had taken over ten minutes to get to the building, eating into a third of Kotler's time. He needed to expedite the rest of this, to make up for the time, somehow.

Inside the building, he had to go through security, like always. He scanned his ID, nodded to the guard on duty, and emptied his pockets before stepping through the scanners. The whole process, from entering the building to getting through security, took less than two minutes, but felt like an eternity. The elevator ride up to Historic crimes only exacerbated the feeling.

While in the elevator, Kotler started sending messages to everyone he could think of, cc'ing half the department to say he needed the manuscript and the decoding packed up and ready to go, and it was an emergency. He gave as much detail as he was able, including the fact that Agent Denzel was injured, and that Dr. Ludlum's life was in jeopardy. It was the first opportunity he'd had to alert the FBI, and he felt he was botching it, fumbling through frantic emails and texts.

By the time the doors opened, he was already getting questioning responses.

Several agents were waiting as he stepped out into the Historic Crimes floor.

"Dr. Kotler, where is Agent Denzel?"

Kotler rushed past them. "He's at the government sealed building. I have less than 20 minutes to get the manuscript and the translations, or Liz Ludlum dies."

"Dr. Kotler!" One of the agents raced to cut him off. "I can't let you do that, sir."

Kotler halted, staring.

He knew this agent. She was one of Denzel's picks. She'd been one of the first that Denzel had recruited when he was assembling Historic Crimes.

"Agent ... Brown?"

"Yes sir," Agent Brown said. "Now, calm down and explain to me what's happening."

"If I don't deliver the manuscript, Liz dies."

"I understand that sir, but we don't do that." She was firm, adamant. Direct.

Kotler opened his mouth to say something, to argue, and stopped.

She was right.

Giving the manuscript to this man would accomplish nothing good, and could potentially put a lot of people in danger. There was no way to know what this man was really after. He was smart, connected. He had access to things Kotler could only guess at.

Kotler blinked.

The man in the balaclava—he couldn't be the one running things behind the scenes. He didn't fit.

Whoever was behind this had managed to stay hidden from

the start, to manipulate Denzel and Kotler and the entire Historic Crimes division with only a few well-timed messages and hints. The man who had attacked Denzel was an enforcer, operating on orders.

We will know when you have it.

"Dr. Kotler?" Agent Brown asked, peering at him curiously.

He looked around at all of the agents gathered, staring at him.

He couldn't blame them. He'd rushed in here like a lunatic, causing quite a commotion.

Or a distraction.

"I need to get to Liz's lab," he said, moving in that direction.

Brown stepped in front of him again, putting a hand to his chest. "Dr. Kotler, I told you ..."

"I'm not taking anything," he said calmly, reaching up to touch her arm. "I don't think there's anything to take."

She gave him a curious look, and then followed him to the lab.

The tech team was hard at work as he entered, still deciphering the rest of the manuscript. "Dr. Kotler!" One of them smiled up at him. "We put together a program that uses OCR to spot the encoded text and ..."

"I'm sorry," Kotler said, holding a hand up. "I need to see the manuscript."

The man nodded and turned his laptop around, showing the scan of the document.

"No," Kotler said. "I need to see the physical manuscript."

The man frowned, exchanging glances with the rest of the team and with Agent Brown.

Brown nodded. "Show him."

The tech shrugged. "I don't know where it is. We've been working from scans all this time. I assumed it was in the archive room."

Kotler turned and hurried to the door of the archive room,

swiping his badge on the panel and entering as soon as the door was open.

There were myriad items in this room, artifacts and documents the FBI was studying in pursuit of a dozen open cases. Each piece was tagged and placed on a shelf, in a cataloged location. Kotler knew the spot for his great-grandfather's paper. He navigated directly to it and stood in front of it.

The space was empty.

He turned to Agent Brown. "Who isn't here?" he asked.

"I'm sorry?" Brown replied.

"Out of the agents, tech staff, and forensic team who had access to the manuscript, who isn't here right now?"

Brown shook her head. "I don't know. I can find out."

"Do it," Kotler said. "And fast. Restrict your search to anyone who has left the building in the past half-hour."

"That's a narrow window, shouldn't be too hard," Brown said, already taking out her phone and calling building security. "What's going on?"

"I'm a distraction," Kotler said. "Liz, Roland, all of this. It's all smoke and mirrors."

"What do you mean?" Brown asked.

"The manuscript has been stolen. It's what they were after all along, and they used us to get it."

"How?" Brown asked.

Kotler shook his head. "There's a mole in Historic Crimes. And they just got what they were after."

16

NEW YORK-PRESBYTERIAN HOSPITAL

Kotler stood just outside the door, peering into the hospital room, watching Liz Ludlum sleep.

He felt someone step up beside him, and looked up to see Denzel, with his neck in a brace.

"Doctors say she's fine, just needs some rest," Denzel rasped.

"You sound like you could use some rest yourself," Kotler replied, smiling. "How's your throat?"

"Bruised," Denzel said. "But fine."

They stepped into the hall, leaving Ludlum to sleep. Kotler would talk to her later. He was anxious to hear her voice. He wanted to hear her story, but more importantly, he needed to hear her voice.

They made their way to a waiting room that had been commandeered by the FBI. Unofficially. The number of off-duty agents and members of Ludlum's forensics team had simply overwhelmed any other presence on this floor of the hospital. Agents had lined up to volunteer for guard duty. The rest were there running support, bringing in coffee and food and reading materials. Ludlum was beloved in the department, Kotler knew. But she'd also been nabbed right out in the open and right under their noses. There was a feeling of guilt and responsibility among the agents. Kotler understood it perfectly. He felt it.

Kotler and Denzel grabbed coffee and sat in two plush chairs in one corner of the room.

"What did you find out, about the man Liz took down?"

Denzel took a ginger sip of his coffee; a move made a bit awkward by the neck brace. After a moment, frustrated, he yanked at the Velcro straps and pulled the thing off, discarding it in a corner of the room. He rubbed his neck with one hand and sipped coffee freely.

"His name was Cameron Ryba. He has a juvenile record, a couple of minor smash and grabs. He was carrying an unlicensed .45 that we recovered from the scene."

"So just hired muscle," Kotler said.

Denzel shook his head, winced slightly, and replied. "I don't think so. The kid came back as a relative nobody, but his brother has a file. A big one. His name's Redmond Ryba. Goes by Red. He's a suspect in more than a hundred hits, worldwide."

"More than a hundred?" Kotler said, his eyes wide. "Wait, just a suspect?"

"He's good," Denzel replied. "Makes things look like common street crime. Muggings, B&E's gone bad, that sort of thing. Never leaves any real evidence behind. Nothing anyone can use against him. But he has a reputation."

"What kind of reputation?" Kotler asked.

"Hundred percent success rate, for a start. He has a business built on referrals. He only takes on clients referred to him by other clients. That's the rumor, anyway. It's hard to find anything solid on the guy. Only a couple of his clients have ever talked, and they met with mysterious, tragic circumstances."

Kotler sipped his coffee, thinking. "So he's a hired hand. Definitely not the mastermind behind this. What about the agent who took the manuscript?"

"Agent Lee Patterson," Denzel sneered.

Kotler thought, struggling to remember. He'd met Agent Patterson a few times. Did he know anything about him? He couldn't recall any deep conversations, anything beyond the work. Kotler occasionally got an icy reception from the agents in Historic Crimes, who sometimes saw him as a power. Or maybe they felt he had too much influence over their boss. As a result, not everyone in the department had warm feelings toward him. There were plenty of people in Historic Crimes that he'd never quite bonded with. Patterson was one of them.

"Do we know his motive?" Kotler asked.

Denzel shook his head. "Not yet. We're looking at his financials, his extended family, that sort of thing. He had a thorough background check before coming in, though. I made sure of that. Not much showing up now."

Kotler considered this. Could Patterson have played a long game? For two years Denzel had built his team from the ground up, vetting everyone, even Kotler himself, well enough to weed out most threats. But there had been breaches before. One of the tech team had been sharing information with Gail McCarthy, as an example. The screenings weren't perfect.

Kotler knew that this would be a wound for Denzel. The agent was likely already kicking himself over imagined failings and dropped balls.

"All of this," Kotler said, shaking his head. "It had to take a lot of planning."

Denzel nodded. "He had this set up pretty well. It must have taken months to pull it together. He knew everything that was happening, and when. While I was getting choked by Red Rybas, Patterson was already out of the building and off the radar, manuscript in tow."

"How did he get it?" Kotler asked.

"When we brought in the tech team, they took over Liz's lab. He checked the manuscript back into the archives, but it never actually made it there. Best we can figure he had it tucked into his coat or something as he left the archive and the lab. He went to the lobby and waited."

"Waited?" Kotler asked, confused. "For what?"

"For you," Denzel said. "When you came through, you sent some messages, and things got moving. The building went on alert. People started to scramble. And Patterson used it as a distraction to get out and get moving. He was miles away by the time you figured out it was all a distraction."

Kotler lowered his chin to his chest, closing his eyes, breathing. "I'm an anthropologist," he said, then looked up to Denzel. "How do I keep ending up in situations like this?"

Denzel chuckled. "I've been asking that question for two years, Kotler. Just face it. This is what you do."

Kotler smiled at that and turned his attention to the room. He intended to stay until Liz was awake, to chat with her for a bit and then go home. He hadn't been back to his apartment in some time, and he could use a shower and a hot meal, maybe some solitude.

It was a hard thing, facing the fact that they'd lost this one —that the bad guy had gotten away.

No less difficult for Denzel, he knew. His friend had been meticulous about vetting the members of his team, sussing out their backgrounds and determining not only who was best suited for work in Historic Crimes, but who could be trusted. After the events surrounding the former Director, Matt Crispen—the man who'd actually brought Kotler and Denzel together by betraying the Bureau and his country— Denzel had become a zealot about screening. Kotler knew that Denzel would take this hard, that he'd blame himself, that he'd ...

Sit quietly and serenely, sipping coffee as if nothing had happened.

"Roland," Kotler said, cautiously. "Why aren't you yelling or cursing or demanding the heads of your enemies?"

Denzel laughed. "Well, my throat hurts. But ... ok." He turned to Kotler, leaning in, and spoke in a quiet, conspiratorial tone. "There's something I didn't tell you. In fact, only Liz knows."

"Secrets?" Kotler said in mock surprise. "From me?"

"From everyone," Denzel said, grinning. "There's a dot on the manuscript."

Kotler blinked. "A dot?"

Denzel smiled and nodded. "A GPS dot. I had it made to look like one of the brass brads. Patterson wouldn't have known it was there. Liz and I put it there after the first round of tests, while she still had exclusive access to it."

Kotler shook his head. "Why?"

"Saw this coming," Denzel said. "Or, well, I figured it might happen. All the spy stuff, the codes and the NSA connection," he waved a hand as if swatting away gnats. "Made me paranoid. I started thinking about why anyone would want to get me into that room, to find that paper, and to see your name on it. They had to know a lot about me, about you, and about FBI procedure. Not hard. You're kind of famous, in your way ..."

"Thanks," Kotler rolled his eyes.

"... and there are tons of ways to learn how the FBI works. I figured whoever was behind this must know me, though, and would somehow have access to the archive."

"Because it would be inevitable that the manuscript would go in there," Kotler said, eyes wide in surprise. "They would know its location, and all they'd have to do was wait. Brilliant. Roland ... I'm sorry. I underestimated you!"

Denzel shrugged, leaned back, and sipped his coffee with a slight wince. "It happens a lot. I find it's kind of useful to let you think you're the smartest guy in the room. Helps me prove my own theories."

Kotler laughed, shaking his head. "Ok, smart guy. So you're tracking Patterson? You know where he is?"

"I am. I do."

"But you aren't circling up, trying to bring him in?"

Denzel shook his head. "I'm waiting. I want to see where he ends up. Who he ends up talking to."

Kotler thought about it. "So, you don't think Patterson is the person behind the scenes?"

Denzel shrugged. "Maybe he is, and maybe he isn't, but he's on the move, I know that. I don't know what he wants with that thing, or where he's taking it. But I think he's just a fish. I think there's a whale out there, so I'm giving him some play in the line."

Kotler huffed. "You're brilliant," he said, holding his coffee cup up as a toast. "Who knew?"

"Well, I'm not a fancy-pants anthropologist, but I get by," he said, meeting the toast.

17

UNDISCLOSED LOCATION

Red watched from a distance, peering through the scope of a rifle to see his brother's body laid to rest.

He had managed to visit the scene, where his brother had fallen, and had avoided the police and the FBI while performing his own sweep. He needed to know the details, to correct for any such failures in the future.

He needed to know how his brother died.

Inside the survey trailer, he found the wire that had tied the woman's feet. Red had tied the wire with the knot accessible to her hands. He should have knotted it in front, where her shins met the top of her feet. More difficult and more painful to reach.

That was his mistake.

He looked then at the desk. A cardboard tube, an open drawer, a pair of nail clippers and a shred of wire insulation. The severed wire had been taken as evidence, though Red was uncertain why the rest was left behind.

He shook his head. The woman was clever. He had underestimated her. Another mistake.

The clippers had been the key to her freedom. Something he had overlooked. A foolish mistake.

He couldn't deny it. He had caused all of this. He had sent his brother into a scenario in which certain variables had not been accounted for, and it had led to Cameron's death.

This was on Red. While he had enjoyed a movie, his brother had died because of careless mistakes.

It was unacceptable. It gnawed at him, made him question himself and his methods. He had maintained his 100% success rate, had come through exactly as the contract had demanded, but had lost a valuable asset—his brother—in the process. Just as the boy was becoming better at this, too. It was a shame. It was disgusting.

When he was a soldier, Red had observed certain rituals after losing a brother in arms. He observed these now. A bottle of Kentucky bourbon sat on the table of the hotel room. He opened it, poured two glasses, and drank one. The other he would leave, along with the rest of the bottle. A toast for his brother, wherever he may be.

He took out his wallet and removed a hundred-dollar bill.

In his military days, Red had done this with ones or fives or tens—sometimes the odd twenty, if he had one. The largest denomination he could manage, in a single bill, at the time. Giving the most to someone who had given everything.

His wealth was greater these days, but even if he'd been poor, he would have found a way to do this anyway. This was flesh and blood. It called for a higher price.

He wrote his brother's name on the bill, in Farsi, to keep it secret. He slid the hundred under the glass. Room service would take it for a tip. The denomination would prevent them from panicking over what they would surely think of as "terrorist writing." It would disappear into an apron pocket and become a story told to the family that night.

The bottle of bourbon might go with it, depending on the temperament of whoever serviced the room.

With the homage paid, Red turned to the task of breaking down the rifle and putting it back in its case. He had used this as an opportunity to clean it, to run through the ritual of disassembling and assembling it. Now the task was done. He placed the gun case into the compartment in the back of his suitcase, zipped it closed, and then tugged it along behind him as he stepped out into the hall.

He would never visit his brother's grave. There was too much risk. But he would honor him in other ways.

His employer had reached out with condolences. That was kind of them. And they had paid Red an additional sum as compensation for his losses. A good client. Red appreciated it but would never have asked.

This was not the client's debt to pay. It was Red's.

The woman had defended herself and had won. Red had a difficult time faulting her for that. This was the game. It was Red, after all, who had made the mistakes that had empowered her. She was innocent of Cameron's death. Merely an instrument.

But Dr. Kotler.

It was a simple equation to balance. Though Red now realized that the timeline and the demand for retrieving the manuscript had been a ruse, he hadn't known that when he'd delivered it. Kotler had been told to bring the manuscript and the decoded message in thirty minutes. He hadn't delivered. He'd failed, breaking their contract. And Cameron had died.

That was an imbalance. It was a violation of the code by which Red lived, and he intended to set it right.

The client had severed communications, but that was fine. Red appreciated the client's ethics, but the job was finished. His loyalty, now, was to his own honor and his own best interests.

He couldn't allow anyone who failed to keep their end of a bargain to simply continue on as if nothing happened. That had to be rectified.

Red was his own client now.

18

FBI OFFICES, MANHATTAN

"He's here," Denzel said, pointing to a blip on the digital map.

Kotler nodded, looking closely. "I know that area. There's an airport nearby. You're not worried about him making a run for it?"

"We're operating under the assumption that he will, but that he has other business to attend to first. We have agents in that airport, and in another one a few miles further, just in case."

"How do we know he hasn't delivered the manuscript to someone and left it behind?"

"He's not the fish we're trying to reel in, Kotler. We're after his boss. If he's the one running this, then we'll find him when we go for the manuscript. If he's not, then we'll nab whoever hired him and go after Patterson later."

Kotler nodded. Lee Patterson was a pawn, then. The real target was the showrunner, whoever that may be.

The plan made sense, but something wasn't clicking for Kotler.

What was Patterson's motive in all of this? Money?

Could be, but Kotler had a hard time with it. The amount of money that would motivate an agent to turn on the Bureau would have to be significant. Huge. Knowing that the FBI would pull out all the stops to find him, Patterson would need the kind of funds that would let him start over somewhere, with an all-new identity and the resources to stay off the radar for the rest of his life.

Was the manuscript worth that?

They had looked over everything they still had, from the initial emails that Denzel had received to the scans of the manuscript. The software that Tech had running was plowing through the pages, identifying the characters that fit with the Baconian cypher and applying the ADFGVX code to translate it. This was taking time—optical character recognition had advanced quite a bit, but training it to differentiate between intentional discrepancies and inadvertent typographical anomalies was tricky. There were a lot of false positives, which required that each translation was reviewed by human eyes.

It was a time-consuming process, yet all of this was much faster than sitting and hand-decoding the entire manuscript. Progress was slow, but it was still progress.

Denzel was briefing his team, pulling together a timeline and strategy, and Kotler felt superfluous at the moment. He decided to use the time. The Tech team had sent him updates with each confirmed translation, and he pulled these up now, reading through it all.

The first few pages read like an inventory and progress report. From what Kotler could gather, someone was using Daniel's paper to help organize an off-site backup of the contents within the government-sealed room. That off-site location would be the Black Chamber, where Dr. Marvin and Dr. Wiley were held captive.

Kotler realized now that what they thought of as the Black

Chamber was just a copy—a replica meant to preserve the work that had been done. This may have become a necessity as the team learned of an impending government seal. It would help to get hold of the records that led to that room being sealed off, though Kotler had little hope of that. With its ties to the NSA, any information about it would surely be classified well above Kotler's level. Denzel's as well.

"Finding anything new?" Denzel asked.

Kotler looked up from his tablet and shook his head. "Really just digging in. Any word on how close Tech is to having the whole thing translated?"

"Could be another day," Denzel replied.

A day. A lot could happen in a day, Kotler knew, and every minute that went by was another opportunity for Patterson to escape and for the mastermind of all this to disappear as well.

"Something that doesn't make sense ..." Kotler started.

"What? More that doesn't make sense?" Denzel asked.

"... whoever was behind this, they sent us that cylinder with the cypher to decode the manuscript. How did they know how to translate the code?"

"And if they knew that, why did they still need the manuscript?" Denzel added.

"There was a photo of the sealed room, in the Black Chamber," Kotler said. "We've assumed that was how they knew about the manuscript. But we really have no way of knowing what else was in that room, prior to it being used as a cell for Dr. Marvin and Dr. Wiley. What if they had more information than we thought?"

"Maybe some photos of pages from the manuscript itself?" Denzel asked.

"But not all of it," Kotler nodded.

Denzel thought about this. "Ok, but if they had a partial, and wanted the whole thing, why not take the scans and the translations we had to date? Why would they need the physical manuscript?"

Kotler sank back, pressing his hands against the bridge of his nose.

He felt out of his depth here.

He wasn't a cryptologist. Not in the modern sense. He was an expert in deciphering ancient languages and pictographs, and that was similar in a lot of ways. It certainly helped. But this level of codebreaking had been more of a hobby than a serious pursuit.

Experts were working on this, though. Denzel had brought in codebreakers who were studying the scans right alongside Kotler and the rest of the team. They were just getting started but had already made a great deal of progress, helping the Tech team with refining its software, working as the eyes to help verify the scans. They were boosting the pace, which was sorely needed.

There were questions that couldn't be answered by the translation, though.

Decoding the manuscript might tell them what their adversary was after, but it might not reveal why. That was too much uncertainty for Kotler.

Kotler glanced over to see Denzel peering at his tablet. The agent had pinched to zoom in on a section.

"Eyes getting old?" Kotler smiled.

Denzel scowled. "Eye doctor says I need reading glasses. I'm resisting."

"Roland, he has your best interest at ..." Kotler froze.

Denzel looked up, curious. "What is it?"

Kotler reached over and took the tablet from Denzel's hands, looking at the image. He touched the screen and zoomed in further. "Damn," he said quietly.

"What is it?" Denzel asked.

"Are these the highest resolution scans we have?" Kotler replied.

Denzel shrugged. "They're the only scans we have, so I'd say so, yes. What's up?"

Kotler pointed to a blob on the screen. It had a generally round shape, and resembled a blurry amoeba or biological cell, such as one might see on a microscope slide. A pattern of squiggles and gaps was visible, but it was difficult to make out any given shape.

"This is the dot on a letter 'i.' Just a random character," Kotler said. "Look at it. What do you see?"

Denzel shook his head. "Couple'a wavy lines?"

"Spaces. Shapes. You know what negative space means?"

"Of course," Denzel said. "Like inverse drawing."

"Exactly," Kotler smiled. "Also like a photo negative. Look at it."

Denzel looked and shook his head. "I can kind of see it, Kotler, but it doesn't make any sense to me. It's too fuzzy. Are you sure?"

"During the Cold War, spies would sometimes use micro-dot cameras to photograph enemy intelligence. They'd send that information back to their handlers in magazine clippings, books, newspapers—anything with printed text. Any dot on the page, from the letter 'i' to the period at the end of a sentence could disguise a message that it would take a microscope to see."

"You're saying the manuscript has messages like these?"

Kotler pointed to the screen. "It does."

"What about the code? The translation?"

Kotler shook his head. "I'm starting to think that was a smokescreen. Or, it may have some useful information, but it wasn't what our mysterious figure was after. They needed the manuscript itself, because it contains another entire level of hidden information!"

Denzel turned back to the other agents in the room. "Get things finalized, now. We have to move earlier than expected."

Activity picked up, agents moved quickly, mobilizing to close in on the last known location of Lee Patterson.

"There are already agents in the area," Denzel said. "I have people watching the location. We're getting an assist from local law enforcement, too. Good work, Kotler. No one noticed this."

"It doesn't do us any good if we can't get that manuscript back," Kotler said. "Roland, all of this has ties to the origin of the NSA. There could be government secrets in this that might shake up the entire nation. Maybe the world. We need to call them in."

Denzel made a disgusted noise, turning his head away, a sour expression on his face.

"Call in the NSA," he said. "Great. This just keeps getting better."

19

NEW YORK-PRESBYTERIAN HOSPITAL

Liz Ludlum pulled on a pair of jeans and a T-shirt that her sister had brought by. Rachel stood against the door of the hospital room, watching as Liz got dressed.

"You're sure you're ok to leave?" she asked.

Liz was moving a little slower than she'd like, mostly due to her hands being wrapped in bandages. Her head still hurt a little, but the pain meds were taking the edge off. Still, bright light bothered her, and she winced from the slight effort as she tugged at the top button of her jeans.

"I'll be fine," she said quietly, smiling at Rachel. "Thanks for bringing this. For being here."

Rachel moved forward and hugged her little sister, kissing her on the cheek. "This job ..."

"Don't start," Liz said.

"I just worry," Rachel replied. She held Liz at arm's length. "You don't look like you should be leaving the hospital."

"They cleared me, and I'm checked out. Time to make this bed available to someone who really needs it. Besides, I think they'll be glad to be rid of all the FBI agents in the waiting room."

"They're a mess," Rachel said, shaking her head. "Shouldn't they be out hunting bad guys?"

"Most of them are off duty, but there's less than a quarter of them here compared to yesterday. I think something's up back at the office."

"And you think you're going back there to help out," Rachel said. Her expression was stern, and Liz knew she'd be in for a fight.

"It's my job," she said.

"It's your life," Rachel replied. "Has been ever since Pappy left you that bag."

"You watch it," Liz said, but smiled, and then winced.

"See?" Rachel said hugging her sister again. "Take some time off, ok?"

Liz started to argue, opened her mouth to say something, but thought better of it. She nodded, and Rachel seemed satisfied.

They left the room, spent a few minutes saying goodbye to the agents in the waiting room, and then Liz took a seat in a wheelchair as she was rolled out of the lobby. She and Rachel shared an Uber back to Liz's apartment.

Rachel hovered over her as they took the stairs, and Liz let her. It slowed things down, but she knew Rachel was just trying to help. She was worried. Liz understood, even if she'd prefer to be left alone.

Liz unlocked her door, and they were inside. Things were just as she'd left them, which was a relief. The only exception was that her grandfather's medical bag was on the floor next to the little hall table. She had requested that someone bring it from the lab, and it was comforting, seeing it there. She picked it up, hugging it to her as she and Rachel entered the apartment and made their way to Liz's bedroom.

"You shower," Rachel said. "I'll make lunch."

"I'm not all that hungry," Liz said.

"Go!" Rachel ordered, and Liz went.

A few minutes later she was standing under the steaming stream of water, grateful that her big sister was so bossy. It was wonderful. She could feel the past few days washing away, along with some of the stress and tension she'd been feeling since being released from the hospital.

And the fear.

She had admitted it to herself while she was still in the hospital. She'd felt it growing since dropping Cameron Ryba's motorcycle to the ground outside of FBI headquarters. Agents had rushed to her, paramedics were called, blankets had been wrapped around her shoulders. Everyone had been on high alert, but her co-workers had dropped everything to make sure she was alright.

She was. Physically. Mostly. But she was also a little shook, and that was harder to get past.

She mentally replayed her encounter with Red Ryba, again and again. She couldn't get it out of her head, really. Opening that door. The disoriented seconds in which she couldn't think of why he was there, or why he was wearing a mask. The sudden terror as he grabbed her. The pain as he slammed her head against the doorframe.

She'd held on to consciousness, struggling to keep track of details, in case they were needed. And then she was in a metal box. Everything went black, and she had passed out until the van stopped, and the man had yanked her out and carried her into the survey trailer.

There was nowhere in that series of events where she could wedge in some idea of how she should have reacted, how she might have escaped. There was no gap in that sequence where she thought she could have fought back and won. Red Ryba was too powerful. He was too fast. He was an overwhelming and irresistible force.

That was what nagged at her now.

Liz hadn't had much direct conflict in her life. She hadn't struggled, beyond the day-to-day struggles of a woman of color working in a field dominated by white males. Those challenges were real, but she'd long ago decided that the only way they could negatively impact her life was if she let them. She had decided that she would not play the role of victim and would instead use her intelligence and her character to build the life she wanted, rather than accept that her die was cast, and her fate was set.

It had worked. She had built a career for herself, followed by a reputation that propelled her upwards in the ranks of the NYPD. And when Agent Denzel had approached her about taking on a similar role with the FBI, she'd taken it because she knew she had earned it. She accepted increasing responsibility as part of her rise, and she'd owned it. And there, among the agents and her own team, Liz Ludlum had become the most empowered version of herself that she'd ever been. She was no victim.

Until Red Ryba had slammed her head into a doorframe.

Now she felt it.

Fear was nagging at her, just under the surface. It ate at her. It burned like acid in her stomach.

Five days ago she had been confident and secure, perhaps struggling to adjust to her role as a leader in her department but certainly not afraid of the challenge.

Right now, though, she felt like she might jump out of her skin. Red Ryba was still out there. He was still a threat. He still loomed over her, in her mind. A man overpowering her, taking her, weakening her.

There was a knock on the bathroom door, and Liz jumped. The sudden movement made her head hurt. "Y-yes?" she asked.

"Just checking on you," Rachel's voice came back. "Take your time. I made a spread for lunch, but it'll keep."

"Thank you," Liz called back, and stood, waiting. She peered through the glass door of the shower, watching the door to the bathroom as if it might creak open and Red Ryba would be standing there. She felt her heart pound, and she swallowed. She squeezed her eyes shut, and let the hot water wash over her face, down over her shoulders.

She needed to do something.

She wasn't sure what. Not yet. But she did have one idea.

Everyone was busy looking for Lee Patterson and the manuscript. They were hunting for whoever was behind all of this. Agent Denzel's entire team was focused on this. Kotler was focused on it.

No one was focused on Red Ryba.

No one except her.

She shut off the shower and toweled herself dry. She stretched, trying to loosen tight muscles in her neck and back and shoulders. Her hands, a bit bruised and scraped, ached but were otherwise fine. She'd skip the bandages. They just slowed her down.

She dressed, casual and comfortable. She needed to look relaxed, at peace. She needed Rachel to see that her little sister was alright. She needed Rachel to leave.

Liz emerged from her bedroom to find Rachel placing a veritable feast on the little dining table. "Your fridge is like the health food section of a grocery store," Rachel said, shaking her head. "I did the best I could."

"You're a trained chef," Liz smiled. "Your worst is better than most people's best."

"Bruschetta. Prosciutto. Olive spread. Eat."

Liz ate. And it was good. She hadn't felt hungry before, but now she was nearly ravenous. And for the next hour, she and

Rachel talked, caught up, shared what they knew about various family members.

"Momma wants you to come see her," Rachel said.

Liz nodded. "It's been too long, I know. I'll go by the home this weekend. Are they taking good care of her?"

Rachel shrugged. "She spends most of her days cackling with the other ladies in that place, playing cards and taking very slow walks around the pond. She misses you."

"I miss her," Liz replied.

"But she's proud of you," Rachel said. "She tells everyone about you. How you're a scientist that works for the FBI. The whole place knows everything you do. I bring them five-star cuisine twice a month but isn't Liz just incredible?" She laughed.

She was teasing, smiling at Liz, but there was a certain bite beneath the surface. Rachel wasn't jealous by nature, but she loved their mother as much as Liz did, and it hurt, Liz knew, to be so accomplished and still be "the other daughter."

Liz hugged her. "If you stopped taking that food by, they'd start appreciating you more," she said.

Rachel laughed. "That's true."

The conversation went on for a while longer, but finally Liz yawned, and Rachel stood and cleared the dishes. She loaded the dishwasher and got it running. And she gave Liz strict instructions to get plenty of rest. "I talked to your boss, that big guy."

"Agent Denzel."

"He said you're off duty for the next week, and longer if you need it. So you're off duty. You hear me?"

"I hear you," Liz said.

They hugged, and Rachel kissed Liz's cheek again. When she was gone, Liz closed and locked the door. For the first time since moving in, she made sure the top bolt was turned. She double checked even before walking away.

Alone, she stood in the middle of her living room. She turned slowly, taking in the details. This place was made to be a comfort to her. It was filled with photos and heirlooms from her past. It was home, and she needed that right now. All that talk of her momma made her feel a little guilty, and a lot homesick. She meant it when she said she'd go visit. Maybe even before the weekend.

But for now, she had work to do.

She went to her grandfather's bag and took out her laptop. She logged into the FBI database, using her credentials, and started sifting through everything she could find about Red Ryba.

There was a lot. Most of it speculation about his involvement in crimes around the world. There were hints of him everywhere, but very little proof.

What she was interested in most, however, was his current whereabouts. Unknown, but again, hints.

She pulled up the security footage of him and passively watched as he attacked her. She looped it, watching it on repeat. She was detached from it. For now. She was focused, being an unbiased observer, trying to find clues. That was what kept her steady.

The truth was, there really was no way to be sure that it was Red Ryba in this footage. They suspected it, because of his brother's involvement, but couldn't prove that he was the one who had grabbed her. The FBI wanted him for questioning, but so far, he was unreachable. Once again, just as he'd been in hundreds of other cases, Red Ryba was a ghost.

She knew that other agents were tasked with finding him. This wasn't her job. She was operating well outside of her purview. She tried to make her searches as passive and discrete as possible, so she wouldn't be flagged, and her access wouldn't be restricted. It was making it tough, like trying to find evidence from a photograph, at a bad angle. She was looking for details that might not even exist. The hope of tracking down Red Ryba was narrow to impossible.

But she would find him.

She would find him.

20

FBI OFFICES, MANHATTAN

The NSA was not cooperative.

Kotler wasn't privy to the conversation, due to not having the right level of clearance. But it was clear enough, as he sat at one of the desks in the bullpen and watched through the glass wall of Denzel's office. Denzel had left the blinds open on purpose, despite the NSA agents request that they were closed. Passive aggressive as ever.

It made Kotler smile to think of Denzel asserting authority over his own window coverings.

Kotler had some proficiency with lip reading, but the angles and the distance made it difficult. He could, however, see the body language of both men clearly, and he was learning plenty. Denzel was furious, agitated, but keeping his cool. The NSA guy was controlled, unreadable.

It gave Kotler the creeps.

Things progressed. Denzel was at first obstinate and defiant, maybe a bit blustery. He was asserting that he had control over this, that it was his case. Over time, however, he began to show signs of resignation and uncomfortable acceptance.

Kotler couldn't know what his partner was hearing, but he could make a guess that the NSA agent was quietly and calmly taking things over.

That hadn't been entirely unexpected. Kotler and Denzel had talked extensively about what to expect, once they'd alerted the NSA to what they'd discovered. There was no delusion here. Denzel was aware that when it came to the level of government secrecy involved, the NSA would want to edge out any element that wasn't entirely under their control. That included the FBI. And it particularly included Dr. Dan Kotler.

Denzel had taken a seat behind his desk now. A sign that he was putting up what barriers he could, between him and the NSA.

A defensive position, Kotler knew. It was settled. They would be asked to hand everything over and stop pursuing the case.

After several minutes of conversation across the desk, Denzel rose and opened the door to his office. He stepped out onto the catwalk and pointed to Kotler, motioning for him to join them.

Kotler was not surprised.

Best case, he'd be asked to remove himself from the investigation and let the secret agents and professional codebreakers take it from here. It also seemed likely that he'd be told, in no uncertain terms, not to mess with the NSA's investigation.

Kotler made his way up the steps and slipped into Denzel's office as the door was closed behind him. Denzel closed the blinds now, and Kotler gave him a quick, surprised look.

Now there would be secrets?

"Sit down, Kotler," Denzel said.

Kotler sat in one of Denzel's chairs, and the NSA agent sat in the other. Denzel dropped into the office chair behind his desk, leaning forward on his elbows.

"Dr. Dan Kotler," the NSA agent said. "I'm Agent Steven Coben, with the NSA."

"Good to meet you," Kotler said, shaking the man's hand.

"Agent Denzel tells me you've been instrumental in this investigation so far. You cracked the code to free Dr. Wiley and Dr. Marvin. And you discovered the microdots embedded in the manuscript."

Kotler nodded. "I've had a great deal of help from Dr. Liz Ludlum and her team, as well as the agents and the technology team here in Historic Crimes."

Agent Coben nodded. "So I've been told. But it seems you're the one person at the heart of all of this, aren't you Dr. Kotler?"

Kotler blinked. "I'm ... not sure what you mean."

"Well, Agent Denzel receives a tip that leads to the discovery of your name on a manuscript, tucked away in a government-sealed room."

"My great-grandfather's name, actually," Kotler replied, cautiously.

"Quite a coincidence," Coben said.

"Not a coincidence," Kotler said. "Whoever is behind this knew about that manuscript, and about the sealed room. They used my connection to Agent Denzel to get their hands on it."

Coben nodded. "And then a gunman attacks a café and tosses you a clue to unlocking the cypher in the manuscript. A clue that, again, literally has your name on it. Why did you take that from the crime scene, by the way? Rather than leave it for the police?"

"I felt we were running out of time," Kotler replied. "Dr. Marvin and Dr. Wiley ..."

"Were still locked in the Black Chamber, yes," Coben interrupted, nodding. "And by all accounts, they still had a good 48 hours of air."

Kotler was silent.

He couldn't read Coben. The man was a blank, as far as his

body language went. He was evidently trained to control even his micro expressions, right down to holding the shape of his eyes during conversation. He was good. Unreadable. It made Kotler uncomfortable, which he assumed was the point.

This was a game.

Coben was casting suspicion on Kotler, trying to rattle him, to see if he'd reveal something about his involvement in all of this. It was possible that Coben even believed that Kotler was behind it. That Kotler was the "mastermind."

The only way to win, Kotler knew, was not to play.

Agent Coben, inscrutable and empowered by the whole of the US government, was playing a game that had no rules. None, that was, beyond the rules of human psychology.

Kotler mentally cursed himself for not seeing this coming. It was a complication they didn't need right now, as the person behind this had what they were after and could escape at any moment. They couldn't afford to play "clear Kotler's name." The person who had orchestrated Liz's abduction—who had endangered several people Kotler cared about as well as a number of civilians, was still out there, and was still a threat. Maybe even more of a threat, now that they had some of the oldest secrets of the NSA.

In scenarios such as this, when one person held all the power and all the cards, there was literally nothing Kotler could say or do that wouldn't be scrutinized and assumed to be incriminating. Agents like Coben were trained to look for even the tiniest hints of hidden meaning. He would assume Kotler had an agenda, and work from that assumption. It was a biased approach, but it was the safest play, in his line of work.

"It piqued my curiosity," Kotler replied, holding Coben's gaze.

This would be Kotler's play. It was a code, of sorts. He was sending a message to Coben, with no assurance that the man would understand it. Although Kotler couldn't get a read on him, Coben was still human. There was still the man's psychology to contend with, and that was the card that Kotler had dealt.

"Piqued your curiosity," Coben said. There was a long pause, and the man smiled, though Kotler could see it wasn't entirely genuine. It touched his eyes, but it was guarded.

Which was a good sign. Coben had let his guard down, for just an instant, giving Kotler a chance to read a hint of understanding in his features. Kotler's message had been received.

"Dr. Kotler, we'd like to request your assistance in the rest of this investigation."

Kotler nodded, "Of course. Roland and I are already ..."

"Agent Denzel's presence, in this case, is no longer required," Coben said.

Kotler glanced at Denzel, who had his hands clasped under his chin. He gave a slight nod.

Kotler turned back to Coben. "Agent Coben, if not for the resources of this department, I'm pretty sure I wouldn't have made any progress on this. Agent Denzel knows everything about this case. I only know the parts I'm privy to."

"You'll be briefed on everything you need to know," Coben said. "But Agent Denzel and his department have been compromised."

Kotler's eyes widened, and he looked to Denzel.

"They say," Denzel said. "They're not entirely wrong. Patterson. Ryba getting to Liz. Data breaches."

"Two years of data breaches," Coben added. "The majority of which seem connected to you, Dr. Kotler. Wouldn't you call that suspicious?"

"I'd call it a reason to pull *me* from this case, and call me compromised," Kotler said sternly. "But Agent Denzel and his department are absolutely exemplary."

Coben pursed his lips, inhaling and exhaling through his nose, and then nodded. "I agree," he said.

"You agree?" Kotler asked. "Which part? Because honestly, I'd rather not be removed from this right now."

"All of it," Coben said. "You should be removed, but you're too much of an asset. And Agent Denzel and the Historic Crimes division have done an outstanding job, despite the obvious liability of having you onboard."

"Ouch," Kotler said wryly.

"Now you hold on one damn minute!" Denzel started, bracing his hands on his desk and rising slightly from his chair.

Coben held up a hand. "No offense. But let's be real, Agent. The bulk of the cases you've closed over the past two years were tied directly to Dr. Kotler. Gail McCarthy and her smuggling network—that was a big win, but it wouldn't have been on your radar if not for him. And it certainly wouldn't have been as complicated, if not for Dr. Kotler. The entire existence of this department is because of him. You do realize that?"

Denzel and Kotler exchanged glances.

"Wait," Kotler started. "Are you implying that Historic Crimes exists because of me?"

Coben studied him for a long moment. "Your great-grandfather ... he was a founding member of the NSA. You've uncovered that."

"Yes," Kotler said.

"Your family history ..."

Kotler frowned, but Coben didn't carry it any further.

"You have to know, Dr. Kotler, that there's more going on here than meets the eye. Haven't you wondered, about all of this?" Coben motioned to the office, toward the bullpen currently hidden by the blinds. "In two years there have been three major upgrades to this division. Funding allocation has been increased multiple times." He turned to Denzel. "Agent Denzel, in your long and varied career in government service, how often have you known any bureaucratic agency to consistently *raise* funding?"

Kotler studied Denzel and noted that his friend was surprised by the question. He hadn't considered it before, Kotler knew. Neither had Kotler. Not really. He wasn't technically a government employee, merely a consultant. He had thought there were conveniences to the charter of Historic Crimes, and an odd sort of accommodation that fit neatly with his own skills, expertise, and interests. He'd thought that perhaps he'd come along at the right time, that someone in the upper echelons of the Bureau had been waiting for an opportunity like this. Was it possible there was something else going on?

"Dr. Kotler," Coben turned back to him. "I do know that neither you nor Agent Denzel is actually compromised."

Kotler studied him, somewhat surprised by his abrupt honesty but once again cautious when he realized that Coben was still guarded, still finely controlling his body language.

Coben continued. "But we need him here, and we need you with us. You may have had help, but it was you who uncovered all of this. And, for some reason, it's you who is at the heart of it. As of right now, your security clearance has been raised. Which means I can tell you certain things. One of those things is that the manuscript isn't just an inventory for the Black Chamber. It *is* the Black Chamber. And the information it contains creates a profound threat to national security."

Kotler shook his head. "I'm sorry ... I want to make sure I follow. This manuscript, drafted decades ago, contains sensitive information that's still somehow dangerous today?"

"That's right," Coben said. He was watching Kotler intently, his gaze steady and signaling how dire all of this truly was.

"How is that possible?" Kotler asked.

Coben smiled. "Well, unfortunately, your clearance level hasn't been raised quite that high."

Kotler slumped back, stunned. He looked to Denzel, who was pensive and grim. "Roland?"

Denzel shrugged. "The resources of this department are here to help, if we're needed."

"You're needed," Coben said. "You have manpower on site. I'll be taking over. If you don't mind."

"Not at all," Denzel said, his voice tight.

"We'll be taking the files and translations you have. But I'd like you to continue investigating Agent Patterson and trying to find the person behind all of this."

"Of course," Denzel replied.

Coben looked to Kotler then. "And I'd like you to come with me."

"Under arrest?" Kotler smiled, half kidding.

"As an asset. We need you to help us retrieve the manuscript."

"I believe there are agents better trained for that sort of work," Kotler said.

"But you're trained as well, aren't you Dr. Kotler?" Coben smiled. "We need you for something else, though. So far, your adversary in all of this has been using not just cryptology but your personal history as a tool. We think there's a connection to you and your past, and we want you on hand, just in case."

Kotler thought about this, sighed, and nodded.

"Good," Coben said, smiling the same half-guarded smile as earlier. "Then let's get moving."

21

LIZ LUDLUM'S APARTMENT

Ludlum had exhausted all of the channels at her disposal. All, that was, that wouldn't get her flagged by the system. It had amassed quite a body of material and evidence, but so far it just wasn't enough.

She had managed to convince several local bodegas to give her any security footage they had from the date and time she was abducted. Many of them kept archives of video going back weeks, thanks to inexpensive digital security systems. Hard drives were cheap these days, and many security companies encouraged their clients to upgrade as much as possible. Ludlum appreciated those upsells, at the moment.

It was easier to get footage from these little storefronts, rather than try for traffic and ATM footage. Those took court orders. Bodegas took kind words, a little flirting, and the occasional twenty. It was a lot of work, canvassing the area, and then expanding as she got more leads. But it was paying off.

From the footage she'd gathered so far, Ludlum was able to piece together the path that Ryba had taken after leaving FBI headquarters. It had started as guesswork, casting around the building block by block until she spotted an image of the truck she recognized from the construction site. It wasn't a perfect shot—it came from an interior camera that happened to have a view of the front window of the bodega. But the truck had stopped for a light there, and she could make out enough details to be convinced that it was the one.

That gave her a direction and an area. The timestamp on the video gave her an exact time.

She had noted these details on her whiteboard—a new purchase that she'd set up in her living room. It blocked one entire wall, including her television, but it helped her to sort all the details she was finding.

The board was slowly filling as she went. From that first bodega, she was able to narrow her search, and she visited even more storefronts asking for video. She used her FBI credentials to grease the wheels, which helped. She could get into serious trouble if that came out, but she wasn't being belligerent about it. She was always sure to be kind, to ask politely, and to be as non-threatening as possible. If it ever came up, she hoped she could mitigate it by saying she was only identifying herself, not abusing authority.

She had about an eighty-percent success rate, which was enough. She could work with the results she was getting.

With the general direction and location established, as well as the timeline, she started making some educated guesses. She knew where they had ended up, having ridden Cameron Ryba's motorcycle from that location. It took time to work out the path that Red Ryba had taken, with her in the back of the truck, but soon she had that all mapped out.

Tracing that route had given her multiple angles of the truck, including the plate numbers and recognizable markings. She could recognize it now, which made it easier to spot.

The real work began then.

She started from FBI headquarters once again, and now she approached stores that lay in the opposite direction, along what she hoped was the path the truck had taken before parking near FBI HQ. To park where he had, Ryba would have had to come from a specific direction, and that helped Ludlum narrow the number of streets he would have used.

It took time, but she finally spotted the van in some of the footage, from a bodega a few blocks away. In the video, the truck was heading in the right direction. A good sign.

She placed it again, on the same street, still further out. And then another.

Block by block, street by street, Ludlum rolled back time, giving bodega owners a timeframe that became more refined as she went. Over the course of days, she traced Ryba all the way back to a specific block. The truck disappeared from all footage in that area, prior to the timeline Ludlum had established. There was no trace of it from any footage she managed to retrieve from the rest of the neighborhood.

That had to be the area where Ryba had first found the truck.

She used her contacts with the NYPD to search for any reports of a stolen truck matching that description, but if Ryba had taken it, no one reported it. It was possible he'd bought it, probably for cash, to keep it off the books. There were plenty of unregistered vehicles on the streets of Manhattan, moving around freely, without much worry about being spotted. As long as the drivers kept their speed down and didn't cause problems, they could get away with it indefinitely.

The plates on this truck were from out of state, but that didn't make them unusual. It mostly made them invisible, especially on commercial vehicles.

She'd convinced one of her NYPD friends to run the license

plate, and it had come back registered to a leasing company in Philadelphia, though the plates were from Florida. The vehicle had been initially purchased in Detroit and had passed through three different owners in New York, Boston, and Mississippi. She called the leasing office and was told that the truck had been sold as part of a liquidation. Bought at auction. No record of who had taken it. The whole thing was paid for with a cashier's check. Untraceable.

In other words, this was a dead end. There was no way to know for sure who had owned the truck before Ryba had gotten his hands on it, and so there was no one for her to question. For all she knew, Ryba may have been the one to buy it from auction in the first place.

This wasn't helping.

Ludlum spent a day canvassing the area where the truck had first appeared on video. She walked ten blocks in a circumference around the first bodega, stopped to ask questions at a couple of potential spots, and walking away with nothing. By the end of the day she was exhausted and hungry, and she found a café where she could get a cup of tea and a sandwich and just sit with her thoughts for a while.

She took out her phone and opened her growing file on Red Ryba.

He was a scary man. Even without the suspicion of being an international "mechanic"—an assassin and fixer-for-hire who took care of problems for the wealthy and unscrupulous— Red's background made it clear that he was both capable and dangerous.

The oldest of three brothers, raised in Russia, Red had left his family to join the military the moment he was old enough to do so. He had trained as a *Morskov Spetsnaz* "frogman"—the Russian equivalent of a US Navy SEAL—and by all publicly available accounts had served with distinction during two tours of combat. And then, for reasons not explained in his public record, he received a discharge.

Ludlum suspected she knew what that meant.

Upon leaving the Russian military, he'd been employed by a security service catering to diplomats and high-powered executives doing business in hotly contested regions. His work was not limited to Russian officials, but extended to anyone who could pay the exorbitant rates of the agency. Ryba excelled at this work and had become a client favorite for his dedication and commitment, as well as his track record.

Over the next few years, Ryba served as a bodyguard for several CEOs and other executives before becoming embroiled in a bit of intrigue. One of his clients had been kidnapped and tortured in Afghanistan.

Reports on this were also vague, but Ludlum had managed to piece the story together through a variety of news accounts and declassified military documents, mostly from US operatives.

The client had been taken while Ryba was charged with escorting the man's young daughter out of the country. That mission went off without a hitch, but in the meantime, the facility where the client had been living was raided by insurgents. The man, a high-level Russian diplomat, was abducted, and almost immediately there were photos and video of him being tortured, broadcast over live television.

Upon learning of the abduction, Ryba returned to the region, apparently commandeering a private plane to get there. Despite a US lockdown on the area, Ryba snuck behind enemy lines and penetrated the compound where his client was being held. In a single-man operation that took only 24 hours, Ryba rescued the diplomat and returned him to Russian soil.

By the news accounts and the diplomat's own profuse public gratitude, Ryba was a hero.

Ludlum suspected, though, that there was a lot more to the story than what the press had been allowed to cover.

And she wasn't alone. Though she hadn't been able to gain access to Ryba's full FBI file, she'd seen enough of it to know that he had a twisted code of honor. In the years since that rescue, his reputation had grown to legendary status. There were whispers and rumors about him. A mythology grew around his skills and his exploits. He was known to have a 100% success rate, and the rumor was that he would do anything, sacrifice anything, to keep that perfect score.

At some point, he had gone freelance, shifting his business model to a referral-only system. This had only enhanced his reputation and garnered an impressive level of loyalty from his former clients.

Ryba had created a closed system of sorts, letting his happy and satisfied clients take a cut of his fees in exchange for well-vetted referrals. It was a lucrative business for everyone, especially Ryba. His clientele trended toward the uber-wealthy, who had specialized needs. Any former client could refer a new client to Ryba and receive ten percent of the fee. It wasn't a bad deal.

The catch was responsibility—if a job went bad, if Ryba found himself betrayed, the referring client would pay the price. And the coin was skin, blood, and bone.

There were very few examples of this, though a couple did come up in Ludlum's research. There was far more information about Ryba's targets. She had a collection of crime-scene photos, victims splayed in all manner of grotesque and obscene poses. They'd all been tortured, that much was evident. And the work had been done with efficiency, if not elegance. The results seemed dependent on Ryba's goal. Pain, if pain was required. Or a quick death, if the client had asked him to supply that small mercy.

That was the story for each method she could spot. There

were commonalities, but each victim's corpse revealed subtleties that hinted at more than routine and process.

Ludlum studied these photos, comparing them, and came away with signs of commonality between each murder. Ryba did have a signature. It was subtle, but she had studied enough of his victims to recognize it.

The trouble was, it was only assumed this was Ryba's work. There was no substantial evidence linking him to any of these crime scenes, and so everything she was learning was tinged with conjecture. Thinking of this as "Ryba's signature" was a convenience.

So far, nothing she'd uncovered could hold up in a court of law. She needed more.

As Ludlum dug further, however, she began to find his signature in things that could be tied to him. His early work, in Afghanistan, the way in which he'd taken out enemy combatants. His interrogation methods. She could see the patterns.

Blunt force injury to the skull, to incapacitate the victim. Ryba was using his physical strength and imposing build to take the enemy by surprise.

Strips of cloth to gag the victim. Silence was key. He was exerting a sort of psychological power over them, by removing their ability to speak.

Hands and feet tied with something difficult or even impossible to snap by brute strength, and something tough to cut— like electrical wire. More incapacitation, more control, more dominance.

Abduction and relocation to remote sites. Isolate the victim, disorient them, surround them with the unfamiliar, so they lose hope of rescue or escape. Make their dominance complete so they will be compliant.

All of it was familiar. Ludlum had lived it, only a few days ago. She'd been part of a story Ryba could weave like a master. Her abduction had his fingerprints all over it.

This was him.

She'd never be able to use that in a court of law. A good defense team would chew through it like it was cotton candy. But it was a start. It settled the question for her, at least. Red Ryba had been the one to abduct her.

The trouble was, none of this helped her to find him.

She'd sipped her tea, and stared out of the window of the café, watching the light fade as evening approached. She'd need to catch a cab or an Uber home. She'd rest and start again tomorrow. Though she was out of leads, at this point. She didn't know what to do next. Ryba was a ghost. He was going to get away.

Maybe she needed to change her perspective.

She'd been searching for Ryba like a detective, finding his last known location, tracing his route backward, trying to track him using the clues she could identify. This wasn't her specialty, though. She was a forensic anthropologist. She specialized evidence she could find on a body. Evidence that wasn't always apparent.

How would she approach this, if it were a murder? If she were examining a corpse and was having trouble finding the cause of death, what would she do?

She turned back to the autopsy photos.

They all shared commonalities, and Ludlum had been able to find Ryba's signature, tracing it from victim to victim, back to his early days. There were only a few autopsy reports showcasing his work at that time, but the roots of his methods were there. He had learned his craft there. Perfected it.

What else had he learned from that training? What other skills had he been taught, that might still be part of his patterns today?

His file hinted at some of what she needed, but there had to be more.

Ludlum called for an Uber, and when it arrived, she left the café and made her way home. Before she'd reached her apartment, however, she'd already made travel arrangements. She needed to talk to someone who knew how men like Ryba were trained. And she had someone in mind.

She'd just have to convince him to talk to her.

22

TARGET LOCATION

Kotler and Coben were *en route* to the location that Denzel had provided. It had been a long, quiet, and admittedly stressful car ride so far.

Rather than drive to the site, Coben had arranged for a car, and the two of them sat in the back seat as they passed through New York streets. Kotler tried to take some comfort in the everyday details of the world streaking past his window, but he had to admit that the silence was starting to get to him. Which may have been the NSA Agent's intention.

Kotler smiled to himself and shook his head. He was letting paranoia have a say, and that would only lead to heightened anxiety. If he had questions about Coben's agenda, and about his presence here, then there was only one practical way to get answers.

He turned to Coben, who was reading something from his phone.

"You said you want my help. What exactly are you expecting me to do?"

Coben continued reading for a moment, then clicked off the

phone's display and slid it into the interior pocket of his suit jacket. He turned to Kotler, and wove his fingers together, cupping them over one knee as he crossed his legs.

"You did an impressive job of cracking multiple cyphers in that manuscript. Not to mention the cylinder. The step rotor keypad. Quite a bit of cryptological work. Is codebreaking something you practice regularly?"

A game. More games. Coben was deliberately orchestrating his body language, taking a pose that was intended to put Kotler at ease, while keeping his facial features and micro expressions under perfect control. It was all meant to manipulate Kotler. And to some extent, it was working.

The NSA would have a file on him, Kotler realized. They would know his skills, as well as his history. They would know things about him that, conceivably, Kotler didn't know himself. So the game was rigged. Kotler couldn't win this.

But winning and losing weren't the only two possible outcomes. There was also playing to a draw.

Kotler wouldn't be able to read Coben, as he could most people. But maybe he could use that as an advantage. Maybe he could learn something from the way Coben masked his body language—learn what he needed from what Coben wasn't saying and doing.

"I've dabbled with it as a hobby," Kotler said. " From time to time. It's not all that dissimilar to my actual work."

Coben nodded, allowing a tight smile. "Anthropology. You study ancient cultures."

"Among other things," Kotler smiled back.

"Quantum Mechanics," Coben nodded. "You have an impressive academic background, Dr. Kotler. Multiple Ph.Ds in multiple disciplines. And not easy disciplines at that."

"I have a wide range of interests, and I enjoy learning," Kotler said. "I was encouraged to explore my interests."

"Your education goes well beyond your university career,

though, doesn't it? You've evidently studied psychology, forensics, body language ... and now codebreaking."

Kotler shrugged and smiled. "I've also studied where to find the best brisket in Manhattan and how to make the perfect cup of espresso. I have a wide range of interests."

"Very wide," Coben said. "That list doesn't even include the military training."

Kotler sighed. "I wouldn't exactly call it military training. I never served."

"No, that's true. You were never officially part of any branch of the military. Though you were courted."

"I had a few offers."

Coben smiled, laughing lightly. "More than a few. Every branch of the US military."

"I never should have taken the ASVAB," Kotler said.

"And, more recently, offers from government agencies," Coben continued. "What made you decide to work with the FBI?"

Kotler shrugged. "Agent Denzel," he said. "He saved my life, in Pueblo."

"He also helped you to remain involved in a joint action against a terrorist threat. The events in Pueblo have put you on an interesting path, haven't they?"

Kotler considered this. "It wasn't the first time I've been involved in some harrowing events, but sure. After we recovered the Coelho Medallion and stopped Anwar Adham's attack on NORAD, I'll admit that things picked up for me. The details that were released to the public helped to get me more invitations to speak and to participate in research and dig sites around the world."

"And the classified work," Coben said, "put you in a high-level position in a brand-new division of the FBI. You gained access to a whole new world of information and resources."

Kotler studied Coben. Everything about the man was strategic, calculated. The comfortable pose, hinting at openness but with a touch of being guarded. The smile, placating but welcoming. Open up to me, his body was saying. Tell me all the secrets and all the true things. Tell me who you really are and what you want most in the world.

That was what Coben's calculated body language was asking, and so Kotler could deduce a few things, make a few educated guesses.

Coben knew Kotler's background. He knew not only Kotler's public history but his hidden history as well. Not just the FBI work—that would have been easy. There were files, reports, video of debriefings. Coben would have access to all of it.

It was clear, though, that he knew some of Kotler's hidden personal background. The details that Kotler had kept off record as much as possible.

Nothing sinister. Nothing Kotler was ashamed of or needed to worry over, if they came to light. But a lot of those details led to parts of Kotler's past that hurt for him to think about. They were avoided out of self-preservation, rather than some clandestine agenda.

Coben was probing into things Kotler had buried, so that he wouldn't think about them, and was using them to imply that Kotler might be playing some sort of long game.

Which meant that despite everything Coben clearly knew about Kotler, he hadn't yet worked out Kotler's motives. He was probing to find out what Kotler really wanted, why he'd moved to position himself as an independent consultant with the FBI, why he had bothered to learn about history and physics, psychology and codebreaking. Coben saw Kotler as an enigma, and the NSA had a long and robust history of finding trouble on the other side of an enigma.

Kotler laughed.

Coben frowned. "What is it?"

Kotler shook his head. "I don't have one," he said.

Coben was confused, and for the first time, Kotler saw a genuine expression flicker across the man's features. "I'm sorry, what don't you have?"

"An agenda," Kotler said. "A plan. I don't have anything motivating me to be part of the FBI or any other agency. I've only ever been after one thing, and it has nothing to do with government agencies. Except that sometimes our interests overlap."

"And what is that one thing, Dr. Kotler?"

Kotler grinned. "The meaning of life, Agent Coben. At least, that's the shorthand for it. I've studied the things I've studied so I could make an effort to solve the oldest riddle in history. I want to know why people are the way they are. I want to know what the purpose of humanity is, what it means to be alive, to think. I study history because I want to find a reason for it to exist. And I study physics because I want to find the cause of it all. That's it. That's all I was ever after. It's a lifelong pursuit. Probably impossible."

Coben waved this off. "I know this already. You don't exactly make a secret of any of this. You say this line in every interview, and you write it into every personal thesis. The whole world knows the 'why' you've chosen for yourself."

"So you know that I'm not after anything that should concern the NSA," Kotler said.

"I'm not so sure about that," Coben replied. "You could genuinely be as idealistic as you seem to be. But you've managed to get yourself into an influential role with one of the most powerful agencies in the country. One where idealism can be disastrous. Idealists do things that put lives in danger." He studied Kotler for a moment, his composure slipping back into place. The mask was back. "I think there's more motivating you than even you realize. And in my experience, it's the motives men hide even from themselves that end up being the most dangerous."

Kotler considered this.

For two years he had more or less sidelined his life's work, the archeological research that he'd decided was his career, in favor of helping Denzel and his new division solve riddles and crimes that had world-changing implications. He had helped to bring dangerous people to justice. Kotler hadn't really considered himself anything more than an anthropologist, even when he was busying himself with tasks that no anthropologist would ever have to worry about. Was it possible that he had some underlying motive for this work? Something he hadn't yet revealed to himself?

He glanced at Coben once more and saw that the man had returned to examining his phone.

The car arrived at the location Denzel had specified. The doors opened, and Coben and Kotler stepped out. They were back to relative silence, broken only by Coben issuing orders and asking for updates.

Kotler was thinking about everything that had happened over the past twenty-four hours, and a detail he'd glossed over now nagged at him.

Coben had hinted that Historic Crimes was the beneficiary of some unknown, special consideration, higher up in the echelons of the bureau, perhaps even in the government itself.

Maybe Kotler's agenda wasn't the one Coben was after.

The Agent was good at hiding his micro expressions, masking what he was really thinking, what he knew and didn't know. He was unreadable.

But he'd slipped.

Kotler realized that without meaning to, Coben had posed the very problem he was trying to solve.

He didn't know who was behind the establishment and funding of Historic Crimes.

But he believed that Kotler did.

RED RYBA HAD BEEN PATIENT, following from afar, but when he recognized what was happening, he pulled back even further.

There was an operation in progress.

The man escorting Kotler was an agent, Ryba was confident, but he was not FBI. The way this man conducted himself, the way he moved about in the world and the manner in which he had arrived and taken command at what was obviously a checkpoint—it all hinted at the man being in a more clandestine line of work. CIA, most likely. Perhaps NSA, though they were not often found in the field.

This complicated things.

Ryba left the car he'd been using and began to move around in the neighborhood on foot. He would come back for his tools, stashed in the trunk. For the moment he needed access to someplace that would give him the proper vantage point but would also allow him a means of escape.

The challenge was the notable presence of FBI and police in the area. They were everywhere. Every rooftop, every empty apartment or storefront.

They were hiding, staying out of sight, but Ryba had been trained to spot them.

He bought a Coke from a street cart and sipped through the straw as he walked casually back to the car. He'd seen enough.

This wasn't the time. For the moment, Dan Kotler had the best sort of protection, though Ryba was certain that Kotler wasn't aware he even needed it. This operation might have provided the perfect distraction, but there was too much activity. Too many risks, with agents everywhere.

Kotler could wait.

Ryba started the car and turned into traffic, leaving the site behind. He would find Kotler again. He knew where he lived. He would find a time when Kotler had his guard down, and he would take care of him then. There was no hurry.

For now, there were other things to deal with.

It took half an hour to get to the lot, and Ryba circled it twice to gather the intel he needed to finalize his plans. The lot closed in an hour. At that point, security would begin its rounds.

There were three gates allowing access to the lot. The first gate was just beyond a squat office with bricks so stained by city pollution it was impossible to determine their original color. Many of the windows were covered on the inside with aluminum foil. A glass door was sheathed in iron bars, with a camera directly above it, aimed at the pad of cement at the entrance.

There was a drive-thru window just in front of the gate, and a short pole with a keypad mounted to it.

This was where tow trucks would bring vehicles in from the streets. The window would be manned during business hours, in case there were questions. Otherwise, city tow trucks had the code for the gate and could make their deposits any time, day or night.

Too public. And too many obstacles. Getting through that gate would bring more attention than Ryba was willing to deal with at the moment.

The second gate had more promise. It was a side gate that ran parallel to a side street. This was a long, ambling gate topped with razor wire that opened wide enough to bring in larger forms of transport. The lot housed a menagerie of seized vehicles one might not expect, including large boats, camper trailers, and even a parade float.

This gate was locked with a simple chain and padlock. It had potential. It was partially blocked from view, from the main street at least, by the eclectic collection of large vehicles parked just inside. The trouble was the street lamp. Directly above the entrance was a large halogen light that would cast a cone of near daylight on the spot. The neighborhood was just busy enough that someone was sure to witness someone cutting that chain.

Still, Ryba noted it, primarily for its proximity to his target. He could solve the problem of the light. There were ways.

The third gate was at the back of the lot. At first glance, it seemed the best choice. It backed up against a lot filled with junk, mostly abandoned cars. The lot beyond was encircled by its own fence, but this was in such disrepair that parts of it sagged inward. Local kids likely used the place as their own personal playground. Red and his brothers had played in a similar lot back home, and the sight of it was enough to inspire some nostalgia. It also reminded him of why he was here.

Still, this gate had promise.

There was some appeal to this gate, but there was also a downside. The alley running between the impound lot and the abandoned lot was strewn with large debris—dumpsters, crates, even the shell of an old car. There was no clear path in or out. He could be boxed in if conditions went against him, and he always worked under the assumption that something unexpected could happen.

Like the side gate, there was a chain and lock, with the chain snaked through the chain link of the gate and the fence. It was loose, though not loose enough that Ryba could slip in. He could cut the chain and leave the gate closed, and it likely wouldn't be spotted.

This was the most vulnerable of the three gates. There were street lights, but they were on the corners of the impound lot, for use on the two streets that ran to either side. This meant the back of the facility was cast in shadow.

Night came upon the neighborhood, and Ryba parked the car several blocks away, in a parking garage that charged by the day. He would retrieve it later, perhaps in several days. He'd just leave his tools in the trunk. It would be safe enough. Later he'd retrieve it and resume his hunt of Dr. Kotler.

He did take one item out of the trunk, stowing it in the inner pocket of his long coat. He then walked back toward the impound lot, taking his time, letting local activity slow to a crawl as people returned home from day jobs and left for night shifts. He lingered for a time with a light crowd outside of a local bar, never really engaging with anyone, leaning against the wall and listening to stories of sexual conquest and American sporting events. Uninteresting stuff, but it was easy to blend in while waiting. Eventually, he left them to their conversations, having made no impression on them whatsoever.

As he walked, he scanned the environment, making sure no one was around. At one point he spotted three drunken frat boys—or what he thought of as frat boys—stumbling and laughing, shushing themselves, taking selfies. They were on the other side of the avenue, and stopped in front of yet another bar, lingering in the doorway. They were the only people out at this time of night, in this area of town. The neighborhood was rough enough to keep most people indoors.

He arrived at the impound lot ten minutes after leaving the bar and almost three hours after leaving the car. The site was now dark and quiet, as he had hoped. He turned the corner and took up a position across the street. He leaned against the wall of an auto mechanic's shop, looking up at the halogen light above the lot's side gate.

He had made his decision on the walk over.

The back gate would mean less opportunity to be spotted, but it was also the furthest from his target, and the debris in the alley could slow him down.

The side gate was less than forty feet from the target and had a clear path to an escape route. He could time things better, exiting onto the street and gone before anyone could stop him.

It was the best option, but far from perfect. He could make it better.

Ryba reached into the side pocket of his coat and slowly removed the pistol. It had a silencer already in place, adding to its length and bulk, but it still felt light and welcome in his gloved hand. He glanced from side to side, looking for anyone who might be on the street. When he saw no one, he raised the weapon in a quick, smooth arc and fired a single shot.

The sound was muffled by the silencer but was still loud enough that it might have drawn a glance from passersby—like firing a compressed air nail gun. The noise from the street helped to further mute the sound of the weapon, however, along with the tinkle of glass as it rained down from the halogen.

He slipped the gun back into his coat pocket. He waited.

If security had noticed the light going out, they hadn't considered it much of a problem. No one came to the gate, no one appeared on the street.

This whole side of the impound lot was now shrouded in darkness, providing precisely the cover that Ryba needed.

He walked across the street, pulling the balaclava over his face as he went.

When he came to the gate, he took out the tool he'd hidden inside his coat—a stubby set of bolt cutters. He cut the lock and let it fall to the ground as he took hold of the chain. He carefully moved this, threading it carefully back through the gate so that it would dangle free, rather than running down the corrugated metal of the gate with a sound like machine gun fire.

He paused again, waited, listened, watched. He then rolled the gate open, as quietly as possible, until there was a gap about four foot wide.

He entered the impound lot, casting the bolt cutters into the weeds.

He knew there would be cameras, but what he was about to

do would be more than enough for authorities to figure out who was responsible. His features were covered, and it would be impossible for anyone to verify his identity. But they would know. His reputation, as well as recent events, would tell them.

He found the Indian among several other motorcycles, lined up side by side on a wide pad of cement. The light here was low, but even in the dimness, Ryba could tell that there was damage. The woman had casually dropped it to the ground, in front of FBI headquarters. A mirror was shattered, and there were dents and scratches. Nothing that couldn't be fixed or replaced. And more importantly, nothing that would prevent it from running.

This had been Cameron's favorite thing. Red wouldn't allow it to be sold at some police auction. He would take it, have it restored in his brother's honor. It would be a memorial to Cameron Ryba. Red owed him that, as blood. His brother had died in the line of duty, and restoring his prized possession would be a fitting memorial.

"Hold it right there!" a voice said from behind him.

Ryba turned, feeling perturbed. This was a moment of reverence. Part of his mourning for the loss of his brother, and a price his code of honor demanded. It was a rare moment of letting his guard down, which he now realized was foolish. Mistakes such as these were the very thing that had gotten Cameron killed. Red was better than this. He had allowed himself to be soft.

Ryba turned to face the man, who was already chattering into a radio pinned to his lapel. He told Ryba to raise his hands, and Ryba complied.

With the same quick, smooth motion as he'd used for the halogen, Ryba raised the gun and fired another single shot, this time hitting the security guard in the chest.

The man toppled backward, his own weapon firing, ricocheting into the night. He was alive but severely injured.

Ryba wasted no time. He leapt onto the motorcycle, using the spare key to start it. The machine roared to life, and Ryba throttled it to high speed, racing through the impound lot, turning down the darkened alleyways between seized vehicles. The bike's headlight reflected crazily from boats and trailers, creating a cacophony of shifting shadows as Ryba passed.

A pulse of blue and white lights snapped on in front of him, and Ryba turned to the side, skidding the bike to a stop.

Another security guard, this time in a small pickup, had pulled in front of the gate.

"Put your hands over your head and get down on the ground, now!"

Ryba heard him, though he couldn't see him past the lights of the truck. He glanced around, looking for any other route. He was hemmed in, however, and had very little choice.

He again throttled to full speed, racing directly toward the security truck, taking his weapon out and firing directly into the lights and windows of the vehicle.

He once again skidded to a stop and slammed the kickstand down, climbing off and moving in a crouch toward the door of the truck. He rose then, casually, without worry. He put the gun back into his coat pocket, stepping forward, peering into the truck.

The guard was slumped over the steering wheel, dead. There was country music playing on the radio. The guard had an unfired revolver still in his hand.

Ryba put the vehicle in gear and stepped aside, letting it roll out of his path until it crashed into the colorful parade float.

He stepped back and swung his leg back over the seat of the Indian. In seconds he was blasting through the side gate, onto the side street and then turning onto the main avenue. He raced down the street at high speed until he disappeared into the canyons of the city.

23

RIKERS ISLAND PRISON COMPLEX, NEW YORK

Ludlum surrendered her purse. She used her FBI identification, which helped move things along. She wasn't allowed to carry anything into the prison, beyond her pen and notepad. That would be enough.

The visitor booths at Rikers were drab, depressing, but everything Ludlum had come to expect thanks to television and movies. She sat in front of a thick pane of glass in what looked like a beige cubicle, and she waited.

The man she'd come to see was escorted into the booth by two large and capable-looking guards, and he was guided to his chair. He waited until the guards left, and then reached up with cuffed wrists and took the handset on his side, holding it to his ear.

Liz did the same.

"Do I know you?" the man asked, his Russian accent thick enough to sound like a stereotype.

His name was Ramzan Peskov, a former colonel in Russia's *Morskoy Spetsnaz*. He was maybe in his sixties, with grey-to-white hair that spiked in a crazy, unkempt pattern on top of his head. His face was long and wrinkled, his eyes sunken. There was white stubble on his cheeks.

Beneath the rolled-up sleeves of his orange jumpsuit, there was a hint of a tattoo. Something written in Russian, beneath a detailed depiction of the skulled figure of death bearing an automatic rifle. It was a common mark for members of the *Morskoy Spetsnaz*.

Peskov had somehow managed to apply for and receive US citizenship, despite his history. He'd enjoyed good ol' American freedom for two years, until he'd robbed a liquor store and shot three people, leading to a life sentence without possibility of parole.

"No," Ludlum said, shaking her head. "You don't know me. But I believe we have a friend in common."

Peskov studied her and shook his head slowly. "I do not believe this is so." He started to hang up the receiver.

Ludlum held up a page from her notebook, with the name Redmond Ryba written in block letters at the top.

Peskov studied it and brought the phone back to his ear. "Is he in trouble? Has he died?"

Liz shrugged. "Yes. And no. He's alive, but he's definitely in trouble. Or he will be when we find him."

Here she was treading on thin ice. She had used her FBI credentials to get in here, but it wouldn't take much for anyone to determine she wasn't operating in an official capacity. The wrong question could unravel all of this. She had to play it close.

"And I suppose you are here to entice me to help you," Peskov said, his expression curious.

"I'm here to ask for your help, yes. But I have nothing to offer you. I can't get you any special favors in here."

Peskov chuckled, shaking his head. "You offer no incentive but wish for my help. Very American."

"I was thinking it was very Russian," Ludlum replied, her

tone hard. "I may not be able to offer you much incentive, but it wouldn't be difficult to cause you trouble. The right call to the right person, and your stay here becomes a lot more unpleasant."

A bluff. Mostly. She thought she might have enough pull to get someone to harass the guy, if she needed. Beyond that, ethics and resources became limiting factors. Whether she could do it was less relevant than whether she would. And she wasn't sure of that at all.

Peskov, of course, had no way to know that. She hoped.

He studied her for a moment, then laughed again, shaking his head. "I do not believe you. But is ok. This place," he waved at the walls of the booth but was indicating the prison in general. "There is little to entertain me here. Your American books, they're so *cheerful*. And so short. American television," he rolled his eyes and let loose a stream of curses in Russian. He leaned in then, locking eyes with Ludlum. "What is it that you need? What can I do to assist my old friend, Red Ryba, in finding hell?"

Liz flipped her notebook to a blank page. "The two of you served together in Afghanistan?"

Peskov nodded.

"I'm looking for information about how Ryba works. How he thinks. What can you tell me about this training?"

Peskov laughed. "His training? It would take years to tell you. We have less than ten minutes."

"Give me something I can use as a starting place then," she said. "A way to figure out how he thinks, so I can track him."

"Track him to do what?" Peskov asked, a smirk on his lips.

Ludlum paused, took a breath, and said, "To bring him to justice."

Peskov chuckled, which led to a slight coughing fit. He patted his chest as if looking for a pack of cigarettes that weren't there. Giving up, he leaned forward and nodded to her hands, then motioned to the wound on the side of her head. "Ryba, he did these things to you?"

"Yes," she said, deciding that honesty was the best policy here. "He abducted me. Bound my hands with wire. Slammed my head against a doorframe. Then he sent his brother to ..." she wasn't entirely sure about this part. "To take care of me. And I killed him."

Peskov's eyes widened, and he laughed, a loud bark. "You killed the brother of Red Ryba?"

She nodded.

"And now you wish to bring him to justice. For his crimes," he said, waving again at her injuries.

"Yes," she said.

Peskov nodded. "My advice is to leave this. If he has not already come for you, then he has decided you acted honorably. He does not blame *you* for his brother's death."

She thought about this. She hadn't even considered that Ryba might come after her again. Which, as she considered it, was a strange thing. Why wouldn't he? She had killed his brother. She had escaped from the confines he'd personally placed on her. She was a loose thread. Wouldn't he want to take care of that?

But Peskov's words made sense, and they opened up another possibility she hadn't considered.

"He doesn't blame me," she said slowly. "Then ... who would he blame?"

Peskov shrugged. A buzzer sounded, and the door opened behind him. Two guards stepped into the room. Peskov ignored them for a moment, holding the phone to his ear and saying in a deliberate tone, "Red Ryba will seek out the one he feels is responsible for his brother's death. You wish to find him? He will be wherever he can have access to this person."

The guards barked orders at him, and Peskov shouted back in Russian, dropping the receiver to the table top.

Liz, still holding her phone, watched as Peskov was guided back through the door, on his way back to his cell. She hung up the phone, and sat back, staring at the notebook that still lay open and face-up on her table.

Who would Ryba hold responsible for his brother's death, if not her?

It took only seconds.

She snapped her notebook closed and raced back to the front desk, retrieved her things, and left Rikers as quickly as possible.

24

TARGET LOCATION

The target building was surrounded, but from the look of it, no one could ever guess.

Kotler was impressed by the level of secrecy and camouflage. Denzel's people were laced throughout the neighborhood, in vans and empty office spaces, on rooftops and on the streets themselves. From what he could overhear from Coben and the FBI liaison, everyone Kotler saw out in the open was a part of this sting, and there were dozens more agents hidden out of sight.

They were in the front room of a closed storefront only a block from the center of everyone's attention. The windows were boarded, preventing anyone from seeing inside. Lights, tables, and chairs had been brought in, setting up temporary office space for the agents.

Coben finished with the liaison and turned to Kotler. "Are you armed?"

Kotler blinked. "No one ever asks me that," he said. Then frowned. "But no."

Coben called over one of the field agents and asked that Kotler be brought a vest and a sidearm.

"Roland never lets me have a gun," Kotler smiled.

"You're not a child," Coben said. "And I've seen your training record. You're a crack shot."

Kotler shrugged. "On a shooting range, sure."

"You qualified with one of the tightest groupings in your class," Coben said. "Impressive."

Kotler felt a bit flattered but realized this was likely all part of the same game. Coben was demonstrating more knowledge of Kotler's past. More manipulation.

The field agent returned with a vest and a weapon, and Kotler donned these quickly as he followed Coben into another room.

"What exactly is my role here?" Kotler asked. The room they'd entered was filled with communications and surveillance equipment. Agents wearing headsets were communicating with men and women in strategic positions all around the target building. On one monitor Kotler could see that the building of interest was a multi-story warehouse, with offices occupying the top floors. There was no sign on the front of the building, but it seemed to be in active use, not abandoned.

"Wait," Kotler said, stopping in front of the monitor. Coben moved on, and Kotler snagged the agent's arm. "Wait!"

Coben turned and gave him a steady look. Kotler held firm. "That building ... it's an active business."

"Yes," Coben said. "The top floors are rented out to business tenants."

"There are civilians in there, then?"

"Yes," Coben repeated. "We're taking precautions to ensure their safety."

Kotler looked from Coben to the monitor, and back again. "And what precautions are those?"

"We have this handled, Dr. Kotler," Coben said, then turned and resumed walking to the back of the room.

Kotler suddenly wondered why he needed a gun. Or a vest.

They were going to raid the building, that much was clear. What was it Coben thought they'd find in there, besides the manuscript?

Something was off, and Kotler couldn't quite work out what it was. It worried him.

He joined Coben and several other agents in the back of the room, which had become the command center of the operation. Kotler didn't recognize anyone in the room, and assumed they must also be NSA agents. No introductions were made.

They were huddled in various conversations, consulting a wall of displays, satellite imagery, and POV footage from agent body cams. Kotler checked the clip from his weapon, then cleared the chamber and engaged the safety. He attached the holster at his side. He hoped he wouldn't have to use it. He also wasn't especially keen on trying out the efficiency of the bullet-proof vest.

Coben finally left the others and pulled Kotler aside. "There are two teams of ten going in from the front and back. The primary target is on the top floor. Support will surround the building, and we have snipers on the rooftops in every direction. I want you to go in with Team Bravo."

Kotler blinked. "You want me in the building? On the raid?"

"We think we've narrowed down the location of the manuscript, and I want you there to verify authenticity."

Kotler thought about this. "And what else?"

"That's it," Coben said. "Put eyes on it, retrieve it, and the men will back you out of there."

"I could verify that from here, after retrieval," Kotler said. "So there's something else happening."

Coben studied him, then nodded. "You're right. There is. And it's classified."

"So classified that you need to send me in there under a pretext," Kotler said. "And endanger the lives of civilians on those other floors."

He watched Coben's features, inscrutable as ever, then shook his head. He unbuckled the vest, tearing away Velcro and pulling the whole thing off over his head.

"What are you doing?" Coben asked, calmly but deliberately.

"I'm not sure what the end game is, but I'm done playing blind. Whatever is inside this building, I need to know about it before I go in. You're risking my life and the lives of the people inside, without so much as giving me a reason." He tossed the vest on the floor and handed his sidearm to a passing agent. He started to walk to the door they'd used to enter.

Coben reached out and put a firm hand on his arm.

"You're going to want to go in there," he said.

Kotler stopped, looking Coben in the eye. "Why?" he asked.

Coben glanced around the room, making sure no one was listening. He took the sidearm back from the agent and nodded for the man to move on.

He turned to Kotler, offering the weapon. Kotler made no move to take it.

Coben shook his head, dropping the weapon to his side and meeting Kotler's gaze. "Because," he said, "your brother is in there."

He waited for the news to register, and held the weapon out one last time. "Now do you want the gun?"

25

FBI OFFICES, MANHATTAN

"He's been pulled into the raid on Lee Patterson's last known location," Denzel said over the phone.

Ludlum was halfway to FBI headquarters, in the back of a taxi, and stopped dead by traffic. The tension was tempting her to get out and sprint the rest of the way. "I think Red Ryba may be after him," she said, knowing that this would raise the inevitable question ...

"How would you know that?"

She sighed. "It's going to be hard to explain, but I've talked to someone who knows Ryba. Someone he served with, in the *Morskoy Spetsnaz*."

"The who-what now?" Denzel asked.

"Russian military. Kind of the Russian version of the Navy Seals. Ryba was an agent who went freelance, and ..."

"Liz," Denzel said calmly. "Have you been investigating Red Ryba while off duty?"

She swallowed, nodding, and then said aloud, "I have, yes. And I've discovered some things."

There was silence for a beat from Denzel's end. Then, "Tell me."

She gave him the details she'd uncovered, glancing up from time to time to see if the cabby was listening. He appeared to be absorbed in whatever talk radio show was blaring from the speakers. She kept her voice low anyway, tilting her head down to keep the conversation as private as possible.

When she'd given Denzel everything she had, he replied, "Get here as soon as you can. There's more happening that you're not aware of."

"Like what?" Ludlum asked.

"Ryba stole his brother's motorcycle from the city impound. One security guard is dead, and another is critically injured. But he made a mistake." Denzel took a breath. "We got his face on camera," Denzel said. "We can positively link him to everything."

Ludlum took a sharp breath, then looked with increasing anxiety at the jammed lanes of traffic. She took some cash out of her bag and threw it into the cabbie's lap. He looked over his shoulder, surprised, as she popped the door open and took to the sidewalk.

"I'm on my way," she said, and started to run.

DENZEL MET Ludlum just as she was entering FBI headquarters. It was clear that he'd been waiting for her, outside of security. "Come with me," he said, motioning for her to follow.

She kept pace with him to the parking garage, and stood beside him, panting slightly, as they rode the elevator to where he was parked.

"You ok?" he asked, concerned.

"Ran here," she panted. "Nine blocks."

He shook his head, and as the elevator opened, they were once again on the move.

"So where are we going?" Ludlum asked.

"To warn Kotler," he said. "I can't get him on the phone. The whole team is on a complete communications blackout. I think they're moving on Patterson and the manuscript."

"You're not worried we'll get in the way?"

"I'm worried they don't have all the information they need." They came to his car, and he unlocked it with the remote. They climbed in, and Ludlum had barely tucked her bag under her feet and buckled her seatbelt before they were passing under the gate arm of the garage.

"We have about fifteen minutes until we get there," Denzel said. "Tell me everything you've uncovered."

She nodded and began telling him all the details, referring to her notebook when she needed to. "It never occurred to me that he might be out for revenge," she said. "Dumb. I just didn't think of it."

Denzel shook his head. "I should have considered it. I was too busy focusing on Patterson, and then this weirdness with Agent Coben."

"Who?" Ludlum asked.

Now it was Denzel's turn to explain.

"You called in the NSA?"

"No choice," Denzel replied. "But it didn't go quite the way I expected. Agent Coben took over, which is fine. I saw that coming. But then he wanted Kotler with him on it, and that seems unusual to me."

"Why would the NSA need an anthropologist on a raid?"

"Kotler has an ... eclectic background," Denzel said. "Coben seems to know everything about him."

"More than I know, that's for sure," Ludlum said.

Denzel shot her a side glance.

She shook her head, recovering quickly. "We aren't just

racing to tell Kotler about Ryba, are we?" she asked. "You're using this as an excuse."

Denzel said nothing but stared straight ahead, navigating through traffic at a pace that Ludlum thought was a little fast.

He was in a hurry. He was worried.

So was she.

26

TARGET LOCATION

Kotler hung back as the Beta team breached the rear door of the building.

This was a warehouse level, with only a few offices, mostly for the workers. Their entrance caused a stir, but several agents rushed in to secure the floor and escort everyone to a safe location. They would stay in the building, for now, where they were easier to corral. The warehouse floor would become a holding area.

Luckily it was getting late, and most people had left for the evening. There were only a handful of people in the building at this hour.

The ten agents of Beta team rushed to the stairs, with Kotler in tow.

Several flights later Kotler wished he had a better cardio routine, but he managed to keep up.

They arrived on the target floor and left two guards at the stairwell door as the rest went up one more flight.

The radio earpiece Kotler was wearing came to life.

"Beta, Alpha. We are in position, over."

"Roger Alpha. Beta in position."

There were a few more exchanges, and then a feeling of chaos as the lower and upper floors were secured and cleared. A smattering of workers, mostly the cleaning crew, were handed off and escorted to the warehouse level.

Kotler felt a lot better with the civilians out of the way, but questioned the decision to wait until this moment to do it. He understood that they were attempting to take the target off guard, but having these people here increased the risk of civilian casualties.

He decided to trust that the agents had good intel and a good plan, and that he wasn't privy to it.

For now, Kotler was focused on finding and rescuing his brother.

Coben had reluctantly briefed him, telling him that Jeffrey was reported missing after he'd failed to show up for a charity event the previous night. Worse, Jeffrey's car had been found, abandoned but still running, only a couple of miles from the event. There'd been blood, and signs of a struggle.

Kotler wanted to call Christina, to make sure she and Alex were ok, but Coben informed him that they were in a safe house, and that there was currently a communications blackout on the mission. No calls, in or out.

Kotler's only choice was to accept the situation and do what he could to help. He was being offered a rare opportunity—to aid in rescuing his brother. Of course, he was only being allowed access because Coben needed him to identify the manuscript.

He'd deal with Coben later.

Kotler followed the Beta team as they moved back to the target floor, and when both teams were set, they burst through the door in the same way as they had on the floor above. The agents shouted commands and trained their weapons on anyone they saw, ordering them to the floor.

Everyone complied, though Kotler could see panic in their eyes.

They moved now through the offices, rapidly clearing the space, section by section, until they came to the door of a storage room. It was locked but took only one hit from the portable battering ram, splintering into bits and slamming open.

They moved, weapons ready, and after a moment called to Kotler.

He had his own weapon out, and when he moved into the room, he was prepared to open fire, if needed. He stopped short when he saw Jeffrey, hands chained to the wall.

Around his chest was a vest laden with what Kotler assumed was C-4. A device was attached dead-center of Jeffrey's chest. A light blinked on, steady.

"We have a bomb," one of the agents reported.

The order went out to clear all civilians from the building.

Kotler heard it all playing out over his earpiece. There was a flurry of activity all around, but Kotler was moving in slow motion, inching toward his brother.

Jeffrey stared at him. He looked a little rough. His chin had a scuff on it, and there was blood drying on the side of his face. His shirt was untucked and stained. Despite all of this, it was good to see that he was not only alive but in generally good shape.

He stared at Kotler, his eyes a little wide, and a little angry, a little frightened.

"Jeffrey," Kotler started, moving closer.

"Dr. Kotler," one agent reached out, putting a hand on his shoulder to stop him, but Kotler angrily shrugged his hand off.

"They said if I made any noise, alerted anyone that I was in here, the bomb would take out this entire floor," Jeffrey said, his voice a bit raspy. "They gave me a message for you."

Everyone in the room went silent. Kotler approached, slowly, cautiously. "What is it?" he asked.

"Rooftop," Jeffrey said. "Five minutes. Alone. Or this detonates."

Kotler looked from his brother to the lead agent, who shook his head. "No sir," he said.

"I'm going," Kotler said.

"I can't let you ..."

"I'm going, unless you're shooting me," Kotler said, and pushed past him.

"Keep your radio on!" the agent said, and then started rattling off commands to other agents, ordering them to follow Kotler but to keep back. "Do not follow him onto the roof. Repeat, no one is cleared to go onto the roof but Dr. Kotler."

Kotler got to the stairs and sprinted up them, two at a time. Five minutes became four, then three, then two. He burst through the rooftop door, lungs and legs burning, in the literal last minute.

He waited, dreading that he might hear the sound of an explosion. He stepped out onto the roof. Out to the horizon, the city stretched like Christmas lights and tinsel.

"Dan Kotler," a voice said. It sounded small, muted and distorted.

Kotler looked around and spotted a phone resting on top of an air conditioner unit. He picked it up, holding it out. He could see himself in a video preview.

"Who are you? Is this Agent Patterson?"

"No, sorry. Agent Patterson's task is complete. He's moved on."

Kotler took this in. "Who are you?" he repeated.

"Not important. Not right now. What is important is that Jeffrey will die, along with anyone left in the building, if you do not do what I tell you to do."

Kotler felt his pulse getting out of hand. He took a breath, let it out. "What do you want?"

"I want you to walk to the edge of the roof," the voice said. "And then I want you to jump."

"Jump?" Kotler asked. "You went through all this just to get me to kill myself?"

"I want you to jump," the voice said, the distortion masking any sign of amusement or other emotion.

Kotler turned, looking at the roofline. He walked toward it, came to the edge, and looked over.

The street was several stories below. From this vantage point, he could see that FBI agents were hurrying people out of the building, getting them down the block and to a safe distance as quickly as possible. Lights from police cars, fire engines, and ambulances cast pulsing strobes on the surrounding buildings.

"Not there," the voice said from the phone. "Other side."

Kotler stepped back from the edge and went to the opposite side of the roof. He looked over.

Below him, approximately one floor down, was a window cleaner's platform.

Kotler took a breath, shoved the phone in his pocket and holstered his gun. One more breath, and he jumped.

He landed on the platform with a solid thud and had to scramble to grab onto the handrail as the platform tilted, throwing him off to one side. He found himself hanging out over open air, his legs kicking wildly until he was able to stabilize and climb back up.

He sat, sprawled on the platform and holding the rail with one hand, huffing, his heart pounding. He fished the phone from his pocket.

"Good work," the voice said. "I was worried about you for a moment there."

"What now?" Kotler asked.

"Open the window. Climb inside."

"Open the window?" Kotler looked. The windows for this building were uniform sheets of glass, not sliding or louvered. It shouldn't be possible to open one, especially from the outside.

Kotler reached out and put his palm against the window, and gave a push.

There was a click, and the window swung inward.

He quickly climbed through, relieved to stand on a solid floor.

Inside, he now found himself in a room with no door or other exits. It seemed the only way in or out was the window—a fact that carried with it some uncomfortable possibilities, about whether or not he was meant to leave this room at all.

The room was a singular space, but in the middle of the open floor was a pedestal. A bright light shone from the ceiling and illuminated an object Kotler didn't recognize. He moved forward and bent to get a better look.

It appeared to be a cylinder made of bronze, with thousands of protruding knots and burs on its surface. At either end of the cylinder there were teeth, as one would find on a set of gears.

"Impressive, right?" the voice asked.

"What is it?" Kotler asked.

"I'm surprised you don't know. You know everything, don't you?"

Kotler said nothing but studied it further. There was something familiar about it.

After a long moment, he had a spark of recognition.

"Is this some sort of platen? Like from a typewriter?"

"I knew you'd get it," the voice said.

The cylinder was the exact reverse of what Kotler would have thought of as a typewriter platen—typically a cylinder sheathed in rubber, meant to help feed paper through a typewriter. This one looked like an amalgam of a platen and the type head used to strike a ribbon and make characters on a page.

"Part of some other coding machine," Kotler guessed aloud.

"Yes," the voice said. "Only it isn't quite ready for use."

"And I can somehow make it ready," Kotler replied.

"You wouldn't be here otherwise," the voice said.

Kotler reached out and picked the object up, feeling its heft in his hands, running his fingers over the raised protrusions.

"Dr. Kotler," a different voice said in his ear. The agents, listening in on him. He couldn't respond. He didn't want to take any chances, give the mysterious voice on the phone any excuse to detonate the bomb on Jeffrey's chest. "We're monitoring your situation. You're in a completely sealed room. Steel casing, all around. We can't get in. The window is the only entrance or exit, as far as we can tell. Tap your earpiece once to acknowledge."

Kotler leaned forward, as if studying the platen closer, and allowed the phone to drop slightly, blocking the view of whoever was on the other side. He casually reached up, as if running his hand over the side of his head, and gave the earpiece a quick, single tap.

"What about my brother?" Kotler asked aloud.

The voice on the phone replied, "Solve the puzzle in front of you, Dan, and Jeffrey goes free. The bomb will be disarmed, and I'll allow the agents to cut his chains and take the vest off."

Buy time. Kotler felt like he was borrowing time, at the moment. And the cost could be higher than he was willing to pay.

From the earpiece, the agent said, "We haven't been able to remove the device. We have an explosives expert on his way. We need you to buy us as much time as you can."

"How do I know I can trust you to keep your word?" Kotler asked.

"Silly question," the voice on the phone said. "You can't really trust me, obviously. But I will let him go. I swear."

Kotler knew he had no choice. He was playing by this person's rules, and his own moves were limited.

He placed the phone on the pedestal and lifted the platen in both hands.

"You have thirty minutes," the voice said.

"What happens at thirty minutes?" Kotler asked.

"Let's not find out," the voice replied.

27

TARGET LOCATION

Denzel and Ludlum arrived just as a crowd of people was being hustled away from the target building. Emergency vehicles were everywhere, and agents were scrambling. One of them recognized him.

"Agent Denzel?"

Agent Danielle Brown approached from the crowd. She was waving people through, getting them out of the street and handing them off to local police officers, who ushered them to safety. "I wasn't expecting to see you here, sir."

"Just got here," Denzel said, side-stepping to let a man pass. "What's happening?"

"The raid went off as planned, but there was a complication. There's a bomb strapped to Dr. Kotler's brother," she said.

Denzel blinked. "Tell me that again. Slower."

She filled him in on everything that had gone down over the past hour, from Kotler's arrival with Agent Coben to his accompaniment with them on the raid.

"Coben sent Kotler in?" Denzel asked, perplexed.

Brown nodded. "I thought it was bizarre, but they gave him

a weapon and a vest. He went in with Beta team. Coben's orders."

This made no sense. Kotler was trained, sure, but he wasn't an agent. Why would Coben send him into a scenario like this?

He was about to ask more questions when Ludlum grabbed his arm.

"Look!" she said, pointing upward.

Denzel looked up to see a figure standing on the edge of the roof, as if preparing to jump.

"Is ... is that Kotler?" Denzel asked, a spike going through him.

"That's him," Brown said, holding a hand to her ear. She shook her head, as if she couldn't fully understand what she was hearing. "There's something going on. He's being told to jump."

Denzel watched for a tense moment, waiting, powerless. Kotler hovered on the edge of the building for a beat, then stepped back, disappearing from view.

"Who do we have up there?" Denzel asked.

"Kotler was ordered to go alone," Brown said. "Whoever is on the other side of that phone has all of this stitched up pretty tight."

Denzel turned to Ludlum. "Find Agent Coben," he said, his voice tense. "See if you can find out anything that's going on here."

"What about you?" she asked.

He stepped around to the trunk of his car, popping it open and pulling out a vest. He shed his suit jacket and pulled the vest on, tightening it, and then checked his gun.

"I'm going in."

28

STEEL CHAMBER

Kotler examined the platen, turning it over in his hands, examining the burs and nodules protruding from its surface.

He'd never seen anything like it. There was no hint of a language or symbology that he could decipher. Nothing about it triggered any sort of recognition. To Kotler, it might as well have been merely a series of random squiggles.

He didn't even know where to start.

"It would help if I had some context," Kotler said. "What sort of device does this go into? Can you tell me anything about its background?"

"You want to use your thirty minutes on a history lesson?" the voice asked.

"I need to know how it's used. You've asked me to solve it. I have no idea what it is or how it works."

There was a pause, then suddenly the pedestal in the center of the room rose a few inches and then split along one corner with an audible click. The front and side panels swung open like a bifold gate, slowly revealing a set of steps that sank down into the floor, disappearing into darkness.

"Where do those go?" Kotler asked, inspecting the stairs with caution.

"Step on down, Dan. You wanted context. It's at the bottom of those stairs."

Kotler stepped forward, but before he took the first step downward the voice from the phone said, "Oh, and get rid of the earpiece. This next part's just between us."

From the earpiece, the agent's voice spoke up. "Dr. Kotler, do not remove ...!"

Kotler never heard the rest. He took the earpiece out and tossed it aside.

"Good," the voice on the phone said. "Now, down we go."

Kotler took the first step, and then started his descent.

As he went down, he saw that he was passing through a passage cut into the thick floor of the building. From the looks of things, it had been added after the building's construction, and hadn't been cut that long ago. It must have been a real job to get all of this set up, Kotler thought. Whoever was on the phone had resources. Money.

Kotler reached the bottom of the stairs and found himself in a room set up like a workshop. There were tools and other objects all around, filling every darkened corner. Workbenches lined the walls. And on one of these was a machine that resembled a typewriter.

Kotler approached, the phone in one hand and the platen in the other.

"This is a Heisenberg machine," the voice said, and even through the digitized distortion, Kotler thought he could hear reverence.

"Heisenberg?" Kotler replied. "As in Werner Heisenberg?"

"I'm absolutely certain," the voice said. A beat later, "That's a joke. It probably didn't translate well through the distortion."

"I got it," Kotler said. "But what is this?"

"It's an encoding and decoding device. A spy telegraph, you

could say. There were only four of them made. I have two. This one, and another, in a secure location. I had to sacrifice one to get what I want, but it will be worth it."

"Sacrifice?" Kotler stared at the machine. "I'm sorry, I've never seen this before in my life. I'm not sure how I can help with this."

"You're a resourceful man, Dan. You'll figure it out in the ..." there was a pause, then, "... twenty-four minutes you have left."

Kotler nodded. He couldn't afford to waste any more time. He needed to get to this.

The voice had told him to "solve" the platen. But what did that mean?

Until he'd been shown the Heisenberg machine, he'd never heard of it. How was this tied to Werner Heisenberg, the father of modern quantum physics? Heisenberg's uncertainty principle was famous enough to be part of pop culture, but beyond that ...

Kotler had been pacing a bit, the platen in his hand. He stopped, astonished. He turned back to the Heisenberg machine and stepped closer.

Cryptographic Applications of Heisenberg's Theory.

It was the title of his great grandfather's paper—the manuscript that had started all of this. The manuscript that Kotler and Denzel had treated as merely a clue, when it was actually the target of whoever had orchestrated all of this.

Dr. Daniel Kotler's theories weren't just fodder for a scientific paper. Someone had taken the time to translate them into a physical machine. A machine for encoding and decoding messages using Heisenberg's uncertainty principle.

But how?

Kotler shook his head. He was running out of time, which meant Jeffrey, and anyone with him was also in danger.

He looked at the platen again, bringing it up close, examining the symbols protruding from it. He looked for anything that might click, that might spark some inspiration.

For the first time, he noticed the seams—one at about every half-inch on the platen, from end to end.

Could it be?

He grasped two sections, divided by the seam, and gave them a twist.

They each turned, separately from the other, and a new pattern of projections emerged.

He tried it again, with two more sections, and got the same result.

The platen was itself encoded.

He went to the machine, examining it.

In most respects, it did resemble a typewriter, with a metal base and a set of alphanumeric keys. It wasn't a QWERTY keyboard, however. The top line was a complete series of numerals, starting at zero and going to nine. The next few rows were alphabetic, beginning with A and ending with J on the top row, then K to S on the second row, and finally T through Z on the last row. There was another key that Kotler assumed was spacebar. No Enter key, however. An L-shaped, chrome-plated bar protruded from a module inside the machine, and Kotler recognized that as the carriage return.

He did a dry fit of the platen, snapping it into place where it should go. The gears were able to line up, with some coaxing.

He struck a key.

To his surprise, nothing moved, but there was a sound, almost like a camera flash. A pop followed by a whine that faded slowly.

"Tick tock, Dan," the voice said.

Just over twenty minutes. This exploration was costing him, but he needed it. He was starting to see how the machine worked, and that was putting him closer to solving this.

He took the platen out, examining it again.

"You have a second machine?" Kotler asked.

"I do," the voice said.

"And you know how they should work," Kotler said.

"I do," the voice repeated.

Kotler thought for a moment.

From what he could tell, the Heisenberg machine differed from a typewriter in one key aspect: It wasn't meant to convey whatever was typed on the keyboard to a piece of paper run through the platen. At least, not locally.

The voice on the phone had referred to it as a "spy telegraph." That implied that it could send messages to a remote location.

Kotler believed the machine used quantum entanglement to convey a message across a vast distance—maybe even infinite distance.

It was incredible, if true. But Kotler had read his great grandfather's work. This was one of the applications he had proposed, using quantum entanglement to build an encryption technology that could never be cracked. The safest, most secure method of communicating sensitive intelligence that had ever been conceived.

In simplest terms, two quantum particles could be entangled, or made sympathetic with each other. Essentially, they'd be locked into sync, sharing each other's fate, as it were. Whatever happened to one—a change in its direction, a shift in speed, an alteration of any kind—instantly happened to the other.

This was remarkable enough on its own, but things got even spookier.

Because the effect of the entanglement wasn't limited by space or time. No matter how far apart the two sympathetic particles were, whether across the room, across the planet, or across the galaxy, they would both behave in perfect unison. The state of one would be perfectly reflected in the state of the other.

This was mostly theoretical, of course. Some experiments had been conducted, with incredible and often repeatable results, but these tests were done on a scale so small they were hardly useful, or conclusive.

The implications of this, however—if it were perfected, if it were expanded, if it were immeasurable.

It would change everything.

At a minimum it would open the door for technological marvels such as instant communication and data transfer, possibly even teleportation, down the way. The world would change in a profound way, virtually overnight.

Endless possibilities. Endless power, for whoever controlled it.

Kotler wasn't sure how this technology could exist, but here it was. It would be the most potent encryption tool ever invented, that much was assured. But the technology itself would disrupt everything. Entire industries would collapse overnight. The balance of power would shift.

Was Jeffrey's life more important than the threat this represented, in the wrong hands?

Was anyone's?

Kotler had paused, time had passed, and finally he shook himself. He couldn't let Jeffrey die. Whatever threat this posed was hypothetical, at the moment. The threat of those explosives, the threat to his brother's life, was real.

Kotler focused.

The platen could be adjusted in six segments. It was clear there was a pattern to it. Something Kotler had to align just right.

The shapes on the platen were complete nonsense, though.

He couldn't make out a single character. Nothing readable. Just a profusion of gnarls, peaks, and valleys. A circuit of gibberish.

He stopped.

Could apply to the stepping maze.

Those words had been written on the cover of Daniel Kotler's manuscript. What did they mean?

Kotler had assumed it was a reference to the step rotors in the device that unlocked the Black Chamber, but what if it was something else? What if it was a reference to this device?

The sound he'd heard—the camera flash—hadn't produced any light or other effect that Kotler could detect. But maybe it wasn't meant to. Perhaps it was the sound of electric switches attempting to trigger but failing. As if something had tried to power up, but that power had nowhere to go.

What if this wasn't a code?

What if it was a circuit?

He stooped to look at the Heisenberg machine and noticed that the modules at either end, with the recesses that could accept the gears of the platen, each had a set of metal contacts inside of them.

Looking at the platen, he saw that there were identical contacts on either end of the cylinder. These would match up with the machine—like inserting batteries into a remote control.

The machine was supplying power, and the platen would complete a circuit. If the circuit was aligned properly.

The protrusions on the platen's surface formed a chaotic pattern. Kotler envisioned what must be under the surface—a series of resistors and transistors, perhaps? Something conductive, for sure.

And like the lines of solder on a computer's motherboard, the protrusions on the platen were meant to form a cohesive pattern. One that would conduct electricity, guiding it through a series of components within the platen, connecting it to the larger circuit of the Heisenberg machine itself.

He started to turn the cylinders, frequently checking, rushing. Time really was counting down. But he had it. He knew he had it.

This wasn't a code. It was simpler than that.

It was a puzzle.

Align the pattern in the right way and ...

He held it up, examining it closely.

He had only a few minutes left. This had to be it.

He turned to the machine, aligned the platen, and snapped it into place.

"So, is that it?" the voice asked. "You got it?"

"I got it," Kotler said.

"Alright then," the voice said. "Let's prove it. Type the word 'Shiva.'"

"Shiva? The Hindu god of transformation?"

"Dan, again with the history lessons. Tick tock, remember? And Shiva was also known as the god of destruction. You can be very optimistic."

Kotler shook his head, but quickly typed the letters into the machine:

S-H-I-V-A

He stepped back. Nothing happened. Then he realized his mistake. He hadn't done anything to initiate the sequence. In essence, he hadn't hit "Return."

He leaned forward and hit the carriage return bar, which made a satisfying ding.

There was the sound of a camera flash again, but this time it cascaded, like a symphony of hums and whines.

"Oh, that's good," the voice said from the phone. "That's very good."

"What happened?" Kotler asked. "What have I done?"

"Unlocked a hundred-year-old code," the voice said. "Good work, Dan."

At that, the phone disconnected, and Kotler was left standing in the silence.

29

TARGET LOCATION

Denzel raced up the stairs, weapon drawn. When he encountered some of the other agents, he was quickly led up to the breached floor. They took him straight to Jeffrey Kotler, standing against the wall of a storage room, his hands chained at shoulder level.

Denzel had never met Kotler's brother, but he would have recognized him anywhere.

For a start, he and Kotler favored each other in that way that only brothers can. They had common features, making Jeffrey seem vaguely familiar. There was no mistaking that they were related.

An explosives expert was examining the device strapped to Jeffrey's chest, using an endoscopic camera to probe and analyze it from all angles, as carefully as possible.

There were two other agents, mulling just outside the storage room, all wearing protective vests and helmets and taking cover as best they could. They weren't bomb squad. Denzel recognized them as FBI field agents.

Denzel stepped closer to the explosives expert, moving deliberately. "What can you tell me?" he asked.

The expert shook his head. "There's no way to get this off of him without triggering it," he said. "Our best hope is to block the signal somehow, prevent it from triggering this thing remotely."

"Can you do that? Do you have what you need?"

The expert nodded. "The rest of my team should be here any minute. They have what we need. I happened to be in the area, and I didn't have much in my truck. Just this gear. And that mobile detonation chamber," he nodded to a large, metal box in the corner. Denzel had overlooked it but saw now that it was made from thick steel, possibly layers of it, and was covered in soot and grime. Residue from detonations past.

The whole thing was on a set of wheels so it could be rolled in and out of a scenario like this one.

"How'd you get that up here?" Denzel asked.

"Elevator," the guy responded. "I'll take it down the same way. But we'll need the building completely cleared by then, just in case it detonates in transit. I don't think there's enough C-4 in this thing to take the building down, but it could create problems."

Denzel nodded. "Understood. What can I do?"

"You can tell me whether my team is close or not," the man said grimly.

"Sorry, I have no idea," Denzel said.

The expert nodded and continued examining the device, looking for a way to disarm it, if possible.

Denzel looked up to Jeffrey, who appeared to be both angry and afraid.

"It's going to be ok," Denzel said.

"I'll believe it when I'm back home with my wife and my son," he said, his voice quiet but firm, his jaw clenched.

Some of Kotler's bite and fight came through in that one

statement. That sort of fierceness that Denzel had seen in Kotler when he wasn't cracking jokes and things had gotten bad enough that even Kotler had to take them seriously.

Denzel was about to say something about this, as a way to break some of the tension, when suddenly there was a beep from the device.

Everyone in the room froze, holding their breath as one.

There was no explosion. No flash of light, no ball of fire. Instead, the little light on the device stopped blinking and went dark.

Denzel turned to the explosives expert. "Did you do it? Disarm it?"

The man shook his head. "Wasn't me. It just shut off on its own."

Denzel turned to the others, just outside the room. One of the agents had a set of bolt cutters. "Get these chains off of him." He turned back to the expert. "What about cutting that bomb loose?"

In answer, the man reached up used a pair of surgical scissors to cut one of the straps. The whole thing sagged, and the man had it pulled away. Walking slowly, he carried it to a large metal box in one corner of the storage room, and placed the device inside, closing the lid over it and locking it down.

"Get him and everyone else out of here," the expert said.

"You heard him," Denzel replied, nodding to the others. The agents helped Jeffrey to move away, surrounding and shielding him while leading him to the stairwell.

Before they were clear, Denzel grabbed one of the men by the arm. "Where is Dr. Kotler?"

"Radio chatter has him in some kind of sealed room, on the top floor. There's a team up there, trying to figure a way in or out."

Denzel left them and started up the stairwell, in the opposite direction. He went up a few flights before entering a set of offices under construction. Here, several more agents were gathered around a large, metal box, the size of a small room.

"What's the situation?" Denzel asked, flashing his ID as he approached.

"This thing is about six inches thick, solid steel," one agent replied. Denzel recognized her. Agent Schumer. Not one of his team, but he'd worked with her prior to taking over Historic Crimes. "It continues on into the ceiling and down through the floor. There's no way in, other than the window Dr. Kotler went through. We have people lowering down to that now, but we were waiting on the all clear for the bomb before making entry."

"You're clear," Denzel said. "Jeffrey Kotler is safe. Bomb squad has the device, and they're taking it down now."

Schumer nodded and relayed this to the team on the roof. She listened for a moment, then said, "Dr. Kotler took out his earpiece. The voice on the phone ordered him to go down through some staircase in the room."

"Kotler's on the floor below us?" Denzel asked.

"I was," a familiar voice said from behind him.

Denzel turned to see Kotler standing in the doorway of the stairwell. He looked a little rough but seemed unharmed.

"Kotler!"

"There was a door out," Kotler said, his voice flat. "It opened as soon as the call ended."

"Call?" Denzel asked. He went to Kotler, putting a hand on his shoulder, steadying him. "The voice on the phone?"

Kotler nodded, staring at the floor, then looked at him. "Jeffrey?"

Denzel nodded. "He's safe."

Kotler seemed to accept that, but there was something off about him. He seemed distracted. Or was he shaken? What had he experienced, in that steel-encased room?

"Kotler, are you ok?"

He looked up at Denzel, his expression hard, concerned. "I am, yes. But I think I just did something horrible, Roland. I think I just gave someone the keys to something. I don't even know for sure what it is."

"You did what you had to do," Denzel said quietly. "To keep your brother safe."

Kotler shook his head. "I don't even know that for sure."

Denzel nodded to a couple of agents, and they escorted Kotler out of the room, down the stairs and to the warehouse. Now that the bomb was secured and removed from the building, they commandeered the space. The bomb squad was moving the device to an empty parking lot nearby, where it could be safely detonated within the mobile chamber. It would be loud, but no one would be hurt.

Denzel took over the scene, ordering agents to get into the steel chamber and start marking any evidence they could find. He wanted to know who was renting these floors, who had authorized construction, where the steel had been purchased —any details he could get, and he wanted them now.

He'd have to debrief Kotler, but for the moment he was letting him have some peace.

Denzel made no move toward them. This was a private moment. A family moment. He couldn't turn away, though. He watched as Kotler made his way across the room.

Orders given, Denzel moved quickly down the stairs, emerging on the warehouse floor. He saw Kotler with a couple of paramedics, waving them off as he looked around the room. He was searching for his brother, Denzel knew. He finally spotted him with another paramedic, on the far side of the room.

Kotler approached Jeffrey, who was sitting on a collapsible gurney as the paramedic tended to some minor wounds.

Denzel watched as Kotler stood to the side. He tried to talk to Jeffrey, placed a hand on his arm. A comforting gesture.

Jeffrey shook it off, angry. He stood, shoving the EMT aside, and marched for the door of the warehouse while several agents and medics tried to get him to calm down and go back.

Denzel watched and made no move. He wasn't sure what he could do. He wanted to help, wanted to be there for his friend. But this was family. He didn't want to intrude.

Kotler stood there for a moment, watching his brother leave, and then turned and walked away himself.

He approached Denzel.

"Kotler," Denzel started.

"I need to be debriefed," Kotler said.

Denzel nodded, and took out his notepad.

30

NSA WAR ROOM

Ludlum eventually found the command center, after asking dozens of agents, flashing her FBI credentials to everyone she met. She entered to chaos as FBI and NSA agents scrambled. Orders flew through the air, transmitted to operatives in the field, and reports came in a cacophony of radio chatter and video feeds.

Ludlum grabbed one man by the arm, halting him as he passed. "Coben?"

"In the back," the agent replied.

Ludlum went through a door in the back of the room and emerged in a dark and dingy space that was absolutely crammed with computer equipment. Large screens were arrayed along an entire wall of the space, and several men and women worked frantically at laptops, consulting each other in quick bursts of conversation. The scene was bedlam.

"I'm looking for Agent Coben," she shouted, as she entered. She had no idea who to address, so she addressed the room.

"Tell me when you find him," one agent replied, holding

aside the microphone on his headset. "I've been waiting for confirmation from him for half an hour."

"He stepped out," another agent replied. "Didn't say where he was going."

Stepped out? Coben was supposed to be in charge of this operation. Who steps out when they're the ones calling all the shots?

Ludlum lingered for a moment, then left the command center, exiting out onto the street. The scene here was much more orderly, now that everyone had been evacuated. Lines of yellow police tape stretched in a web around a large area. Barricades had gone up at every street.

In the sky above, news helicopters were pushing the limits of allowable airspace. Reporters on the ground pressed against the barriers, cameras and lights in full bloom, microphones extended toward anyone close enough to answer shouted questions.

Where was Coben in all of this?

She moved away from the command center and walked until she was nearly back to Agent Denzel's car. She would have to let him know she'd been unable to find Coben. She didn't know what it meant, that the NSA agent in charge had more or less abandoned his post, but it couldn't be good.

She reached the car and considered her options. She wasn't about to sit, waiting. There was too much going on here, too many questions that needed to be answered.

She looked toward the target building and saw a man emerge, trailing a wake of paramedics and FBI field agents behind him.

Kotler? she thought.

But no. He *looked* like Kotler. Remarkably similar. But it wasn't him.

Kotler's brother, then. Jeffrey.

If Jeffrey was safe, that meant the building would be clear. She decided she would go in, find Agent Denzel and maybe Dan Kotler himself, and try to work out everything that was happening.

She started walking but stopped when she saw something unexpected.

Two men were moving away from the crowds, toward one of the storefronts. Though no weapons were visible, it was clear that the man in front was being driven under duress. That might have been enough to pique Ludlum's interest, but it wasn't what had initially caught her attention.

The man in front was Agent Lee Patterson.

She raced forward, trailing them, drawing her weapon. She was far enough back that she worried she might lose them in the chaos. If they turned into a building while out of sight, she'd never find them.

She managed to catch up enough to see Patterson and the other man duck into an alley, and she followed, cautiously.

Ahead of her, the men hid on the other side of large recycling dumpsters—the sort used to crush cardboard. Patterson turned to face the man who had practically bum-stepped him into the alley. Ludlum pressed against the wall of one building, taking cover behind a set of large, metal circuit boxes. She inched closer, as she could, staying quiet.

They were talking, and if she was still, she could make out the words.

"You have it on you?" the other man asked.

"I ... yes," Patterson replied.

"Show it to me. Slowly."

Patterson reached into his coat and took out a rolled-up ream of papers. Even in that condition, and from this distance, Ludlum recognized them.

The manuscript.

"Put it on the ground, and then step back with your hands on your head."

Patterson did as he was told, backing away so that the man could stoop and pick up the manuscript from the ground.

"Agent Coben, please believe me ... I did this because he threatened my family."

Coben? It looked like she'd found him after all.

Coben nodded. "I know all about that, Lee."

There was a pause, and Patterson said, "Are you him? The one on the phone?"

Coben didn't respond but instead brought up a weapon—a pistol with a silencer.

Ludlum felt her heart thump. She gripped her sidearm, then turned into the open space of the alley and leveled her sights on Coben.

"FBI! Lower your weapon!"

She was not a field agent, but she'd had training, both with the FBI and with the NYPD. Still, this was her first time aiming her weapon on another human being. She felt herself shaking but took a breath to get steady.

Coben and Patterson both turned to see her. Patterson, his hands on his head, squinted. "Dr. Ludlum?" he asked.

Coben stared at her. His weapon was still on Patterson. "Dr. Ludlum, my name is Agent Steve Coben, with the NSA. If you'll allow me, I'll show you my identification."

"I know who you are," she said. "Put the weapon down, now!"

"I'm afraid I can't do that," Coben replied.

"Lower your weapon or I *will* fire!" Ludlum shouted.

Coben seemed to consider his options, then nodded and placed his weapon on the ground before straightening and raising his own hands to his head.

Ludlum fumbled in her pocket, retrieving her phone. She

prayed the communications blackout was over and called Agent Denzel.

To her great relief, he answered.

"Ludlum? Where are you?"

"I'm in an alley, not far from your vehicle. I need backup! I'm taking Agent Patterson and Agent Coben into custody."

31

FBI OFFICES, MANHATTAN

Kotler sat with a hot cup of coffee warming his hands, across the table from Agent Coben. The manuscript was between them. Agent Denzel was standing, leaning on his fists, staring the NSA agent down.

"Tell it to me again," he said.

Coben never showed signs of stress. He had an infuriating half smile on his face that made Kotler want to punch him, more for the knowledge that it was entirely contrived than for anything else. Even now Coben kept himself completely masked. Kotler wasn't sure what that told him about the agent, but he did know that it pissed him off.

"I can tell you everything in detail for a second time, Agent Denzel, but it's not going to get us any further than right here. My people will eventually be here, and we will leave, with that manuscript. And all the details of this will still be classified well above your pay grade."

"But you're perfectly willing to tell me all about Lee Patterson and that muffed handoff?" Denzel asked.

Denzel was angrier than Kotler had ever seen him. The

events of the past few days had been stressful in many ways, but here at the end, with no real way to know the facts of all this, it was just impossible.

"Agent Patterson was coerced into stealing the manuscript. A threat to his family. He took it to the location he'd been given, and as ordered he waited."

"Waited," Denzel said. "So after all of this, after orchestrating this whole thing to get his hands on that manuscript, the person behind this never even picked it up?"

"Actually, he did," Coben said.

Denzel blinked. "What do you mean?"

"That manuscript is missing some pages," Coben replied, nodding to the document on the table. "Specific pages, which tells me that this person knew exactly what it contained and where to find it. They had Patterson leave it in a drop, and then had him pick it up again an hour later. They returned the manuscript to throw us off. To buy time."

Kotler shook his head. "None of this makes any practical sense, Coben. Who would even know about this?"

"Whoever first located the Black Chamber," Coben said.

"Here's what I think," Denzel replied, leaning forward and staring menacingly at Coben. "I think that person was you. I think you are the one behind all this, pulling all the strings. I think you wanted to get your hands on this manuscript, and you set up this circus to cover your tracks."

"That would be a neat and tidy ending," Coben said, nodding. "If a bit cliché. But you're wrong. I only became involved when you called me. When Dr. Ludlum found us in that alley, I was retrieving the manuscript from your agent. I could make a profoundly solid case that you were the one behind this, Agent Denzel. Though I'd favor Dr. Kotler for it if I'm being honest."

Denzel scoffed. "Won't wash, Coben. We have you dead to rights, in that alley, with a weapon trained on Agent Patterson and the manuscript at your feet. You took him there to kill him so you could escape without anyone even knowing you had this thing."

Coben again nodded. "Plausible. And I'll admit, killing Patterson might actually have been the outcome. I took him there so no one else would hear our conversation, which admittedly didn't work out as I'd hoped. I spotted him on one of the surveillance monitors. He was using his FBI credentials to try to make an escape in all the chaos. And, he says, he took the manuscript with him hoping he might be able to trade it for some sort of immunity, in a trial against him."

"He says the same," Denzel replied.

"Corroboration then," Coben smiled.

Kotler watched all of this unfold, growing more frustrated as time went on. Finally, he asked, "How did you know pages were missing?"

Coben turned to him.

"Liz says that Patterson threw the manuscript down, and you never picked it up. He had it on him the whole time. It's unlikely he took the time to examine it before trying to make his escape. So how did you know?"

Coben watched Kotler for a long moment, then said, "That's classified."

"You knew because you took them," Denzel said.

"I can't answer any of these questions, Agent Denzel. But I can tell you that I am not the one behind this. I know it would fit the narrative you're building, and I also know how much this case has cost each of you, personally. But this wasn't me, and you'll be wasting time and resources if you pursue it. However, I do have a suggestion."

Denzel shook his head. "And what's that?"

"Follow the money," Coben said. "That building, the steel walls, hiring the Ryba brothers. It's all very expensive. Who has that kind of money? Who could operate at that level, while knowing all of the history involved, including how to decipher codes?"

With this, he turned and looked squarely at Kotler.

Kotler blinked, then laughed. "Are you implying that I'm behind all of it?"

Coben smiled. "I'm telling Agent Denzel to follow the money. Wherever it leads."

There was a knock on the door, but before Denzel could answer two men burst in, flashing IDs that indicated they were NSA. Without a word, they scooped the manuscript from the table.

Agent Coben rose then, pulling on his jacket. "There's my ride," he said.

Denzel stood aside, arms folded, watching Coben with a hard stare. Kotler knew they were sewn up for this. There was nothing to say. They'd come in here knowing that they wouldn't be able to hold Coben for long, and that something like this was the most likely scenario.

Coben paused in front of Denzel before leaving with his two agents. "Ask yourself about the string of coincidences here, Agent. And notice who is at the very center of all of it."

"Implicate Kotler all you want," Denzel said, staring into Coben's eyes. "But he could have gotten his hands on whatever was in that manuscript at any time, and no one else would have ever guessed it was there. Setting all this up? Strapping a bomb to his own brother? Going through all this nonsense to get something he already had access to? None of that makes any sense, and you know it."

"A lot of things don't add up," Coben said. "But trust me. Follow the money."

With that he and the other NSA agents left the room, with Denzel and Kotler slumping, feeling defeated and unsure of what came next.

KOTLER FINALLY RETURNED HOME.

He felt as if he'd been gone for months. Even when he'd actually *been* gone for months, he'd never felt so ready to see his apartment. All he wanted was a shower, a hot meal, and a warm bed. He'd order food. He didn't want to leave the place, now that he was here.

As he walked into the lobby, Ernie greeted him.

"Welcome home, Dr. Kotler," the doorman smiled. "How's tricks?"

Kotler shook his head and forced a smile. "Same as always, Ernie. Mostly. It's good to see you."

He started to move past and make his way to the elevator banks.

"Oh, Dr. Kotler, your FBI friends never came by, but I did get that footage you wanted."

"Footage?" Kotler asked.

Ernie held out a thumb drive. "I had it put on this for you," he said.

"Oh!" Kotler replied. "I nearly forgot about this. Thank you, I appreciate you going to the trouble."

"No trouble," Ernie smiled.

Kotler left him then and rode the elevator to his floor. He used his keycard to gain access, and moments after stepping out of the elevator he had shed his jacket, hanging it on the rack by the door, and slumped into his sofa.

He sighed.

From this vantage point, he could see the New York Skyline. It was early morning, though Kotler was only just getting home, and the sun was starting to rise. Maybe he'd have a sandwich and hit the sack. He was feeling the exhaustion of the past several days washing over him.

He watched as sunlight started to glint and reflect from the windows of hundreds of buildings, stretching to the horizon. He felt himself dozing.

The thumb drive fell from his fingers and clattered to the floor, waking him.

He was groggy, and a little disoriented, but didn't want to crash on the couch when he had a warm bed waiting. Food, shower, and everything else could wait until tomorrow.

He stooped, picked up the thumb drive, and stood. He had intended to drop it on the kitchen counter, where he would spot it later. He was about to do so when he remembered that he hadn't yet forwarded his written statement to Denzel.

Feeling a little out of sorts, he almost decided it could wait until later. But he fully intended to blow the entire day in bed and didn't want to catch grief for not doing the paperwork.

He fished his laptop out of his bag and powered it up at the kitchen counter. He had the report ready, and so all he had to do was drop it in an email and fire it off. Done.

And since he was here ...

He put the thumb drive in one of the laptop's USB ports and opened it up. There was only one file—a video with a thumbnail that depicted the downstairs lobby. He clicked on this and let it play.

Whoever had grabbed the footage and done him the kindness of cutting it to the segment he needed. There was little preamble as a man entered the lobby, approached Ernest, talked for a few minutes, and then left.

It was nothing, then. Probably unrelated to all of this. It may have been someone from the press, here to pester Kotler about his role in one FBI case or another.

Kotler was about to shut it off, close his laptop, and go straight to bed, but stopped. He rolled back the footage and looked closer. He was able to capture a still frame and zoom in on it.

He rubbed his eyes, uncertain that he was seeing what he thought he was seeing. Suddenly Kotler was wide awake.

He forwarded the image to Denzel, and then called him immediately.

"Kotler ..." Denzel answered.

"Check your inbox," he said as he grabbed his coat. "I'm on my way back to your office."

"Stay where you are," Denzel said.

Kotler shook his head. "Listen to me, I've just found something. I can be there in ..."

There was a loud knock at the door.

"Roland, hold on, there's someone ..."

Another knock.

Kotler opened the door to see two of Denzel's agents, identifying themselves by showing their IDs and badges.

"Dr. Kotler," one of the agents said. "Please hang up the phone sir. You'll have to come with us."

32

FBI OFFICES, MANHATTAN

Kotler had been locked in an interview room for the past hour, which really pissed him off. Over the past two years he'd been on both sides of this enough to recognize that someone was trying to sweat him out—give him time to stew, so that when he was questioned, he'd make a mistake.

That someone, Kotler knew, was Denzel.

Finally, the door opened, and Denzel entered.

"Roland, what the hell is going on? Did you get the file I sent you? Why am I here?"

Denzel sat across from him, looking somehow angry and disappointed all at once. He had a folder in his hands, and he placed it on the table between them.

"Agent Coben said to follow the money," Denzel said quietly.

Kotler blinked. "Ok. And what did you find?"

Denzel opened the folder and slid it across the table. "We found you, Kotler."

Kotler shook his head and then looked at the top sheet in

the folder. He read it, then flipped through. "I don't understand. This looks like bank records."

"Your bank records," Denzel said.

Kotler shook his head, examining the pages. "Not mine. At least, not for any account I'm aware of."

"You're saying you don't know anything about this account?"

Kotler shook his head.

Denzel pointed at a highlighted series of numbers. "This is your social security number?"

Kotler looked and nodded. "Yes."

"Date of birth? Address?"

"Roland, what is this? Where did this come from?"

Denzel took the folder back, closing it. He leaned back slightly, looking at Kotler, then shook his head. "I shouldn't be the one talking to you," he said. "Our relationship compromises me."

"Can you just tell me what the hell is going on?" Kotler replied.

Denzel tapped the folder. "When we dug into the rental records for that building, the lease showed the name of some dummy corporation. They had paid a year's worth of rent up front, paid for city permits, paid for materials and construction, all from what turned out to be a private account. Your account."

Kotler stared. "Roland, this ... I don't know anything about this."

"You don't know how a private account with millions of dollars was set up in your name and used to pay for all of this?"

Kotler shook his head. "No, Roland. I don't."

"Kotler, we've known each other for a couple of years now. I've come to trust you. But this ..."

"I agree. This looks bad. But I have nothing to do with it."

"So how did it get here? Who would have opened this account? And why?"

"To set me up for this, obviously," Kotler said. He pointed to the folder. "May I?"

Denzel slid it back across to him, and then watched him as if Kotler might pull some trick.

Kotler felt sick. Denzel had been his friend, possibly his best friend, for two years now. Whatever this was, it wasn't just making Kotler's life difficult. It was fracturing a relationship that Kotler had come to depend on. Being here, now, under a veil of suspicion, was just sickening.

Kotler opened the folder and started to look through the records.

None of it made sense.

All of his personal information was there. Everything he would have needed to start an account, all neatly typed into each field.

"This account says it was opened a year ago," Kotler said, leaning over the pages as he would have done with some ancient manuscript.

"Yes," Denzel replied.

Kotler looked up. "I haven't opened any new accounts in years." He looked back down, studying further, shaking his head.

The transactions were mostly outgoing, but there was a series of electronic transfers, at a rate of about once every three months. They were for large amounts, but always different. Irregular.

"What are these?" Kotler asked, pointing to one of the deposits.

Denzel looked. "Bank transfers. They're coming in from a portfolio management service. Payouts from investments. The managing firm is called Finely Investments."

Kotler shook his head. "I've never set up anything like that. I have a portfolio, but this isn't the firm I use. I've never heard of them."

Denzel paused, and sighed. "Kotler ..."

"Photos?" Kotler said, throwing his hands wide. "Video? Is there anything that shows me setting up these accounts? Anything beyond a paper trail?"

"Could have been done online, or over the phone."

"I'd have to sign something," Kotler said. "Is there anything with my signature? And a photo ID, that would be a requirement."

Denzel reached out and flipped the pages to the back.

A form, with a signature, and a photocopy of a driver's license. It was a New York State license, and the photo was definitely Kotler. Though in Kotler's estimate it looked a bit more like one of his former headshots than a photo taken at the DMV.

Kotler laughed.

"What's so funny?" Denzel asked.

Kotler pointed to the page, "First, that isn't my signature. It isn't even close."

"Doesn't prove anything," Denzel said. "Maybe you faked it, in case you were caught later."

Still smiling, Kotler said, "And then there's the fact that I don't have a driver's license."

Denzel frowned. "Wait ... you don't have a license? I've let you drive my car."

Kotler shook his head. "We'll ... discuss it later. But third, there's this," he pointed to the driver's license.

Denzel looked and shook his head. "I'm not seeing anything."

"Nothing?" Kotler said, shaking his head. "Roland, you wound me."

Denzel looked again, and glanced up, annoyed and confused.

"Look at my name," Kotler said.

Denzel looked back down and frowned. "K-O-L-T-E-R," he said, leaning back. "Your last name is spelled wrong."

Kotler nodded. "People do that all the time. In fact, I had a professor who used to do it. Annoyed the hell out of me."

"So what do you think this proves?" Denzel asked. "You're a smart guy, Kotler. You might have thought of things like this."

"Well, for a start," Kotler replied, "it proves you haven't looked at your email yet."

Denzel glared, then reached into his pocket and produced his phone. He flicked the screen, tapped it, and then stared. He looked up at Kotler. "What am I looking at?" he asked.

"That's a picture of Dr. Robert Wiley," Kotler said. "He came to my building on a night he was supposedly locked in the Black Chamber."

THEY WERE in Denzel's office now, and Kotler sat in one of the two chairs in front of Denzel's desk. They were watching the screen on the agent's wall, as he once again fumbled with the remote. A red cursor appeared, wobbled around erratically, then finally circled and highlighted some of the information onscreen.

"These are debit card records from Dr. Wiley. Transactions made the night *after* he was abducted. We already had these, as part of the investigation."

"Any ATM video footage?" Kotler asked.

Denzel shook his head. "We're waiting on a court order, but it could be awhile. But we do have something else." Denzel advanced the presentation. The red dot wobbled again, this time dancing over a screenshot of a social media post. Two women, presumably a mother and daughter, based on their likeness to each other, were smiling for the camera with a stretch of lake behind them.

"Dr. Wiley's wife and daughter went on an impromptu vacation to their lake house, a few days before his abduction. He was supposed to join them but stayed behind. He says he was finishing up some grading and advising some students on their dissertations. I made some calls. No one saw him on campus during that time, and none of his students met with him to talk about their work."

"So not really proof of anything," Kotler said, shaking his head.

"No. But I did get some interesting information from the registrar's office," Denzel said.

Kotler looked at him and noted that the agent was suppressing a smile. It made Kotler feel a strange sense of relief, though he wasn't at all sure what Denzel had up his sleeve. It was just good to see trust in his eyes again.

"Cheryl Lanning is the head of that office," Denzel said.

"I remember Cheryl," Kotler smiled. "She worked there while I was attending, years ago. I liked her."

"Apparently she liked you, too," Denzel said. "Because she remembers vividly when Dr. Wiley came to her office, about a year ago, and requested your records."

"My records?" Kotler said. "My grades? Courses?"

"That," Denzel said, "and the rest of your file. Including your personal information." He changed the screen again, and there was a scan of Kotler's student profile, complete with a record that included his social security number. Attached to the document, with a paperclip, was a canceled check.

"The check had apparently come to their office instead of being mailed to you," Denzel said. "The story that Mrs. Lanning gives is that you left right after graduation, going to some remote archeological dig for months. Out of contact."

Kotler nodded. "I was in Egypt, helping open and explore a newly discovered tomb. It wasn't my first dig, but it was my first as a graduate. I was there for a year."

Denzel continued. "They kept the check with your file, in case you ever checked in about it. Over time it was just forgotten. But this is how Wiley got enough information about you to steal your identity."

Kotler looked at him, sharply. "He opened an account in my name," he said.

Denzel nodded. "And apparently bought a very convincing fake ID," he replied, bringing up another screen that showed the driver's license photo they'd already seen, side-by-side with a headshot of Kotler on the back of one of Kotler's early books.

"Unbelievable," Kotler said quietly.

"I've got requests in for everything I can get on him, including his financials. But he's in the wind. Disappeared almost as soon as he was released. His wife says he called her and told her he'd feel better if she and their daughter stayed in the safe house a while longer. That's the last time anyone spoke with him."

Kotler felt numb. This was all so much. He'd always had a good relationship with Dr. Wiley. At least, he thought he did. Their conversations had been pleasant, when they'd spoken. Wiley reached out to him occasionally with some note of congratulations, or a comment about the latest news story featuring Kotler. After the events in Pueblo, Wiley had sent dozens of emails. Even more, after news of the events in London, with the discovery of Sir Isaac Newton's underground lab. Each subsequent event seemed to spur a few notes and comments, and Kotler was happy to share everything he could. He had assumed that Wiley was just a fan, maybe feeling a sense of paternal pride for having helped to nurture Kotler into his career.

To learn that it might all have been some ruse, that Wiley had been plotting against him, even stealing his identity ...

"Why did he do this?" Kotler asked.

Denzel had been watching him, Kotler realized. "To gain access to your money," he said.

Kotler inhaled deeply and blew out a breath. "That's disconcerting. I admit, I don't monitor my finances all that closely, but I do have an accountant and a financial advisor. No one ever mentioned anything unusual."

"Wiley was pretty tricky about the whole thing," Denzel said. He pulled up another slide, this time a set of Kotler's financial records.

Kotler had given permission for this, but still felt a slight tingle of discomfort. Money wasn't something he thought about. It was just there. A tool. A resource that enabled his lifestyle. But it still felt private to him, and seeing a list of his spending habits onscreen made him uneasy.

"Wiley took advantage of the way you spend," Denzel said. "He mirrored transactions you made, mostly withdrawals. If you gave a thousand dollars to a charity, he'd later withdraw a similar amount, marking it as another donation to a different charity. One that didn't actually exist, except on paper."

"And my accountant never noticed?"

Denzel shrugged. "It blended in. Don't be too hard on the guy, Kotler. It's clear that Wiley was playing this smart. He never made transactions that would be too noticeable. And all of this money went into a portfolio. Since he used your identity to open it, we were able to get our hands on it."

The screen changed again, and now there was a statement for Finely Investments.

Kotler peered at it, then chuckled.

"What's funny?" Denzel asked.

Kotler shook his head. "He did better with my investments than I did," he said.

"Yeah, he definitely had a knack for it," Denzel said. "Over two years he quadrupled the amount of money he'd stolen from you. Congratulations, Kotler, you have more millions."

Kotler laughed, and shook his head. "Under the circumstances, I can't seem to think of it as a windfall."

"You might if you still had the money he's spent and withdrawn over the years. We don't know exactly where this money went. We're waiting on his financials, to see if there are any unusual deposits. But the outgoing cash totals somewhere around thirty million."

Kotler had been sipping from his coffee, and choked, nearly doing a spit take. "Thirty ... thirty million dollars?"

"On top of the two million that's left in the account."

Kotler stared at the screen for a long moment. "Can you send this list to my investment firm?"

"Focus, Kotler. Roll around in your money later."

Kotler laughed. "Ok, so we can assume that he spent that thirty million on everything we just dealt with. Renting those two floors, the steel room, the secret entrances and staircases, all of that. And the Heisenberg machine."

"That one may not have been a purchase," Denzel said. "Something like that wouldn't just be on eBay. It's possible he could have found it on the black market, but it seems unlikely. We think he stumbled onto it, somewhere."

Kotler thought about this. "You're right," he replied. "He did. In the Black Chamber."

"How do you know?"

Kotler shook his head. "It's a hunch, but think about it. He orchestrated the kidnapping of Dr. Marvin. That was cover. He needed Marvin's wife to call the police, panicked, because he'd already arranged for his own wife and daughter to be out of town. He needed them out of the picture because they would know the truth about his abduction. He was never abducted at all. He'd gone to that room voluntarily and had the Ryba brothers grab Marvin. He arranged all of it. Which means he knew about the Black Chamber in advance. That's where he'd found the Heisenberg machine, as well as records and photos about the government-sealed room. It gave him everything he needed to be three steps ahead of us the whole time."

Denzel considered this, then said, "When you were on the phone with him, in that steel room. Did he say anything that might indicate what he was up to?"

"He had me solve the Heisenberg machine. He was ... well, he was very familiar with me, the whole time. Kept calling me 'Dan.' I didn't click to it at the time, but now I remember. He knew me. Knew how I thought and what I could do. He set all of this up to get me to that machine." Kotler thought for a moment, then shook his head. "I think the manuscript pages were a bonus," he said.

"Bonus?" Denzel replied. "How so?"

"I think he was after the solution to that Heisenberg problem. The manuscript was meant to get me involved and get me to solve it for him. He had me enter a word. Shiva."

"Shiva?" Denzel frowned. "Sounds familiar."

"Shiva is part of the pantheon of Hindu gods, and is the god of both destruction and transformation. Or rebirth, from a different perspective. The name is familiar to westerners for a lot of reasons, but the most famous is a misquote of Oppenheimer. After the first detonation of the nuclear bomb, Oppenheimer quoted the Bhagavad-Gita. 'Now I am become death, the destroyer of worlds.' It gets misquoted as 'I am become *Shiva*, destroyer of worlds.' Wiley had me type that word in after I completed the circuit on the device, and he was pretty pleased with the results."

"What did he get out of it?"

Kotler shook his head. "He told me that machine is part of a set. I think it uses quantum entanglement to send and receive signals." He huffed. "I've handed over the world's most secure and uncrackable encryption tool. The word 'Shiva' may have been the key he needed to unlock all of it. He told me there were four of those machines in existence, and that he had two. He was sacrificing one to get what he wanted."

"So there's another set out there," Denzel said.

"Probably in the hands of someone we don't want to have it," Kotler replied.

"And now they have a way to turn it on," Denzel said.

Kotler said nothing but slumped slightly in his chair.

Denzel watched him for a moment. "This wasn't you, Kotler."

"I gave him the key."

"True, but under duress. And what I'm saying is, I believe you." Denzel waved a hand toward the monitor on his wall. "This wasn't you. I believe you."

Kotler nodded. "I appreciate that, Roland. But what good does this do us?"

"We know who we're looking for now," Denzel said. "I've got requests in, court orders on the way. I have people already digging in and asking questions, trying to find where Wiley disappeared to. We'll find him."

Kotler thought about this. "Have we checked the lake house?"

Denzel's eyebrows went up. "It was cleared after his wife and daughter were retrieved from there," he said. "We wouldn't have had any reason to go back there."

"Sounds like we have a reason now," Kotler replied.

Denzel stood and pulled on his coat. "Let's go. And I'll be driving from now on." He shook his head in wonder. "I can't believe you don't have your license."

33

HISTORIC CRIMES FORENSICS LAB

Ludlum was relieved when Denzel emailed her to say that Kotler was cleared. Of course, she'd never believed for a moment that he was guilty. It was just good to know that the matter was settled.

She'd come back to the office, insisting that she was fine to return to work. And it was true. She was fine. But more importantly, some things needed to be tended to. There were tests she needed to approve and test results she needed to sign off on, that sort of thing. Just because she'd been abducted didn't mean the work stopped. There were other injustices in the world. She had to do what she could to help right them.

That was the way she framed it, to herself and to anyone who might ask. She knew the truth, however, and she could admit it herself.

Her real motive for coming back so quickly was that she needed access to resources she didn't have at home.

She was still hunting for Red Ryba.

Since he'd broken into the impound lot and killed a security guard, he'd become more of a priority for law enforcement, but he'd also gone completely off the radar. Both the NYPD and the FBI had traced his path from the impound, tracking him and the Indian through the city streets using footage from traffic cameras and other means. They had gained footage much faster than she had when begging it off of bodegas and convenience stores. But Ryba had turned into an alley with a blind spot, a part of the city that had very little video coverage, and had disappeared entirely.

Police were combing the area, knocking on doors, questioning locals and searching for any clue about Ryba, and they were finding nothing.

Ludlum had warned both Denzel and Kotler about Ryba's likely motives, but she worried that they'd both let it fall down on the list of priorities. With everything else that was happening, a hypothetical hitman with a grudge wasn't at the top of their list. Even if Ludlum thought it should be.

The NYPD and FBI hadn't given up on finding him, of course. Now that they could positively ID him in conjunction with a murder, interest was on the rise. And Ludlum was pleased when Denzel told her that she'd been given clearance to access the files from the investigation.

It made things a lot easier.

Ryba had a history of going underground when suspicions were high. If there were any chance he'd be so much as questioned over any incident, he tended to end up in a whole other country, far enough away, in a short enough timeframe, that he could claim an alibi and usually leverage non-extradition loopholes. He had managed to keep a veil of doubt around his involvement in every crime he committed, by hiding his features and distancing himself from all of it. And when that veil was pierced, he'd lay low someplace that couldn't care less about having another murderer on its beaches, as long as they bought plenty of rum drinks.

Ryba had a system, and it made it nearly impossible to catch him.

But this time he'd made a mistake.

She opened the file and found the video clip.

It was surprisingly clear and crisp, for night footage taken on a mobile phone.

Ryba, wearing the exact clothing that could be seen later in security footage from the impound lot, was standing with his back against the wall of a bar. He had his hands in his pockets and was looking around, monitoring the crowd but never engaging with anyone.

The footage was from one of the bar's patrons, who had been shooting video of his friends laughing and enjoying themselves. Everyone in the video was a little drunk, save Ryba. He was definitely sober, and as the man who shot the video put it, "A little creepy and uptight."

Ryba left the scene, walking in the direction of the impound lot, and the man behind the video, along with two of his buddies, decided to follow him.

It had been a lark. They were drunk and being stupid. They thought maybe Ryba was gay—something they thought was funny, for whatever reason—and maybe he was out trying to hire a male prostitute. It happened a lot in that part of town. The guys behind the camera thought it would be funny to get video of it.

They followed from across the street, managing to keep their giggles and conversations low enough to be masked by street noise. Ryba never seemed to notice them, though he did periodically scan the environment, ensuring that he was alone. He must have taken the guys as some drunk imbeciles making their way home from a bar.

And in fact, they stopped at one of the local bars, a dive that had indie band stickers plastered over its windows and an array of neon casting colorful light out onto the sidewalk and the street. The footage shifted for a moment at this point, with the guys holding the phone up, aiming the camera at themselves, arms over shoulders and loudly yelling "Cheeeeese!"

A selfie. Or a pretend selfie, at least. It was clear from the video that the guys thought Ryba had noticed them. This was camouflage. It appeared to work, and Ryba moved on.

The guys followed him again, giggling, making crude jokes, speculating about physical actions that would be anatomically unadvisable. Ludlum turned the volume down and watched the rest of the video with the sound barely audible, just in case something was said that she might need to hear.

When Ryba turned the corner by the impound lot, the three guys hid behind a collection of trash cans and parked cars. They were waiting for Ryba to get some distance on this side road, intending to follow him further. They were pretty sure of what he was doing at this point—the area was known to be a hotspot for hookers.

To their surprise, though, Ryba stopped and looked around. They ducked, hiding, but kept the phone raised, propped on top of one of the trash can lids and still capturing footage.

Ludlum leaned in and enlarged the window, making the video full screen.

In a quick and smooth motion, Ryba raised a silenced pistol. It was clearly visible in the shot, illuminated by the halogen lamp across the street.

In one quick and impressive shot, Ryba took out the light over the impound lot's gate.

The guys shooting the video were swearing and panicking, but thankfully kept the video running. Even though it was dark, Ryba could still be seen moving quickly across the street. At this point, all details of his features were lost, but it was still obviously him.

The guys were frozen in place, and Ludlum could hear them whispering to each other, deciding what they needed to do. One of them suggested calling the police, which Ludlum thought was their best idea of the night. The others practically whisper-shouted him down, calling him an idiot, claiming that they might get in trouble themselves.

As all of this was happening, the camera eventually picked up the sound of a motorcycle starting, and moments later the flashes of pulsing blue light from the security truck. There was a pause in the activity from the impound lot, followed soon after by the scream of engine noise as the motorcycle flew from the impound gate, out on the street, and off into the night.

Ludlum backed the footage up, pausing it. On screen, only a few feet from the camera, was a man wearing a long coat and a balaclava, straddled on Cameron Ryba's restored Indian motorcycle.

The figure looked just as he had when he'd grabbed Ludlum. It was him.

She grabbed a screenshot of the frame, sending it to herself. She did the same with footage that showed Ryba's face.

She turned then to the bolt cutters, recovered from the scene.

These, along with the slugs taken from the security guard's body were the only physical evidence they had in this case. It wasn't enough. The video was damning, but a good attorney could punch holes in it. Ryba was implicated, but he could still wriggle out of all of this.

They needed more.

And he was still out there, still gunning for Kotler. They needed more, and they needed it fast.

She looked to the database, combing once more through the evidence, the reports, the statements. She wasn't a detective. All of this made a kind of sense to her, but some of it just didn't click. This wasn't quite the same as examining a body, looking for clues in the anatomy, in the bones. With a body, she could run tests, compare results, find markers and traces that could let her use her experience and background to draw conclusions.

Maybe she could apply that here, but she wasn't quite seeing how.

Some of the information she had on hand was the comparison of the bullet from the scene with the database. There were no useful hits. The gun had been stolen from a home in Naples, Florida, two years earlier, and had so far never been linked to any known crimes. Ryba could have picked it up from anyone, anywhere, any time.

But the bolt cutters ...

Ryba had cast them into the weeds, after cutting through the chain on the side gate. She'd already tested for prints and found nothing. No help there.

But there was some promise in the bolt cutters themselves.

The brand was a store brand, specific to a chain of home improvement stores. It happened that there was only one of the stores in all of the state of New York, near Manhattan. A lucky break, in Ludlum's opinion.

She made a call to the store, identified herself as a Lead Forensic Specialist for the FBI, and made fast progress on requesting video as well as sales records.

She got lucky.

Only one set of those bolt cutters was sold within the past month. And in fact, it had been sold just a couple of days before the incident at the impound lot. They had a specific time and date for the sale, and with this Ludlum was able to narrow down her video search.

The head of store security was more than happy to send her a file, via email. She opened it while still on the phone, and watched it with him listening. She then thanked him profusely.

It was Ryba.

He was even wearing the same coat. And in his hand was

the stubby set of bolt cutters that now had a spot on Ludlum's examination table.

She had him.

Now she just had to find him.

SHE WROTE UP HER FINDINGS, included her photo evidence, and updated the case file. She emailed both the lead detective from the NYPD and the FBI agent running the investigation from their end. Everyone was pleased, even excited. She was getting congratulatory emails and text messages at a high volume.

But Ryba was still out there and was still on the hunt for Kotler. He was highly trained and relentless. He was also highly motivated by the death of his brother. His honor would demand that he take out Kotler.

Ludlum had brought this on Kotler by killing Cameron Ryba. This was on her. She had to do something. Something more than link Ryba to the crime.

She sat back from her computer, rubbing her eyes, yawning. It had been a very long day. She stood, taking her empty coffee cup with her, and wandered to the break room. She took note that outside the windows of Historic Crimes the city had darkened, night had fallen. It was late.

She poured the last of the coffee into her mug, splashed some cream into it, and sipped.

People were hunting Ryba. She could trust them to find the man. That security guard he'd murdered was retired NYPD. The Blues had a stake in this, and they'd do whatever they could to find the guy. The FBI also had a keen interest in Ryba, for more reasons than Ludlum could count.

She didn't have to worry about this.

But she felt it as her responsibility. And that meant she had to do something.

What did she know about Ryba?

If Ludlum were examining a body or a blood stain or any evidence collected from a crime scene, she'd start by looking at the knowns. If the splatter formed this pattern, it meant this sort of injury, this angle, this timeframe. If there was a bullet, the striations could be measured and matched to a database, the angle of entry could tell her the shooter's position. If a victim was stabbed, the cut could tell her the shape of the blade, the angle of attack, the force of the thrust.

The knowns were details that could let her make intuitive leaps. She could piece together the rest of the story from these tiny shards, by examining the end result and working backward.

What did she know about Ryba's hunt for Kotler?

She had details on the man, from his file. She knew his background and his training. These might be helpful, but she wasn't entirely sure how. She wasn't a profiler. She couldn't really discern what Ryba would do based on what he'd already done. Not really.

But that wasn't the way things worked for her anyway. She was a forensic anthropologist. She dealt with end results. She worked backward, building the story from its end to its beginning.

What was the end of this story, as Ryba would have it?

She realized that was an easy question.

Ryba intended to kill Kotler.

And the only way he could get that result was to get to Kotler when he least expected it. Isolate him. Take him out in such a way that he'd never see it coming, that Kotler would have no means of escape, and that Ryba could disappear, unseen and unconnected.

Ludlum froze.

She knew how to find Ryba because she knew what he was after. She knew, as well, that he wasn't going to just give up on this. He had a code, and that dictated that he get the job done. A 100% success rate. Even if Ryba were being his own client at the moment, he'd want to keep that record.

Kotler was with Agent Denzel. The two of them were on their way to Dr. Wiley's lake house.

That was where Ryba would be.

She put her coffee mug in the sink and raced back to her office, grabbing her phone. She dialed Kotler and got no answer. She dialed Denzel, and it went to voicemail. The area they were in was remote. They might not have a signal.

She needed to warn them.

She raced out of her office and went straight to the elevator. On the ride to the ground floor, she called for an Uber, and then made arrangements for a rental car. Before she reached the lobby, it was done.

From the backseat of the Uber, she pulled up a map to the lake house, based on the address in the file Denzel had compiled.

It would take four hours to get there, if she obeyed speed limits. But they were only two hours ahead of her. She might be able to catch up. And she could also arrange for some backup.

She called another number on her phone. "Detective Holden?"

"Liz?" Detective Peter Holden was an old friend from the force, and knew both Kotler and Denzel, having worked with them on the Ashton Mink murder investigation.

"I need your help," she said. "I need you to make some calls. And I need to run some lights."

34

ADIRONADACK LAKE, NEW YORK

The drive to Adirondack Lake had taken almost four hours. Kotler tried to admire the scenery as they closed in on the lake house of Dr. Wiley, though there wasn't much to see in the dark. Still, the lights from the homes here made the place seem warm and inviting. The reflection of moonlight from the lake gave the whole area a mystical energy. It was beautiful here. The kind of place where evil things should never happen.

They slowed.

"The address is up ahead," Denzel said, checking his GPS. "I don't want to alert him to our presence, if he's here."

Kotler nodded.

His phone vibrated, and he looked down to see he had a voicemail from Liz Ludlum. There was no sign of a missed call, so it was likely she had tried reaching them while Denzel and Kotler were in a dead zone. Out here, as they'd closed in on the lake, service had gotten spotty.

Denzel had taken his own phone out. "Ludlum," he said.

"She called me, too," Kotler said, looking up. "We'd probably better check."

They each played their voicemails, holding their phones to their ears and then turning to each other.

"Ryba?" Denzel asked.

Kotler nodded, then looked out of the windows into the dark, as if Ryba might appear and take his shot. For all they knew, that was precisely what the man had in mind.

"We'll have to keep an eye out," Denzel said. "But there isn't much we can do about it now."

Kotler agreed.

Denzel paused for a moment, then opened his door and walked to the trunk of the car, popping it open. Kotler joined him.

Denzel opened the locked case in which he carried a veritable arsenal. He pulled on a vest, and then handed one to Kotler, minus the large yellow "FBI" insignia.

"You still have the weapon Coben gave you?"

Kotler shook his head. "Confiscated when you brought me in."

Denzel nodded, then reached into the case and took out a .45 EAA Witness, handing it to Kotler along with a hip holster.

Kotler turned, checked the clip and the chamber. "This is a switch," he said.

"You're apparently cleared for a weapon," Denzel said. "The NSA says it's so."

"Not exactly a source I'd trust," Kotler said.

"Good enough for now. And we don't know what we're walking into here. With Ryba in play, it's better to be safe."

Kotler agreed. "Should we call for backup?"

As if on cue, suddenly a pulse of red and blue appeared. They turned, and both put their hands out and to their side. Kotler hoped the large "FBI" emblazoned on Denzel's vest would be enough to keep any local deputies with itchy trigger fingers from shooting them out of panic.

To Kotler's relief, the officer stepped out of his cruiser and immediately greeted them.

"Agent Denzel?" he asked.

"That's me," Denzel replied.

"We got a call from a Detective Holden, with NYPD?"

"Holden?" Kotler asked, leaning toward Denzel.

Denzel put his hands down and walked over to the officer. Kotler followed.

They talked for a moment, exchanged information. Ludlum had made some arrangements, it seemed.

"We have a couple of units on the roads going in and out of this area," the officer said. "Looking for anything suspicious. We have a description of Ryba. We'll keep our eyes open."

"I appreciate that," Denzel said.

"Agent Ludlum is on her way," the officer said.

Kotler's eyebrows raised, and he looked to Denzel. "Agent ... Ludlum."

"That's good," Denzel said. "And I'm glad you're here. Can you cut the lights?"

The officer reached into his cruiser, and a moment later the lights were off.

"We think our suspect is in a lake house less than a mile from here. I was planning to go in on foot. It would be helpful if we could keep anyone from driving through here for the next couple of hours."

The officer nodded. "I can head back up the road, block it further up the shore. There are only three houses out here, and this is the only road in or out. It ends in a turnaround a couple of miles past the Wiley place. I can't say for sure if anyone is home, down the way."

"Do you know them?" Denzel asked.

"One of them. I can have Dispatch put me through to the other. I'll make sure they stay put."

Denzel nodded, then turned to Kotler. "Ready for a hike?"

Kotler smiled. "Are we sure we don't want to wait for Agent

Ludlum?"

"We'll fill her in later," Denzel said.

LUDLUM SAW the flicker of police lights up ahead, and took a breath. She patted her pocket, found her ID, and had it ready as she pulled to a stop and rolled down her window.

"Agent Ludlum," the officer said.

Ludlum blinked. "Y-yes," she said, smiling. She hadn't claimed to be an agent, but it was easier just to let him assume.

"The other two are already at the property," he said, smiling. "I have this route blocked for incoming traffic. If you pull over to the shoulder, you can pass by." He pointed to the rear of his cruiser, where the shoulder was indeed wide enough for her to drive.

"Has anyone else come through?" she asked.

He shook his head. "No ma'am, not since I've been here."

She thought for a moment. "Is this the only road in?"

He nodded. "This is the only way to get a vehicle to this part of the lake, unless you're on an ATV."

"ATV?" Ludlum asked.

"Four-wheeler," the officer explained. "Or a dirt bike. Something small enough to get through the forest trails."

Ludlum felt her pulse quicken. "How public are those trails? Are they on a map?"

The officer frowned, thinking. "I'm not sure." He straightened then and picked the radio from his lapel. He spoke into it while Ludlum picked up her phone and once again tried Kotler and Denzel. Again, it went straight to voicemail. If they were making their move on Wiley, they'd have the phones off.

The officer stooped again, "I'm sorry Agent Ludlum, I never even thought about those trails. They connect this area with a park, east of here. The public trails there have a map, and it's possible it includes a route all the way through."

"Can they be blocked off?"

He nodded. "I already have someone headed that way."

She huffed. It might be too late. Ryba might already have found that route, and he could be in the area right now. "Where do those trails lead? Where do they come out?"

He nodded to her phone. "Can you pull up a map?"

For the next few minutes, he took her through the area where the trails met the road. She marked the spot, setting it as a destination. "Is there anyone who can go there? Check it out?"

"I could," he said, "but it would mean leaving the road open here. It'll be an hour before anyone else can get out here."

An hour? By then, Ludlum knew, it could be too late. Ryba might already be there, as it was.

"I'll go," she said.

The officer nodded.

Ludlum pulled around, driving onto the shoulder and then merging back to the road once she'd passed the cruiser. She picked up speed, frequently checking to see her position on her phone's GPS.

Her headlights reflected from a vehicle up ahead, and she slowed.

Agent Denzel's car. Dr. Wiley's lake house was close.

She checked GPS again.

The trails emerged a short distance past Wiley's house, from a patch of forest that encircled the property. The road continued on from there, ending at the lake.

She cut her headlights as she came to Wiley's property. There was a light at the gate here, which made it possible for her to see the road. She noted that the gate was standing open.

Once she was beyond Wiley's property, she had to turn her headlights back on or risk driving off of the winding road and into the steep ditches on either side. The forest had thickened here, blocking the moonlight and making her feel closed in on all sides. It was amping up her anxiety, and she breathed through it. She reached over and opened her grandfather's medical bag, taking out the pistol she had tucked inside. She placed this close. Just in case.

Up ahead she saw a flash of red as her headlights bounced from a reflector.

She slowed, and eventually stopped.

In her headlights, parked in a curved patch of gravel just beyond the shoulder of the road, was a motorcycle.

A vintage Indian.

She cut her headlights and pulled over, turning off the engine. She huffed, breathing heavy, feeling her pulse in her throat. Reaching for her weapon, she opened the door and stepped out into the night. She quickly turned back, leaning in and digging through the medical bag until she found her small flashlight. She straightened, closed and locked the door of her car, and moved to the motorcycle, her weapon ready.

It was exactly as she remembered it. There was a small bit of damage from where she had let it drop to the street, but nothing that couldn't be fixed. She reached out and gingerly put her hand on the engine, then jerked it away.

Hot.

Ryba hadn't been here long.

She hadn't seen him on the road, but this spot was close enough to Wiley's property that he may already have gotten there. She turned, looking back the way she'd come.

Should she drive?

She didn't want to risk it.

She decided to walk back, weapon ready, keeping it hidden. If she needed it, she'd use the flashlight. But for now, she'd rely on the slivers of moonlight making stripes on the road.

This was by far the dumbest thing Ludlum had ever done, but she couldn't think of another plan.

She marched through the darkness to try to find Red Ryba.

35

ROBERT WILEY LAKE HOUSE, NEW YORK

The gate at the front of the property stood open, allowing Kotler and Denzel to enter the property without much obstruction. They moved quickly now, ducking low and sprinting across the property, taking cover in a small stand of trees in front of the house.

The place was impressive. Two stories, but wide enough to accommodate dozens of rooms, up and down. It stretched along the lakeshore like a palace. Moonlight reflected from its white walls, giving it an eerie sort of glow.

The place was dark except for one set of rooms on the southern end of the structure. Light from the windows cast a warm glow on the grounds. If Wiley was here, this was the most likely place.

They made their way to the house, slowly and cautiously, until they were standing against the ground floor wall. Above them, light glowed warmly from the upstairs window.

"What's the plan?" Kotler asked.

"We need to verify that Wiley is here. And determine if he's alone."

"Place looks pretty empty," Kotler said, glancing down the length of the house. "We should move around to the lakeside. If he's hiding out here, there's a higher probability of him being out by the lake."

Denzel nodded, and the two of them inched along, following the contour of the house until they came to a short, brick wall. There was an iron gate embedded in an arch—an access point to the back of the property. Through the gate, they could see a path leading down to the lake, along with hints of some sort of outdoor patio. This was well lit, and there was the smell of grilled meat.

"He's having steak?" Kotler asked, shaking his head. "He's a lot bolder than I would have thought."

"He may not know we're after him yet," Denzel said.

"Let's get him, and then confiscate the steaks. As evidence."

"Not the time, Kotler."

"We skipped dinner, that's all," Kotler said.

They checked the gate, found it unlocked, and moved through it quietly. The ground was covered in dry leaves that crackled with each step, and they stayed to the path to minimize noise.

From here they could hear music, growing louder as they approached.

They rounded the corner, weapons raised and stopped.

No one was there.

An engine started somewhere, and they looked to see a boat come to life at a dock on the lake.

"He's running!" Kotler shouted.

They raced down the path as the boat pulled away from the dock, speeding out onto the lake.

They stopped at the edge of the dock and Kotler, huffing, said, "Now what?"

Denzel raised his weapon, took aim, then fired two shots.

The engine of the boat made a sputtering and popping noise before going silent, drifting out on the darkened waters.

"You got the motor!" Kotler said, grinning.

"Of course I got the motor," Denzel replied.

Kotler laughed, then stood straight, watching the water. "Now what? How do we get to him?"

Denzel was looking around, checking the area. "I don't see any other boats." He took out his phone. "Keep an eye on him," he said. He started walking back up the path, toward the house, waving his phone as if looking for a signal. "I'll call local PD, have them bring out a boat."

Kotler nodded and walked along the shore as Denzel made the call.

He was watching Dr. Wiley as the boat drifted. He could just make the man out in the darkness.

"Why'd you do it?" Kotler shouted to him.

From the boat, Kotler heard Wiley laugh. "You know, I really don't know? At first, it was the money. I have a daughter. I wanted to give her the kind of education she deserved. A wedding. That sort of thing. That's what I told myself. But there was also this place, this house."

Kotler glanced back at the house, nodding. "It's a nice place," he said. "Was it worth it?"

"Oh yes," Wiley said. "For a while, it was worth it. But you kept showing up. You kept appearing on the news. You were out there, having these ... well, these adventures. I'm a physicist. I was never going to see that kind of action. I was never going to discover a lost city or a buried treasure."

"So, what, you were jealous?" Kotler asked. "Was this some kind of mid-life crisis?"

"It was more than that," Wiley said, a note of disgust in his voice. "You were always smug, Dan. Multiple Ph.D.s. All that money. All the fame and recognition. Even when you were my student, I felt like you were outshining me in everything. It was petty, I know. But it led to me obsessing over what you were doing. It led to me trying to ... I don't know ... replicate your career? I started looking into historical mysteries myself. Started doing research, on my own time. I used my sabbaticals to travel and look into some of the leads I found. When that wasn't paying off, I used my access to government databases to start following leads. I was inspired by the underground lab you found. Isaac Newton's lab. I started following any lead that even hinted at something like that. And that's when I found the Black Chamber."

"And you discovered the Heisenberg machines," Kotler said.

"And the government-sealed room. And the manuscript. All of it. It was the photos of that manuscript that led me to the Black Chamber, actually. I traced your family tree, Dan. When I found your great-grandfather, I started following his work. He was a physicist, like me. He did work I could understand. It revealed a lot, actually. About you. About your history."

"Maybe you can tell me all about it," Kotler said. "I'll visit you in prison."

Wiley laughed. "Funny," he said. "You were always funny. But I don't think I'll be in prison," he said.

"I'm pretty sure you will," Kotler replied.

He wasn't sure if Wiley responded, because at that moment he felt a gun pressed against the back of his head.

"Say nothing," a man's voice said. "Move."

KOTLER STUMBLED ALONG, occasionally pushed by Ryba as the two of them moved deeper into the woods.

This was bad.

Kotler's mind raced with possibilities, and he knew what

was happening. The only reason Ryba hadn't shot him by the lake was that Denzel would hear, even with the silencer on Ryba's gun. It would compromise Ryba's escape. And though Ryba might have been able to take out the Agent, the risk of being shot himself, or incarcerated, would be higher.

Ryba played a game of odds and minimized risk. The safe play was to take Kotler off into the woods, shoot him in a spot where the sound would be further muffled by trees and undergrowth, and then make his escape the way he'd come in.

It was a clever bit of deduction, Kotler decided. Too bad he was working out the details of his own murder.

"Here," Ryba said, stepping away from Kotler. "Turn around."

"Don't want to shoot me in the back?" Kotler asked, not moving. His hands were raised above his shoulders. Ryba had removed his weapon and tossed it into the lake. Kotler wasn't confident that the trained hitman would make the mistake of shooting him in the bulletproof vest.

"I will do so, if you leave me no choice. Honor will not prevent it. But I would prefer that you face me, Dr. Kotler. For your honor, more than mine."

Kotler turned, slowly.

Could he make a break for it? Dive behind one of the trees, run deeper into the woods?

This spot was more or less cleared, with very little brush. The trees were thinner here, about half of Kotler's body thickness. There wasn't much cover. He'd be dead in seconds.

He faced Ryba.

"I'm sorry for your brother," he said. He meant it. Recent events had triggered deep feelings within Kotler, concerning the relationship of brothers. Jeffrey wasn't answering Kotler's calls, and apparently wasn't allowing Alex to talk to him, either. That hurt.

Ryba shook his head. "My brother was new to this life. He was learning. He had great potential. But he made mistakes. He got himself killed. But I must still honor him. There must still be a price."

"Will it end with me?" Kotler asked.

"You worry for the woman. And for your friend," Ryba said.

Kotler waited.

"You have my word," Ryba replied.

Kotler nodded, took a breath, and lowered his hands to his side. "Can I remove the vest?"

"No need," Ryba said. "I prefer a headshot. It's immediate. You will not suffer."

"Thanks for that," Kotler said, and closed his eyes, waiting.

When the shot came, Kotler's body was thrown backward, landing on the loamy, leaf-strewn ground.

His chest hurt. A lot.

But he wasn't dead.

Ryba had shot him in the chest after all.

Kotler lay still, not sure what he should do. He felt like someone had rammed a truck into his chest. His breathing was a little labored. But he was otherwise fine. Maybe he could pretend to be dead. Maybe Ryba would just assume and make a run for it.

How had Ryba missed that shot?

"Dan?" It was a woman's voice. Familiar. And in seconds someone was kneeling next to him, frantically pulling at his vest, trying to remove it.

Kotler cautiously opened one eye, and saw that the clearing was lit from below by a flashlight, making the leafless treetops resemble veins branching into darkness.

"Liz?" he asked, and coughed. The action made his whole body hurt, and he groaned.

Liz Ludlum was leaning over him, opening his shirt, feeling his chest with her fingers.

"Be still," she said. She shook her head. "Bruised. No broken ribs. But you're going to be fine." She smiled down at him, relief plain on her face.

"Liz?" Kotler asked again, confused, but returning her smile.

She helped him to sit up, and then get to his feet.

He leaned on her for support as he steadied himself. His chest did indeed feel bruised, but he was so glad to be alive the pain of it was starting to pass.

Liz left him for a moment, stooping, and when she stood once again the light from her flashlight danced over the trees, the ground, the body.

The body of Red Ryba.

"I shot him," she said.

"I see that," Kotler replied.

Suddenly she put her arms around him, hugging him in a tight embrace that made his bruised chest protest. He ignored it, returning the hug, letting the moment be.

She leaned back from him, and her face was suddenly lit by a beam of moonlight.

Kotler studied her for a moment, then leaned in, pressing his mouth to hers.

She dropped the flashlight, and for a few minutes, nothing mattered but the kiss. Not the pain in Kotler's chest. Not the events of the past few weeks. Not even the body of a hitman at their feet.

Then someone cleared their throat.

Kotler and Ludlum looked up to see Denzel, his weapon in hand, resting against his other forearm and aimed lazily off into the woods. "Sorry to interrupt," he said.

Kotler and Ludlum stepped away from each other, but not far. They turned to face Denzel, looking at him across Ryba's body.

In the distance, muffled by the trees, they could hear the sound of police sirens approaching.

"That's backup," Denzel said.

Kotler nodded. "I figured."

There was a pause. "They're bringing a boat," Denzel said."

Kotler smiled, then laughed. And Ludlum joined him.

EPILOGUE

KOTLER WATCHED FOR A MOMENT BEFORE STEPPING OUT OF THE alcove. The wind picked up out here, mostly a breeze but chilly, even in the bright sunlight. He shoved his hands into his coat pockets and crossed the street. He followed for nearly a block, waited, then turned into the building.

There was construction in progress. Workers carried building materials into the space as saws and pneumatic tools provided a continuous, near-painful chorus. The building, nearly a hundred years old, was getting an update right down to its bones.

It held onto its history. Kotler could feel that, and could appreciate it. This was good work.

He saw his brother talking to some of the workers.

"Jeffrey," he said, raising his voice to be heard over the noise.

Jeffrey looked back, and Kotler felt his stomach clench as he saw his brother's expression change. Kotler didn't need to be a master at reading body language to know what Jeffrey was thinking—he made no attempt to hide it.

Jeffrey moved away from the workers and walked past Kotler. "What do you want?"

"I've been trying to reach you since ... for a couple of weeks," Kotler amended.

"I've been busy," Jeffrey said.

"I can see that."

They came to a room with no door. Inside, a makeshift desk had been set up with saw horses and a sheet of plywood. Blueprints were spread over this, weighted with tape measures and other tools.

A coffee maker was set up in one corner, and Jeffrey went straight to it. He poured coffee into a Styrofoam cup and offered it to Kotler.

Kotler accepted, grateful for any amicable gesture at this point.

Jeffrey picked up a second Styrofoam cup, dropped a tea bag into it and poured hot water over it, letting it steep.

"What do you want?" he repeated, dunking the tea bag in and out of the water.

"Just to talk," Kotler said. "To say I'm sorry for what happened."

"Wasn't your fault," Jeffrey said.

"I feel like it was," Kotler replied.

Jeffrey sipped his tea. "You didn't have those men grab me. You didn't strap a bomb to my chest. None of that was you."

"It was done because of me," Kotler replied.

"Because of what you do," Jeffrey said.

And it hit Kotler for the first time. "Yes, what I do. My work."

"With the FBI," Jeffrey said.

Kotler shook his head, confused. "Is that what this is about? You ... are you upset that I'm working with the FBI?"

"You're an *anthropologist*," Jeffrey said. "You're supposed to be out digging in the dirt, finding old bones, old pieces of pottery. Not hunting down terrorists or disarming bombs."

"Technically I didn't have anything to do with disarming that bomb ..."

"Why can't you just do your job and let the FBI do theirs?" Jeffrey said, his voice fierce.

Kotler shook his head. "I don't have a good answer for you," he said. "For a while, I was thinking the same thing. I was going to walk away from it, after ..."

He paused. He hadn't told Jeffrey about the events in Antarctica, and about the death of Gail McCarthy. He couldn't tell his brother. Details of all of it were still classified.

"It's just ... this came to me," Kotler continued. "This work, with Historic Crimes, with the FBI. I'm ... I'm needed. I was going to leave, but I'm needed."

"I'm sure they could get along fine without you," Jeffrey scoffed.

Kotler felt himself growing angry. "Look, it's my work. Part of it, anyway. And I do think about leaving it, sometimes. But for now, it feels important. It ... it feels like something I have to be a part of. I'm sorry you feel jealous about this, but ..."

"I'm not jealous, you idiot!" Jeffrey shouted.

Kotler blinked. His brother was always so level-headed, so calm. Of the two of them, he was less emotional by far. Hearing him this upset was new. It was disturbing.

"I'm *worried* about you," Jeffrey said, still tense and angry.

"Worried?" Kotler hadn't even considered this. His relationship with Jeffrey had always been a little strained. They cared about each other, but it was in that tolerant way that brothers tended to care. Aloof, distant, reluctant to share their feelings. Despite sharing parents and a bit of childhood history, Kotler and Jeffrey had never had much in common. The gap had only widened when Kotler left for college.

And Jeffrey seemed to disdain everything Kotler did, everything he was. He'd even gone so far as to live a lifestyle exactly opposite of Kotler's—a silent judgment of every choice Kotler had made with his own life. Or that was how Kotler had always read it.

What if he'd been wrong?

"You don't have to worry about me. I'm fine."

"Oh, fine," Jeffrey said, laughing and shaking his head. "Shot at. Kidnapped. Manipulated. You're just great."

Kotler shook his head. "I can't deny any of that," he said. "But there are things you don't know."

Jeffrey studied him for a moment, then tossed the Styrofoam cup into a large trash bin. "I need to get back to work," he said, and then he marched out of the room and back into the bustle of the restoration.

Kotler called after him, trying to calm him, to open the conversation again. But it was too late. He knew Jeffrey would dig in, refusing to talk.

He needed time.

It wasn't just about worry for his brother, Kotler knew. It was about Jeffrey's family. It was about Kotler's life intruding on Jeffrey's, cracking the shell of what his brother had created. Marring something beautiful.

Kotler left, walking back out into the cool and sunny day. Denzel was parked nearby, and Kotler climbed into the passenger seat of his car.

"Didn't go well?" Denzel asked, his voice filled with genuine concern.

Kotler shook his head. "He needs time. He needs to feel safe again."

Denzel nodded. "What about you?"

Kotler smiled, "I could use better coffee," he said, holding up the Styrofoam cup.

They pulled away, merging with traffic.

"So," Denzel said. "You and Ludlum."

"It's ... complicated," Kotler hedged.

"Everything with you is complicated," Denzel said. "But I get it. Just ... you know the old adage? Don't crap where you eat?"

Kotler grinned. "I've heard it slightly different."

"I'm trying to offer some advice here, Kotler," he said, pained.

"I get it," Kotler said, nodding. "Liz and I have talked about it. A little. We'll take it slow."

"Is that because you want it to work out? Or because you're still cautious, after Gail?"

Kotler didn't answer, and instead watched the streets go by. The homes here, in his brother's neighborhood, were nice. Quaint. It was a middle-class neighborhood, with no idea there was a multi-millionaire living among them, using his wealth to make the place better.

Jeffrey was a hero, Kotler realized. Unsung, unknown, unpraised. Maybe the best kind of hero.

"ALL THAT MONEY that Dr. Wiley made," Kotler said, after a moment. "What's going to happen to it?"

"It's your money," Denzel shrugged. "We have the paper trail and everything we need for evidence. This has to go to trial, and we'll have to show that Wiley's actually guilty of stealing from you. That's going to be a slow process. But once he's found guilty, that money will go to you. Do whatever you want with it."

Kotler nodded. "I can wait. Actually, I don't have to wait. I'm thinking I'll set up a foundation. Something that helps neighborhoods like this, maybe. Something that makes life normal and safe for good people. I'll put up the funds now, and later I'll add that money to the pot, once it comes my way."

Denzel was quiet for a beat, then said, "Good idea."

Another few miles passed and the two of them made a stop for better coffee. When they were rolling again, Kotler asked, "What about Dr. Wiley? Did we find out what he was up to? Who he was working with?"

Denzel sipped his latte and said, "We found the second Heisenberg machine in his lake house. Still no idea who he was dealing with. We assume he delivered the pages he took out of your great-grandfather's manuscript, but there's no way to know what else he handed over. Wiley isn't talking. I think he's afraid."

"For his family?" Kotler asked.

"For himself," Denzel scowled. "He was planning to leave them. He told us that much. He had a plan in place. If we hadn't gotten to him when we did, he was going to disappear. Start a new life. Whatever deal he was making, it was going to make the money he'd stolen from you look like pocket change. Billions."

"Billions?" Kotler asked, astonished. He shook his head. "That's not good," he said.

"I'd take billions," Denzel said, smirking.

"I mean, if someone was willing to give him billions of dollars for what he had or what he'd learned, it can't be good for anyone."

Denzel considered this. "You're right," he said. "We'll keep working on it. Wiley will break eventually."

Kotler hoped so. But he couldn't help thinking that whatever it was that he'd helped Wiley to unlock, it was something very, very dangerous.

"Shiva," Kotler said quietly.

"What?" Denzel asked.

Kotler shook his head, tried to let the tension ease. Whatever it was, people were working on the problem. For now, their immediate issues were settled. Jeffrey and his family were safe. Kotler was safe. Liz was ... Liz.

"Nothing," Kotler said, shaking his head and smiling. "It'll keep."

"Looks like things are pretty clear right now," Denzel said. "You going back to the dig? To Egypt?"

Kotler raised his eyebrows. "I can't believe I hadn't considered that." He thought for a moment. "Maybe? I actually have invitations from other projects, plus some speaking engagements. I also have a book to finish. My publisher has been trying to reach me. I think I may be in trouble."

Denzel nodded. "That kind of trouble usually works out for you. Sounds like a busy schedule, though. That's good. Keeping busy means keeping out of real trouble."

Kotler didn't respond, but instead sipped his coffee and watched Jeffrey's neighborhood pass out of view. Manhattan loomed before them, and in a short time, they were surrounded by the concrete canyons and the constant activity of the city. He felt a sort of relief, as they closed on his apartment.

Whatever he did next, and wherever he went from here, Kotler decided, he was up for it. This wasn't exactly the life he'd planned on, but he was needed. Maybe now more than ever.

Shiva, whatever it turned out to be, was surely coming.

A NOTE AT THE END

I once compared Dan Kotler and Roland Denzel to Sherlock Holmes and Watson. I was wrong about that.

I meant well. I was trying to frame their relationship with each other in a way that was relatable for readers, so that it would be easier to understand their dynamic. But I was slightly off track.

In the relationship between Sherlock and Watson, there's this vibe of "superiority." Throughout the Sherlock Holmes stories we see that Sherlock becomes fond of Watson, learns to trust and depend on him, even admires him for his own skills and his progress and growth. But all of this is a little like a parent praising their child. There's a sense of uneven equality —respect, but Sherlock is still clearly the "head of household." Respect on Sherlock's terms.

Kotler and Denzel have a different dynamic, in my opinion.

There are times when Kotler has the upper hand in their relationship, particularly when he's on a roll with something about which he's an expert. Kotler shifts into a sort of professor mode, filling in gaps of information (or providing exposition ... I'll admit to using Kotler for exposition), and we get to see the other characters react to this. Denzel tends to be tolerant of it, the way someone tolerates a talkative old-timer in a coffee shop, or the way one spouse tolerates the other when hearing the same story for the thousandth time. My wife, Kara, is fantastic with this.

The thing is, Kotler is smart. Very smart. And more than that, he's clever. He uses his knowledge and expertise to figure things out, in a way that is useful to Agent Denzel. So it's easy to tolerate diatribes and occasional rabbit trails, knowing they're leading somewhere. Kotler has just enough ego to enjoy hearing his own voice, but he's earned it. His intelligence is useful.

Denzel is by no means the "dumb one" in their relationship, however.

What makes Denzel fun for me is that he's often a bit of bumbling. He's constantly getting names and foreign words wrong. He fumbles with technology, tending to prefer old-school methods, but willing to admit the usefulness of modern tech, and equally willing to embrace it. Still, he'd rather jot notes in a pocket notebook and use an old-fashioned slide projector than fall back on his phone or smart tablet and use a fancy display for presentations. He'll do it, but he's going to do it with splendid awkwardness.

Despite this, Denzel is at least as smart as Kotler, though specialized in entirely different areas. Denzel is the type of quiet intelligence that can sometimes be intimidating but is almost always deceptive. It sometimes gives the impression that the person isn't all that sharp. But this couldn't be more wrong.

Denzel keeps his mouth shut and lets other people talk because he knows this is the best way to learn things they may not have intended to share. He also knows that it's better to let the other smart people in the room use their smarts, to help solve problems faster. He can let Kotler go off on tangents because he knows Kotler is a genius, and it's

Denzel's *own* genius that he knows how to channel that brilliance.

Denzel lives by the wise principle of "Never be the smartest person in the room." And even if you are the smartest person, pretend you're not. It usually leads to better ideas and more rapid results.

So these two are not really like Holmes and Watson at all. They're far more equal than that. Kotler doesn't need Denzel for inspiration, to help him "dumb down" a problem so that a solution becomes obvious. And Denzel doesn't need Kotler to do all the intellectual heavy-lifting, solving the riddles because "no one else can." Denzel isn't Kotler's sidekick, he's his partner. And he sees Kotler as a shortcut—a tool to get to the answers faster.

One of the most common comparisons I get with these books is Indiana Jones.

I can see why. The elements of archaeology are a given, as is the gun-toting action, the struggle between a clever and charming protagonist and his equally clever and charming antagonists. The only thing missing is a whip. And a stylish fedora.

This comparison is pretty accurate, I think, but I don't believe that Dr. Dan Kotler is a one-to-one replica of Dr. Indiana Jones. What I believe is that Kotler and Denzel *together* have a dynamic that's reminiscent of Indie.

Kotler could be compared to Dr. Jones, the college professor who has all the co-eds writing love notes to him on their eyelids. He's the professor, spending hours poring over ancient texts and maps and translations, writing papers, publishing. He also goes out into the field, working in or supervising digs and excavations, crawling around in tombs and making charcoal rubbings of etchings in ancient stone monuments. All of that is Kotler.

Denzel, on the other hand, is more like Indiana Jones,

adventurer. Or, maybe less adventurer and more "guy getting into gunfights with the bad guys." The rough but capable side of Indie, facing dangers down with a gun and a badge rather than a whip and a fedora. Denzel shares Indie's tendency to appear less intelligent than he really is. He leverages the fact that others underestimate him, using that to his advantage.

Together, the two of them could give Indie a run for his money. Maybe. I'd pay to see that movie, though. I'd even buy popcorn.

Of course, another common comparison for these books is Dan Brown's *Da Vinci Code*. Or the Robert Langdon series in general. And I'm not going to bother denying the connection there, because it's totally real and totally intentional. Dan Kotler is even named for Dan Brown, in part. He's an homage. I'm hoping Mr. Brown would find it flattering.

In fact, something that I only became aware of recently was the fact that *The Coelho Medallion* pulls heavily from the structure of Ron Howard's film adaptation of *The Da Vinci Code*. It's not a shot-for-shot remake, but it shares a lot of similar story beats.

This was not intentional. I never set out to borrow from the structure of that film, or from the book (which I read just prior to the film's release). I was trying, with that first thriller, to pay respect to the genre that Dan Brown helped to revitalize. But it had been a few years since seeing that movie or reading that book. I guess it made a deeper impression than I'd realized, at the time.

Considering it was my very first thriller, and was more or less an homage to Dan Brown's work, I'm only surprised that I hadn't done it intentionally. Also, it's weird that the subconscious is such a powerful thing. It makes me wonder about how many other "homages" I have floating around in my work, completely unintentional.

What Brown's character, Robert Langdon, inspired in me

was the academic side of Dan Kotler. The idea of an intellectual who becomes embroiled in mystery and action is intriguing and exciting. It opens up lots of possibilities for stories.

Unlike Langdon, however, I wanted my character to have someone he could always rely on. I wanted him to have a relationship that could highlight some of Kotler's weaknesses and vulnerabilities while supplying him with a source of strength.

Kotler and Denzel aren't in love, but they do have a romance. I jokingly refer to this as a "bromance" in the books, and I base it on relationships I have with some of the good friends I have in my own life. Other authors, like Nick Thacker and Ernest Dempsey. And good, lifetime friends like David Dodson and Bob Beaver. And, of course, the real-life Roland Denzel—another fellow author who has become a good friend despite distance and infrequent communication. I have a lot of experience with bromance, and I wanted to explore that with my two protagonists. It's led to some fascinating interactions, between two characters who are very different, in a lot of ways, and yet share some very poignant similarities.

So that's Kotler and Denzel, in a nutshell. I'm still exploring these two, still finding out who they are and what they believe in. I'm sharing as I go. Each book reveals a little more.

Also with each book, I'm branching out and exploring ideas that have fascinated me for years. For Stepping Maze, I brought in an element of cryptology, which has always intrigued me.

Codebreaking is something I've always found captivating, and I've written about it from time to time. This time, however, I wanted it to be a central part of the story.

I did a great deal of research into codebreaking and cryptology before starting this book, but one of the best sources of information and inspiration came from Jason Fagone's biography of Elisabeth Friedman, *The Woman Who Smashed Codes*. It was here that I learned about the American Black Chamber and its connection to the founding of the NSA.

Fagone did an excellent job of introducing and simplifying various ciphers and cryptological methods, and he made even some of the densest and most intimidating processes accessible.

The history of the Friedmans, Elisabeth and William, is fascinating reading. I highly recommended picking up the book, reading it thoroughly, and giving it the best possible review.

My choice to link all of this to Kotler's past was made in part because I found it necessary to start answering some questions about Kotler's personal and professional life, as well as the existence of Historic Crimes.

There are things I put into previous books that hint at Kotler's past, but this was the first time I'd actually used that past as a springboard for a storyline. Discovering that Kotler's great-grandfather was a founding member of the NSA is intriguing. Even more intriguing are the questions I'm only thinking to ask myself, and that the characters themselves should have asked long ago: Why is Historic Crimes even a thing? How does it keep getting funding? Who is advocating for it, higher up in the food chain? And why was it called "Historic Crimes" instead of "Historical Crimes?"

That last one has an easy answer: It's because I wrote that and didn't quite click to the goof until I'd already published the book in which I introduced this new division. By then, I figured it was better to own the mistake and write it into the mythos. Though it took three more books before I got around to it.

At any rate, now here we are. Dan Kotler has a past. We knew it was there, but we're starting to see it emerge. And we'll see more over time.

The same is true for Denzel. We got some of his background in *The Girl in the Mayan Tomb*, learning the origin of his claustrophobia (which, apparently, was one of the subconscious things I borrowed from Robert Langdon). As these books go on, I expect we'll learn more about Denzel, as well as other characters.

Including Dr. Liz Ludlum.

I'm most excited about Ludlum. Because she represents an opportunity to write a female protagonist who isn't the cliché, not-really-strong, only-there-to-be-rescued heroine we usually see. She's also not the over-the-top, overly masculine female protagonist that Hollywood seems to think is "good enough." Ludlum is smart—maybe even smarter than Kotler, but at least on par with him. And she's tough, but without losing her femininity. She's not a man with breasts, in other words. She's a woman. And what a woman.

I admit, I'm a tiny bit in love with Liz Ludlum. She's the female protagonist I've longed to see.

I plan to avoid more clichés with this character, but you can count on some classic male-female relationship stuff making an appearance. Mostly because I want to explore some of that in these books, as well.

What effect does having someone stable and good and caring in his life have on Dan Kotler? How does that change the character? When we first met Kotler, he was pretty adamant that he didn't want to be tied down. Has that changed? Or will it? And what about the trauma he suffered in his relationship with Gail McCarthy? What impact does that have on his relationships?

Lots of gold to mine there.

For now, however, we've reached the end of another tale. I'm going to admit, this one is my new favorite. I think this is the best book I've written to date. And I know, I say that with every book, and I always mean it. But this one does feel special. I think it has nuances and levels that I've never included in my other works. I love it.

It's not up to me, of course. You'll have to let me know if you love it or hate it. I'd appreciate it if you'd leave a review, if you loved it. And you can also email me at kevin@tumlinson.net. I love getting those emails, and I try to answer every one of them. Send away.

Until then, and until the next book, I wish you well and pray for your health and happiness. God bless you and thank you for your support.

Happy reading.

Kevin Tumlinson
Sugar Land, Texas
December 20, 2018

ACKNOWLEDGMENTS

This book wouldn't have been possible without the help of some amazing and wonderful people, including Geoff Symon, a Federal Forensic Investigator and the author of an amazing set of books called *Forensics for Fiction*. Whether you have any desire to write for a living or you just have an interest in how forensics works, these books are amazingly informative and very accessible. Read them. Then criticize Hollywood at length for getting almost everything wrong, all the time.

I'd also like to thank Patrick O'Donnell, police officer and author, and an aficionado of good cigars. He's been a great purveyor of insight into police procedure, even if I've been very poor at putting his suggestions to work in my books. I'll get better.

And finally, I owe a great debt of appreciation to Michael Anderle and Craig Martelle, who set up the 20 Books to 50K conference in Vegas (among other things). It was at this conference that I got a much-needed burst of inspiration, leading me to leap back into these books with renewed gusto.

There are many more names that rightfully belong on this list, and I'm terrible for not spending a proper amount of time thanking them. But I love them all just the same.

ALSO BY J. KEVIN TUMLINSON

Dan Kotler

The Coelho Medallion

The Atlantis Riddle

The Devil's Interval

The Girl in the Mayan Tomb

The Antarctic Forgery

The Stepping Maze

The God Extinction

The Spanish Papers

The Hidden Persuaders

The Sleeper's War

The God Resurrection

The Demon Core

Dan Kotler Short Fiction

The Brass Hall - A Dan Kotler Story

The Jani Sigil - FREE short story from BookHip.com/DBXDHP

Dan Kotler Box Sets

The Book of Lost Things: Dan Kotler, Books 1-3

The Book of Betrayals: Dan Kotler, Books 4-6

The Book of Gods and Kings: Dan Kotler, Books 7-9

Quake Runner: Alex Kayne

Shaken

Triggered

Compromised

Aftershock

Historic Crimes Crossovers

The Man Below

The Outsiders Gambit

Evergreen

Evergreen: Book 1

Evergreen: Trace Contact

Citadel

Citadel: First Colony

Citadel: Paths in Darkness

Citadel: Children of Light

Citadel: The Value of War

Colony Girl: A Citadel Universe Story

Sawyer Jackson

Sawyer Jackson and the Long Land

Sawyer Jackson and the Shadow Strait

Sawyer Jackson and the White Room

Think Tank

Karner Blue

Zero Tolerance

Nomad

The Lucid — Co-authored with Nick Thacker

Episode 1

Episode 2

Episode 3

Shorts & Novellas

Getting Gone

Teresa's Monster

The Three Reasons to Avoid Being Punched in the Face

Tin Man

Two Blocks East

Edge

Zero

God Mode

Collections & Anthologies

Citadel: Omnibus

Uncanny Divide — With Nick Thacker & Will Flora

Light Years — The Complete Science Fiction Library

Dead of Winter: A Christmas Anthology — With Nick Thacker, Jim

Heskett, David Berens, M.P. MacDougall, R.A. McGee, Dusty Sharp &
Steven Moore

YA & Middle Grade

Secret of the Diamond Sword — An Alex Kotler Mystery

Wordslinger (Non-Fiction)

30-Day Author: Develop a Daily Writing Habit and Write Your Book In
30 Days (Or Less)

Watch for more at kevintumlinson.com/books

HERE'S HOW TO HELP ME REACH MORE READERS

If you loved this book, you can help me reach more readers with just a few easy acts of kindness.

(1) REVIEW THIS BOOK

Leaving a review for this book is a great way to help other readers find it. Just go to the site where you bought the book, search for the title, and leave a review. It really helps, and I really appreciate it.

(2) SUBSCRIBE TO MY EMAIL LIST

I regularly write a special email to the people on my list, just keeping everyone up to date on what I'm working on. When I announce new book releases, giveaways, or anything else, the people on my list hear about it first. Sometimes, there are special deals I'll *only* give to my list, so it's worth being a part of the crowd.

Join the conversation and get a free ebook, just for signing up! Visit https://www.kevintumlinson.com/joinme.

(3) TELL YOUR FRIENDS

Word of mouth is still the best marketing there is, so I would greatly appreciate it if you'd tell your friends and family about this book, and the others I've written.

You can find a comprehensive list of all of my books at http://kevintumlinson.com/books.

Thanks so much for your help. And thanks for reading.

ABOUT THE AUTHOR

Kevin Tumlinson is an award-winning and bestselling novelist, living in Texas and working in random coffee shops, cafés, and hotel lobbies worldwide. His debut thriller, *The Coelho Medallion*, was a 2016 Shelf Notable Indie award winner.

Kevin grew up in Wild Peach, Texas, where he was raised by his grandparents and given a healthy respect for story telling. He often found himself in trouble in school for writing stories instead of doing his actual assignments.

Kevin's love for history, archaeology, and science has been a tremendous source of material for his writing, feeding his fiction and giving him just the excuse he needs to read the next article, biography, or research paper.

Connect with Kevin:
kevintumlinson.com
kevin@tumlinson.net

f facebook.com/jkevintumlinson

X x.com/kevintumlinson

instagram.com/kevintumlinson

BB bookbub.com/authors/kevin-tumlinson

a amazon.com/Kevin-Tumlinson/e/B007POXGEG

KEEP THE ADVENTURE GOING!

GET MORE THRILLS FROM AWARD-WINNING AND BESTSELLING AUTHOR, KEVIN TUMLINSON!

★★★★★ "Half way through I was waiting for Harrison Ford to leap out of the pages!"
—Deanne, Review for *The Coelho Medallion*

★★★★★ "Kevin has crashed onto the action-thriller scene as only an action-thriller author can: with provocative plot

lines, unforgettable characters, and enough adrenaline to keep you awake all night."
—Nick Thacker, author of *Mark for Blood*

★★★★★ "Move over Daniel Silva, James Patterson, and Dan Brown."
—Chip Polk, Review for *The Atlantis Riddle*

★★★★★ "Move Over Indiana Jones, there is a New Dr. in Town!"
—Cycletrash, Review for *The Coelho Medallion*

★★★★★ "[Kevin Tumlinson] is what every writer should be —entertaining and thought-provoking."
— Shana Tehan, Press Secretary, U.S. House of Representatives

★★★★★ "I discovered Kevin Tumlinson from The Creative Penn podcast and immediately got his novel, Evergreen. I read it in like 3 seconds. It's the most fast-paced story I've encountered."
—R.D. Holland, Independent Reviewer

★★★★★ "Comparison to Clive Cussler is a natural, though Tumlinson's 'Dan ' is more like Dan Brown's Robert Langdon than Dirk Pitt."
—Amazon Review for *The Coelho Medallion*

FIND YOUR NEXT FAVORITE BOOK AT
KevinTumlinson.com/books